SHAPESHIFTERS

Fate has brought them a gift—immortality—and a curse—growing insanity. The longer they live, the madder they become; the more they evolve, the more vicious their acts.

Caught between heaven and hell, the shapeshifters have one last chance to escape their doom, one last hope to survive.

But they are running out of time—time to stop the horrors that will devastate them—time to stop the enemies who will use them to control the world—time to stop a holocaust of mayhem and murder that will destroy all mankind.

THE OTHERS
D.M. Wind

THE OTHERS

—D. M. WIND—

LEISURE BOOKS NEW YORK CITY

A LEISURE BOOK®

November 1993

Published by

Dorchester Publishing Co., Inc.
276 Fifth Avenue
New York, NY 10001

Printed in the United States of America.

THE OTHERS

Chapter One

Sperry Hollow, Virginia. May.

The exit from the highway came sooner than he expected. Downshifting and hitting the brakes at the same time, Aaron Blaine swerved onto the ramp.

At the bottom of the exit was another sign. He followed the bright red arrow onto a small road barely wide enough for two cars to pass each other.

The halogen headlights sliced through the dark Virginia night. Parallel to the road was a chain link fence. Posted on the fence, every quarter mile, were succinct black and white No Trespassing signs stamped from government issue presses.

The fence ended at the base of a hill. At the top of that hill was the familiar sign of the golden arches that no longer adorned the fast food place other than as a graphic illusion.

Aaron rolled down his window and breathed in the Virginia night. The air was reflective of the late spring—warm and perfect. He pulled the car off the road. Five minutes later, when the glass section of his roof was stowed away and he was on the road again, fresh Virginia air filled the car.

He found the McDonald's 100 yards past the Welcome to Sperry Hollow sign. There was one other vehicle in the parking lot—a late-model pickup truck. Inside, a man with salt and pepper hair sat at a table, drinking coffee, smoking a cigarette and staring out the front window.

Aaron ordered his food from a busty redhead with wide blue eyes.

"Jus' passin' through?" she asked. Her accent was thickened by the throatiness of her voice.

"That's all, Frannie," he said, looking at her nameplate.

"Yeah, I figured so." Turning away, she went to the counter and picked up his order. "Ya'll eatin' here, or takin' it with you?"

"Here."

After she put the food on a tray and he paid for it, he took his meal to a booth. While he ate, he felt the girl's eyes on him. He finished, used the bathroom, and when he came out, the restaurant's only other customer was gone. He started toward the door.

"Hey thar!" the girl called.

Aaron glanced over his shoulder at her.

She smiled. "I get off'n an hour. I'd sure like a ride in that 'Vette."

Aaron thought about it for a good five seconds before he shook his head. "Sorry, Frannie, I've got to get to Dallas."

"You don' know what ya'll are missing."

Aaron locked on her gaze. "I think I do."

Outside, since the sky was still cloudless and clear, he decided to leave the top open.

Slipping into the cocoon-like seat, he closed the door and pulled on the seat belt. Halfway out, the release mechanism jammed. He spent a few minutes fiddling with it before he gave up and started the engine.

Driving out of the parking lot, he turned toward the highway. When he reached the first turn on the mountain road, he had not yet shaken the pretty redhead from his thoughts, but when he crested the mountain and took the oncoming S turn at ten above the limit, he began to enjoy the feel of the car and the road.

The way he felt about the car was totally illogical for him, but he didn't care. His whole life had always been well ordered, rational and productive. His one weakness, his one truly unreasonable moment had been in buying the red ZR-2 Corvette. In everything else, Aaron

Blaine was much too logical.

He reached the beginning of the chain link fence.

Two more fast turns came and went. He took them smoothly, feeling a sense of excitement and power. He started the next turn at 50, but instead of breaking, he powered into it, shifting from third to second. The tach's readout showed the 7000 mark; the protesting rear tires screamed above the thunder of the engine.

Aaron shifted into third and then into fourth while maneuvering the car toward the next turn. His eyes flicked to the readout—80. Then he was on it. The bright halogen cut through the absolute country darkness, and the tires howled. Aaron's hands fought the wheel.

The rear end broke loose. Countering the spin, Aaron kicked down on the accelerator.

The tires found traction, sending the 'Vette out of the curve like a pellet from a slingshot.

His smile was frozen, and his heart pounded with equal amounts of fear and exhilaration.

Sperry Hollow was a mile and a half behind him. His speedometer showed 90, and the next curve came up fast. With a combination of brakes and gears, he hurdled into it as if he'd driven this road all his life. A second later, he was barreling out of the turn.

"Back off," he said aloud and eased his foot back. The car obeyed instantly. When he went through a dip in the road the wheels of the car left the ground for an instant. Then he was into another curve, sharper this time. He slowed the 'Vette, downshifting to third. When he reached the end of the curve, he goosed the accelerator.

And then he saw it.

A large animal, feral. His impression was of a large gray dog, but the image wavered. Aaron blinked, trying to focus his eyes. Then he saw a figure rising to its feet. When he was closer he realized it was a woman, naked. She turned toward the car and, centering herself in the lane, spread her arms as if welcoming the 'Vette.

He jammed the brake pedal. She was 100 feet ahead of him when the night exploded with light. Powerful beams blossomed from nowhere, blinding him.

Afterimages of orange, red and black continued to blot out his vision. He couldn't see the woman, but he knew she was somewhere in front of his hurtling car.

Some of the dancing colors faded from his eyes, and he spotted her. She was 30 feet away, still centered in the lane, and he knew he wouldn't be able to stop in time.

Working his brake and accelerator simultaneously, Aaron jerked the wheel to the right, putting the car into a controlled turning skid. The steering wheel fought him, and the car continued to hurtle toward the woman.

He manhandled the wheel and sent the car off the road. The rear tires lost traction in the dirt, and the low-slung front end hit the steel chain link fence and cut through it like a knife. He made it only 50 feet before he struck the first tree a glancing blow. When his left side rammed against the door, his arm went numb and useless. Still, he fought hard to control the car and keep it on the ground. He almost succeeded, until the right side lifted.

Then the car was airborne, doing a slow barrel roll. His hands were torn from the wheel when the car hit another tree. His headlights illuminated the leaves in a kaleidoscope of color and motion; he heard the sound of his engine peak past endurance. He felt himself torn loose from the seat. He was flying, spinning, cartwheeling.

And then there was nothing.

Four minutes after the accident, 20 uniformed men stood around the unmoving body. "Goddamn it!" screamed a red-faced man. "Call it in!"

The radio man spoke into his phone as five other men came up, dragging the woman between them.

The captain turned. His eyes raked her face. "You did this, you goddamned freak!" he said, pointing to the bloodied face of Aaron Blaine.

The woman looked down at Aaron, her wide eyes fixed intently on his face. Golden flecks within green irises took on a faint glow. She stayed like that until the captain motioned to the men holding her, and they forced her toward a waiting vehicle.

The Others

As she was led away, the radio man lowered his portable phone and looked uncertainly at the captain. "An ambulance and state troopers are on the way. Mr. Aldredge wants to speak to you," he said, handing the captain the phone.

"Aldredge?" the captain said.

"Get those men out of there before the police arrive. You wait for them, alone, and make sure we're kept out of it."

Nineteen minutes after leaving the accident, the red and blue volunteer ambulance arrived at the hospital. The waiting medical team met the vehicle and, seconds later, the paramedics had the gurney on the ground and assisted the hospital staff in rushing the injured man inside. The state trooper who had led the ambulance to the hospital went over to one of the doctors.

The paramedics were telling the E.R. doctor what they'd discovered. While the emergency man listened, he motioned to several others.

The trooper nodded his head when he heard the doctor order the man into surgery. There was no time for releases to be signed—not if the man was to live, which to all concerned seemed doubtful.

The doctor looked at the waiting trooper. His eyes were hooded. "'Lo, Glen, what happened this time?"

"Looks like he lost control over by Sperry Hollow. Crashed through the government fence, hit a tree. He was lucky though, thrown clear before the car went over the edge."

"Who is he?"

"Aaron Blaine," the trooper said. "His I.D. says he's a cop from Dallas."

"We'll do our best. Give Bessie the information so we can contact his family. I'm going to the O.R."

"He's going to need you, Ned. His head's messed up bad."

"Yeah," Ned Sallen replied. Shaking his head, he started after the E.R. team while the trooper, a veteran of too many highway accidents, began to fill out the forms at the desk.

Inside the scrub room, a paramedic briefed him. By the time he had his greens on and the nurse pulled on the gloves, the head of neurosurgery for Mount Holly Hospital was examining the x-rays of Blaine's skull.

"Bone fragment in the lower occipital region," he mumbled. "Any leakage?"

"Not yet," replied another of the team.

"Vital signs?" Sallen called.

"Barely," said the nurse monitoring Aaron's signs. Without a pause, she read off the numbers.

Sallen inspected the prepped area. His stomach spasmed the way it always did when he saw a wasted life. As always, he knew he would do his best, but he didn't like the way this one looked. He didn't like it at all.

Chapter Two

Aaron knew he was dying. He heard the voices of the medical team, but they were distant, fading. A spasm of fear passed through him. Then he was calm. He heard a machine start and sensed vibrations from where the doctor placed it on his head.

There was a sharp and twisting sensation.

An instant later he was pressed against a barrier, and then he was through it and floating above the table. He looked down, staring at himself and the operating team.

"We're losing him," the woman sitting at the monitors called.

"Give him . . ."

Aaron missed the rest of the words. Something was calling him. It wasn't a voice; it was something more. He looked up and saw a bright light. It was pure and magnificent and did not hurt his eyes.

He was oddly at peace and unafraid. Willing himself to rise higher, Aaron floated toward the light. Beneath him, the doctors worked frantically.

He wanted to tell them to stop, to thank them and tell them that he had a better place to go. For an instant he wondered what was happening and why he was so complacent.

That thought disappeared as the light grew closer, welcoming him, caressing him with a warmth that centered within him. He realized that he was traveling through a multicolored universe where galaxies abounded, wheeling in jeweled magnificence.

Aaron moved toward the center of the universe, heading effortlessly toward the purest light he had ever known.

But abruptly he was stopped by another force. He tried to thrust it aside, but he could not get passed the presence. Beneath him, one of the doctors shouted, "He's gone! Flat-lined!"

Aaron struggled against the thing that was blocking his way to the light. "I have to go," he said, knowing that he spoke the words in his mind only.

"No."

The power within the response staggered him. Struggling, he strove to reach the warm white glow.

"It is not your time." With that thought came the most intense sensation of warmth and love he had ever experienced. It filled him with an essence of intimacy he'd never before known. He faltered between the light's offering of peace and welcome and the caress of the unknown force that held him back.

But it was not unknown, he realized. There was something familiar about the voice.

Then surprisingly warm and gentle hands caressed him. The bright light was blocked, and he saw her face. Gold-flecked wide green eyes held him in thrall. A small mouth with generous lips formed words, even as her hands soothed his face.

"You must live for me," she said.

"No," he told her, again feeling the invitation of the light and wanting the release it offered.

"Yes, for me."

Her eyes turned luminous. The very fabric of time wrenched all about him. In the next instant, he was spiraling back to his body. And at the very moment that he reentered his body, he knew exactly who she was. He had seen her once before, framed within his headlights on the Virginia road.

"Who are you?" he asked.

"You gave me my life. Now I give you back yours."

Just as the voices of the medical team rose excitedly, he sensed her presence grow over him. And then he felt her mouth on his.

His body arched at the contact. An instant later she was gone, but her voice lingered within his mind. *"Find me. Help me."*

"He's back! Get to work, Ned!" called the E.R. doctor who held the paddles, staring at the man while he tried to understand what had happened. A tenth of a second before he'd touched the man's chest, his body had spasmed with electrical current. He'd heard it; he'd seen the muscles on his chest and abdomen twist as if they'd been hit with 400 volts. A second later, the monitors had come alive.

Aaron was swimming across a river, but the river grew wider with each stroke. He paused to take a breath and look around. On the far shore, a woman signaled to him. Again he tried to reach her, but the current changed, sweeping him downstream.

He was tired. His muscles hurt. There was a spike being pounded into his head. A cocoon of darkness encased him. Fight! he ordered himself. Taking a deep breath, Aaron ignored the pain and pressed on. He felt hands on his chest. He heard a voice.

Opening his eyes, he found soft brown eyes gazing at him. "Take it easy."

Disoriented, Aaron blinked several times. His mouth was cottony dry, his tongue swollen. He looked at the woman who was dressed in white. Her hair was swept back in a bun, and her face was set in concerned lines that were softening now that he looked at her.

"That's better," she said.

Aaron became aware of the tubes in his nose. He turned his head, but it wouldn't move. "What . . ." The word came out with a dry and brittle rasp.

"Easy. You've had a severe accident. Your car went off the road. You've been unconscious for five days, but you're all right now. I'm Anne Morgan."

Aaron stared at her. He knew he wasn't all right. If he was, he'd be able to move his arms. He tried again.

The nurse saw what he was attempting and placed a gentle but restraining hand on his chest. "Try not to move. Both arms are in casts. They were broken. Just rest. I'll get Doctor Sallen."

After the nurse was gone, he did his best to absorb what she'd said. Unable to move his head, he forced his eyes as far over as they would go. He saw the white blob of a cast hanging near him. Looking at the other side, he saw the same thing.

A dream? he asked himself. Closing his eyes, he tried to remember. Reality harshly returned. He was back on the dark Virginia road behind the wheel of the 'Vette. He was barreling out of the curve when he saw the . . . when he saw *her*.

Then the night had exploded with light, blinding him. He had crashed through the fence. That was all. No, there was more. He remembered the operation. He remembered dying and rising toward the light. He remembered being stopped. He remembered *her*.

She had been there with him. She had stopped him from dying. She had given him life, and . . .

"Welcome back to the world of the living. My name is Ned Sallen."

Aaron opened his eyes and saw the doctor who had operated on him. Aaron licked his lips with his cotton swab of a tongue.

The doctor smiled like all doctors and held a bottle with a straw toward his mouth. "Just moisten your mouth. You're still hooked up to the I.V.s."

"Thank you," Aaron said after releasing the straw.

"It was close," Sallen stated. "Whatever possessed you to drive like a maniac?"

Aaron stared at him, puzzled. "I don't understand."

"You drove your car off the road and almost killed yourself."

"No, there was a woman in the road, and I turned to miss her."

"A woman?" Sallen's brows knitted, meeting in the center. "There was no report of a woman."

"She was there," Aaron insisted.

"It was late. These mountain roads can be tricky at night, especially with all that fencing.

Probably a reflection from your headlights."

"She was there."

"It's unimportant right now," Sallen said soothingly. "And before you pass out on me again, which will be pretty soon, are you in any pain?"

"A little."

"I'll order some codeine."

"No."

"It will help."

"If it gets any worse I'll ask for some. I died on the table, didn't I?" he asked suddenly.

Again Sallen's eyebrows knitted. Then he nodded his head. "For a few seconds. But that's happened to a lot of people before you."

"It was longer than a few seconds. What happened to my head?"

Aaron watched Sallen's eyes as the doctor spoke. "A fragment of bone lodged in the occipital region. I had to go in and get it out. There doesn't seem to be any permanent damage. You also herniated your third cervical vertebra, broke your left arm and your right collarbone."

"That's not too good."

"It would have been worse, but you were thrown clear of the car before it went over a small cliff."

Aaron thought of the jammed seat belt mechanism. The malfunction had saved his life. "There was a woman in the road," Aaron repeated.

Aaron read sympathy on the doctor's features and heard a weary patience in his voice. "Perhaps you did see one. As I said, the night can play tricks on you. But the only person who was around was Captain Lowell. He was driving toward you when you went over. He was worried that it might have been his headlights that possibly blinded you."

"Someone was driving toward me?"

"He saw you go through the fence and called the ambulance. Lucky for you he had a car phone."

Aaron stared at the doctor for a long time. "Yes, lucky. How long will I be here?"

"Until you're able to leave. Mr. Blaine, you had a severe accident."

"How long?" Aaron said.

"At least another month. Then you'll have to convalesce at home for two more months, maybe longer. You'll need physical therapy. Oh, your brother is here at a motel. He'll be by later today."

Darkness edged into his mind. He fought it away, but he was getting weak.

Sallen stood and walked to the door. "I'll stop by later."

"There was a woman."

Chapter Three

Dallas, Texas. Mid-September.

"I don't really give a damn whether you believe me or not. There was a woman on the road!" Aaron sat up straighter, trying to ignore the way the walls of the office kept closing in on him. He fought the claustrophobia by concentrating on the round face of the police psychiatrist sitting directly across from him.

"Aaron, you were in a critical accident. You received a severe trauma, and your heart stopped for a short time. It isn't easy to face what happened. To help you cope, your subconscious created a situation that makes it more acceptable, but you've become fixated on this imaginary woman," said the even-voiced man.

"Like hell I have." Aaron knew that he was overreacting to the police department shrink, but he was unable to stop himself.

The heavyset man leaned back, his hands clasped across his stomach. "In the two and a half months since you've returned to work," the shrink said, "you've violated every security regulation the department has—regulations that you helped to draw up. You're guilty of criminal violations that would have landed anyone else in a federal prison. You've accessed information from the F.B.I. without permission, you broke into army intelligence's computers, and last week you went against a direct order of Captain Morse's and accessed top security information from the Department of Defense."

"I know what I did."

"But you don't know why you're doing it, do you?" asked Doctor Reed.

"I know exactly why. I intend to find her."

"And just how do you find a person who doesn't exist?"

Aaron looked out the window, working hard to control his temper. "She exists."

"Does she? Aaron, you're too logical a person to be doing these things. Don't you find it a shade convenient that you don't have her name? Without a name, your computer can't help, can it? How can a computer find a person who doesn't exist?"

"She exists, doctor."

"A fact you've yet to establish."

The Others

Perhaps it was the frustration that made Aaron answer, or maybe the self-satisfied expression on the shrink's putty-like face that Aaron wanted to wipe away. Whatever the reason, it caused Aaron to speak carelessly. "Consider the possibility that it's you who doesn't see the facts, doctor. Consider this," Aaron snapped. "The accident occurred at a government installation near Sperry Hollow. She's either connected to the installation, or she's from Sperry Hollow. Those two facts give me enough information to use the computers to find her. There's a record of her somewhere, a file in a government computer. Governments like records. They thrive on them. That's why I'm going into those data bases. When I find the Sperry files, I'll find her."

"The Sperry files?" the doctor asked with a shake of his head that told Aaron he'd said too much. "Aaron, you're being irrational. And all you're going to find is a jail sentence."

"What makes you so certain about that?" Aaron asked as he glanced at the full wall of degrees that proclaimed Julian Reed to be a master of the mind.

"Criminals go to jail, especially those who try to steal information from the government."

Aaron fixed the doctor with a hard stare. His lips were drawn, and a muscle ticked on his cheek. "I'm not so sure that I'm not rational."

"I've seen this happen before."

"Really?" Aaron asked without blinking.

27

"Yes. Think about it. You try to avoid hitting a woman who was in the middle of the road—a woman who a reliable witness, an army captain, said does not exist. You were seriously injured with substantial neurological trauma. Your subconscious is looking for an excuse to justify your losing control of your car."

"What you're saying is that she's a manifestation of my guilt for driving carelessly and having an accident? You think it's that simple?"

"It's not simple at all. What I'm attempting to do is to simplify a difficult situation. The human mind is a vastly complex organ. There are so many things that can go wrong just in normal day-to-day life. In this instance, your brain suffered an extreme trauma. Your mind is coping with it in the best way it can."

"And how do you plan to help me deal with this?"

When Reed spoke, Aaron heard the edge of victory in his words. "I'd like to set up three sessions a week."

"To what purpose?"

"Good question. Let me answer it with one of my own. If I can prove that this woman does not exist, will you agree to stop using the computers to look for her?"

"The only problem we have, Dr. Reed, is that she does exist." Aaron caught the twitch on Reed's face. "What if I won't go into therapy?"

"Then you go home."

"I'll be fired?"

He shrugged. "Suspension or medical leave."

Aaron glared at Reed, his anger rising. "Whose idea is that?"

"Mine. You need help Aaron, my help."

"You can't help me," Aaron said softly.

"I believe I can, but why don't you tell me why I can't."

"Because there's something happening in Sperry Hollow, and she's involved with it."

"Aaron, be realistic. You're just beginning what everyone believes will be a very promising career. If you persist with this delusion you'll destroy your life."

Aaron laughed and gained a shard of satisfaction by catching the shrink off guard. "My brother spoke to you, didn't he? Those were almost the exact words he used last week."

"He's worried about you, yes."

"But he doesn't believe me either."

"He believes you need my help. Don't you think that by starting therapy we can change this situation?"

"You mean change the situation to what you and everyone else wants it to be. No, thank you." Aaron stood and looked down at the seated man. "I know what happened in Sperry Hollow."

"Don't leave, Aaron. We have to schedule your appointments."

"Doctor Reed, why don't you take your appointments and shove them up your pompous ass!" Turning, he started to the door.

"Don't walk out on me, Aaron. I don't want to put you on leave, but if—"

"Save it for your regulars," Aaron said with finality.

A half hour later, Aaron had his personal belongings packed and was looking around his office in police headquarters. Strangely, he didn't feel bad about leaving; rather, he was looking forward to the freedom to look for her.

He knew the shrink was wrong. It was true that he was fixated on the woman, but not in the way the shrink thought. And she wasn't a delusion built by his subconscious. Aaron knew what his problem was. He had to find her. She needed him, and he needed her.

He paused by the phone on his desk. Shrugging, he picked it up. He was in such deep trouble already that one more call on the Dallas P.D. wouldn't hurt him.

He dialed the ten digit number. It rang four times before it was answered.

"I need your help. I'm coming to Phoenix."

Chapter Four

Michael Noriss rolled to a stop in front of the Western Airline terminal. He got out of the jeep, went to the front fender and hoisted himself up onto it.

Because it was Friday, it wasn't a busy day for arrivals at Phoenix airport. Most of the business was outgoing, which suited Michael just fine. He disliked being in the center of a milling crowd of people who expanded energy pointlessly.

He exhaled, listened to a plane taking off and again wrestled with the unknown. For several weeks he'd been trying to find out exactly what had happened to his friend. It had started with a phone call from Aaron's brother, Richard.

Michael had always liked the easygoing man who was 13 years Aaron's senior.

When he and Aaron were in college, they had spent a good deal of time with Richard and his family. But when Richard had called, Michael had sensed his nervousness. He learned about the aftermath of Aaron's near fatal accident and of his wild claim about what had happened in his brief period of death. Richard believed that Aaron was having serious psychological problems. Both Richard and the police shrink even thought the problem severe enough to put Aaron on indefinite medical leave from the department.

That was where Michael came in. "You have to help him. Please, Michael, you're his closest friend," Richard had pleaded.

"As his friend, or as a shrink?" Michael had questioned.

"Any way you can. Michael, he's bent on ruining his future."

"I'll do what I can," Michael had promised. Then he'd gotten all the information he could from Richard. The next morning he'd called the hospital in Virginia and spoken with the surgeon who'd operated on Aaron, explaining that he was Aaron's new doctor. The surgeon had promised to send him a full report, which had arrived two days later.

Included in the report was a notation concerning Aaron's persistence that he had returned from the dead and that some presumed entity had saved him. The doctor's report confirmed that they had lost the heartbeat for almost a minute and a half before recovering it and successfully completing the operation.

Once he'd finished studying Aaron's case, he'd tried to figure out a way to get Aaron to Phoenix. That problem had solved itself two days ago, when Aaron had called him.

Michael tensed when the automatic doors opened and Aaron stepped through. The tall man, his body well-proportioned, looked as fit as always. He held his head proudly, his dark hair combed neatly, efficiently hiding the scars. He looked the same as always.

But when he got near the car, Michael saw the difference. Dark shadows formed listless half-moons beneath his blue eyes. Within them, Michael saw a haunted and faraway look.

Seeing Michael waiting on the fender on his car, Aaron waved and went over to him.

"Long time, White Man," Michael said.

Aaron put down his suitcase and looked into his friend's face. His smile came slowly, but for the first time in months, it wasn't forced. "Hello, Michael."

The full-blooded Navajo psychologist eased his wiry frame off the fender and drew Aaron into his arms.

"It's good to see you," Aaron said in a voice as tight as his grip.

Michael's eyes swept Aaron's face. "Let's go. We've got some catching up to do."

Aaron tossed his suitcase into the back of the jeep. Three minutes later they were driving toward the Navajo reservation.

The drive to Michael's house took two hours. Neither man spoke of anything except memories of times shared together. Although their friendship was strong, an undertone of wariness filtered into the conversation. It was Aaron who asked questions and Michael who responded by bringing Aaron up-to-date on his life.

Once they were at the house and Aaron's suitcase was unpacked, they settled into lounge chairs on the flagstone patio and sipped Coors.

Sitting across from Michael, Aaron held the cool beer can in one hand as he studied his friend's face. He took in all the subtle changes of the passing years. Michael's features were more heavily defined now, and it seemed that his face had finally matured enough to make his large nose a part of it, rather than being an extra appendage stuck above his mouth. The only other sign of change was in the grooved crow's feet at the corners of his eyes. They had always been there, but now they were chiseled deeper by the Arizona sun.

Aaron took a long pull of beer and then rolled the can between his palms. He didn't speak right away; he wanted to think one more time about what he had to say. Ever since returning to Dallas, Aaron had wanted to call Michael.

He had wanted to tell him what was happening and ask his advice. He believed deeply that Michael Noriss was possibly the only person in Aaron's world who might be able to help him without thinking him crazy.

"You want to know why I'm here?" Aaron asked almost offhandedly.

"When you called, you didn't exactly sound like you were coming out for a vacation."

"I was in an accident."

Michael nodded. "I know. You wrote me about it."

"Only about some of it. There's more."

"I heard."

Aaron stared at Michael, shunting aside the unexpected sensation that Michael had betrayed him. "Richard spoke to you."

"He's concerned."

"He also asked you to help me, right?"

"Does it matter?" Michael asked.

"No." Aaron laughed bitterly.

He broke off his grim laughter, knowing that he was sounding as crazy as people said. "I'm okay." He shifted his eyes to the silver can of beer. "Actually, it makes it easier. I guess Richard also told you that I've become obsessed?"

"I discounted most of what he said," Michael replied in a low voice.

"It's really funny, you know," he said in a rush that released five months of pent-up emotions. He closed his eyes. Too late, he realized. His eyes snapped open, but the image of the woman remained. "They think I'm crazy."

"Are you?"

"I don't know." He laughed again. This time the manic edge was gone, and only a hollow edge of bitterness remained. "But one thing's for sure."

"Yes?"

Aaron held back for a second; then he smiled, a genuine smile. "Richard screwed this one up real good."

"How's that?"

"Because when I tell you exactly what happened to me—the things I haven't told Richard or the shrink—you're going to save my life."

"Aaron—"

"No, don't say anything until I'm finished." He met Michael's steady gaze and held it until Michael finally nodded. Aaron drained the can of beer and held it aloft. "I need another to keep my throat wet. It's a long story."

Michael stood, stretched and went into the kitchen. Aaron watched him, wondering if he really could tell Michael all of what had happened to him. He had tried to call Michael before the other day, but something within him had held him back. Fear?

And now? Now it didn't matter. Things had gone too far, and he needed help. He had to trust someone, and beside being his friend, Michael had one other important asset.

The Others

When Michael returned with the cold beers, Aaron studied the label for several seconds. "How's your hobby? Still dabbling in ghosts and goblins?"

"Parapsychology," Michael said dryly.

"Same thing. Christ," Aaron said, shaking his head, "when I think of all those theories you used to come up with, and all the hours of lectures and seminars . . . Anyway, I've got a hell of a ghost story for you." The popping of the beer can accented Aaron's words. He killed another five seconds with a deep drink before he began to talk.

He spoke for an hour. When he finished, the sun had set and the magnificent Arizona dusk had arrived. The sky was streaked with gray, cinnamon and violet. The shimmering waves of heat rising in the distance pulled the landscape out of focus.

"Interesting," Michael said at last.

Aaron smiled. While he'd spoken, he'd seen Michael's eyes dancing. He'd known, minutes into his story, that Michael was as deeply enmeshed in it as he himself was. When he'd finished, he had sensed Michael was trapped.

"But you know what's the funniest thing of all?"

"I'm sure you're going to enlighten me," Michael said dryly.

"Naturally. The funniest thing of all is that

Richard asked you to help me! You!"

Michael couldn't stop his smile. Aaron's words were true—it *was* funny. But when Michael spoke, there was no amusement in his voice. "Do you want my help?"

Warmth and friendship rushed through Aaron. Gratefully, he nodded his head. "It's more than wanting your help, Michael. I need it!"

They had eaten dinner outside, two thick steaks grilled over charcoal, accompanied by a salad and two more cans of ice cold beer. The stars were out and the sky was still as clear as it had been that afternoon. The intense heat had vanished, replaced by the desert's cool night air.

As Aaron gazed at the sky, he felt a little of his tension diminish. "Are you happy here?"

"Happy is a relative term, but yes," Michael said with a nod.

"You're helping your people, which is what you always wanted to do."

"I'm trying to help."

Aaron picked up the disillusionment in Michael's voice. "They don't want to be helped?"

"They don't think they do. The Dinee—the Navajo—have a hard time admitting their problems."

"They're no different than anyone else."

"Yes, they are, but I can't explain it."

Aaron shrugged. "Where do we go from

here? Are you going to shrink me or help me find her?"

"Both, maybe. How long has it been since you roughed it?"

Aaron thought back. "Since the last time we went camping."

"I've got a great spot picked out in the mountains."

"Nature and all to heal me?"

"Is that what you came here for? To be healed?"

Aaron's mouth went dry. He let several seconds slide by before saying, "I want to know if I'm crazy or if she's real. And if I'm not crazy, I want to find her."

Michael put his hand on Aaron's. "I know you, Aaron, better than anyone else. You're not crazy."

"Thanks. At least that's two of us who think that way."

Michael dug into his shirt pocket. He withdrew two thin white cigarettes, lit them both and handed one to Aaron.

Aaron took the joint and stared at it. "I'm a cop, Michael. I can't smoke this."

"You're on medical leave under my professional care. And besides all of that, this is Indian land. White man's laws don't reach this far," Michael said, taking a deep poke of the grass.

"Michael . . ." he said, staring at the joint. He'd never been much for smoking grass.

D.M. Wind

He'd experimented a few times but had never needed artificial means to alter his mood. But then again, he told himself, he'd never needed Michael's help either.

Aaron took a pull from the joint. He drew the smoke deep into his lungs and held it for a long time. When he released the smoke, he felt the THC's entrance into his mind.

"Tell me about your dreams," Michael said.

Aaron closed his eyes, letting the lightness of the grass further ease his tensions. He willed himself to see her, and he did. When he spoke, his voice was distant against the night sounds.

"Usually the dreams are similar—at least they start and end the same way."

"How do they start?" Michael prompted in a gentle and well-modulated voice.

"It's at night, usually windy but not cold. The wind is gentle. I can see the branches of the trees bending gently. There's a special fragrance—nothing I can name—but whenever I smell it, I know she's near.

"It's as if I'm walking on a layer of clouds, floating. Then I'm walking through trees and I can hear the leaves rustling in the breeze. It's a soothing sound. Delicate.

"When I reach the center of the copse, the fragrance becomes stronger. I turn. She's about twenty feet from me. There's no moon, but I see her perfectly because the night has a golden sheen, like the point in an ocean sunset just before the edge of the sun touches the horizon. The trees and the grass and the woman are illuminated by the sheen."

The joint, forgotten as Aaron spoke, had gone out. He took several seconds to relight it. "I stand still. Maybe because I'm afraid that if I move, she'll disappear. I wait until she comes to me. When she does, the wind tosses her hair. It's long and coal black and perfectly straight.

"She's wearing a dress, but I can make out her body within it. She has a narrow waist, high breasts and a long neck. When she gets closer I see her eyes clearly. They're almond-shaped and very large. The irises are green, jade green and not quite opaque. They're dotted with flecks of gold.

"Her lips are full and her nose is straight. Her cheekbones are prominent, and her skin is porcelain or perhaps alabaster. She's beautiful, Michael, but it's more than the beauty that I see.

"When she reaches me, we just look at each other for a long time. Then I take her hands in mine. I can feel the warmth of her skin, the blood moving through her veins." Aaron paused to take a breath and to order his thoughts. "I know that I'm dreaming, all the while it's happening, but, Michael, it doesn't feel like a dream.

"Then she releases my right hand and strokes my cheek. It's a motion that combines a loving gentleness with strong sexual desire. It's something I've never experienced before. Then her hand goes to the back of my head. She cups my head and draws it to her. We kiss and I seem to fall into her. Her lips are soft. I can feel her body pressing against me. Her breasts push into my chest. Jesus, Michael, I can even feel her nipples stiffen.

"I don't know how long the kiss lasts, but when it's over, it's as if every desire I've ever had has surfaced. But I have full control over myself. I know that nothing more will happen, and while I accept it, I don't like it.

"Finally she steps back. She looks at me, and her eyes become luminous. It's as though she's trying to speak to me with her mind, but I can't hear her. Then her eyes widen, and I see fear come into them. She opens her mouth, but no words come out. Her lips form a surprised 'O', and she begins to fade."

Aaron's breath rattled in his throat as he fought to finish what he was saying. "The scent in the air changes, too. It becomes offensive. I can sense another presence, something harsh, something . . . bad."

Aaron opened his eyes and met his friend's stare. "Maybe I *am* crazy."

"Is that the only dream?" Michael asked.

"There are others. They're similar, but like I said, they always start and end the same way. In some of them we just walk along a grassy plateau. In others, we hold each other and make love. Can you imagine that? I don't know who the hell she is, but I can make love with her in my dreams."

"Have you been with anyone since the accident?"

"Been with a woman?" Aaron asked, grinning.

"Have you?"

"No."

"Why not?"

"I guess that's what convinced the shrink in Dallas that I was loco. I have no desire to be with another woman, just her."

"Not loco. I believe he thought you were fixated on a subconscious fantasy figure derived from brain trauma and guilt."

"And Richard believes I'm obsessed. What do you think?"

"I'd give a hell of a lot to meet this lady," Michael said, his eyes riveted on Aaron's.

"So would I."

"Richard also mentioned something about unauthorized tapping into computers."

"You could call it that. I went into several government computers trying to find out who she is."

"Fill me in."

Aaron shrugged. "I started with the F.B.I. data base, at first to find out what the hell was going on at the government property in Virginia. I found nothing. Then I went into their CCNI network. It's a missing person information network available to all police departments. I fed in her description and came up with a zero.

"I was okay up to that point, but then I stepped over the line. I broke into the C.I.A.'s data base. Before I was caught, I found a cross reference to Sperry Hollow. It's a D.O.D. project. But nothing else."

"You broke into the C.I.A. computer?" Michael said. "I thought that was impossible."

"Hard, not impossible. But I wasn't thinking ahead. An hour after I'd gotten off line, the chief had me on the carpet. I told him I'd made a mistake in programing. He bought it and smoothed things over with the spooks."

"Why didn't you stop there?" Michael asked.

"Would you? The next day I went into the Department of Defense computer. I was careful this time, but when I called up the file, I got kicked out. I did it three more times, until I worked out the password."

"And?"

"And nothing. There was a secondary password needed to access more than the directory. I tried, but I stayed on line too long. I got caught good this time—red-handed as they say, no pun intended. That's when I had to start seeing the department shrink."

Michael nodded slowly. "What did you learn?"

"Nothing. The D.O.D. is using the Sperry enclave for a research project called Doorway. That's all I know."

"Doorway?" Michael said.

The Others

Aaron stared at Michael, puzzled by the sudden tightness in his friend's voice. "Does that mean something?"

Michael stood and looked up at the sky. A moment later he said, "It may."

Chapter Five

Michael handed Aaron a fresh can of beer. "Tell me what happened when you got home from Virginia."

Aaron followed the tail of a shooting star. "I wanted to find out whether I had imagined her when I was on the operating table, or if she was real. It was the dreams that made me believe. They didn't start right away; they came later, about a month after I got home. But, Michael, something inside me was changed.

"When the dreams came, I couldn't stop them. I tried staying awake. I used uppers, anything. But the minute I dozed off, she was there." He shook his head. "I was so damned desperate that I confided in my brother. You know what he did?"

When Michael remained silent, Aaron went on. "Halfway through my story, he turned away. He couldn't face me."

"That's when he asked you to go see the department shrink?"

"He didn't ask. He ordered me to go. He went over my head and had a department memo issued. Then he told me that he'd done it for my own good.

"When I had my first session with Doctor Reed, I decided to be open about what happened. Do you know what that got me?"

Michael nodded. "I read his reports."

"Neurotic was his first thought," Aaron continued, as if Michael hadn't spoken. "A month later the good doctor decided I was becoming psychotic, fixated with my delusion of the woman on the road. I knew it was hopeless then."

"Nothing is ever hopeless."

Aaron looked up from the beer can. "That's why I'm here, isn't it? To find out?"

"Yes," Michael said. "And to be with someone you can trust." Michael's eyes went distant. "Did you ever think we'd end up as friends?"

Aaron shook his head. "I suppose you call our becoming roommates fate?"

"Better than what you called it. The random selection of the university computer, wasn't it?"

Aaron smiled. "Yes. It's funny, isn't it? Two more opposite people don't exist."

"Two more like-minded people don't exist either," Michael said pointedly.

D.M. Wind

"Like-minded, not like-thinking." When they'd met, Aaron had known that they had a lot in common. Time had proved him right. Both had quick minds and found studying easy. They disliked the immaturity of college life and enjoyed getting away from people.

Their differences were in their interests. Aaron was a totally logical person. For everything that happened, Aaron found a reason. On the other hand, Michael had always professed a belief that there were things that happened for which there was no explanations based on concrete fact. This Michael accepted; this Aaron refused to concede.

They were perfect foils, keeping each other sharp, intellectually and physically. When they graduated—Aaron with a degree in computer science, Michael with his first psych degree— they both returned for post-graduate courses.

While Michael entered a special Master's-Ph.D program, Aaron went for his Master's in computer science and then for a second Master's in forensic science. During those tough three and a half years, they shared a small two bedroom apartment off campus.

Their only ongoing argument was in Aaron's contention that there were no supernatural or paranormal happenings. Everything, he believed, could be attributed to some form of reality.

Yet he watched Michael spend hours in the parapsychology labs or attending whatever seminar or lecture was available on the paranormal. They had argued constantly, but Aaron never put down Michael's interests even though he didn't believe in them.

"Whatever the reason behind our friendship," Aaron said, picking up the conversation again, "I'm glad." Then, feeling worn out by the effects of the trip and half-drunk on the combination of grass and beer, Aaron said good night to his friend and stumbled off to bed.

Morning came—and with it the hated consciousness. It was the worst time of day for Aaron, for as usual he had dreamed of her again. And even though the dreams always ended with that other hostile force, Aaron hated to face the day knowing that he would spend it fighting the overwhelming need to go back to Virginia and look for her.

He gazed out at the strong Arizona sun. The brightness of the new day lent Aaron hope that Michael might be able to help.

Until yesterday, when he'd sat across from his friend, he had wondered what was happening to his life. Now he knew. He was going to find her, no matter what obstructed his way. He and Michael would find her.

"Hey, White Man, you up?" Michael called from the doorway.

"I am now," he replied, stretching and throwing the light sheet from him. "What time is it?"

"Seven. Coffee's on." Aaron used the bathroom and decided against shaving. He dressed in jeans and a tee shirt. When he stepped into the kitchen, he smelled the coffee. Michael was already at the table, drinking from a steaming mug. Through the doorway, Aaron saw camping equipment piled in the hallway.

"Where are we going?" Aaron asked, pouring himself a cup of coffee.

"To a special place, if I can get permission."

"That sounds ominous."

"No. But it's a place I want you to experience. Hungry?"

"The coffee'll do fine."

Michael nodded. "I've got the jeep loaded. All you'll need are a couple of shirts and another pair of jeans."

Aaron sipped the coffee. "Michael," he began, but paused, searching for the right words.

"It'll work out," Michael said calmly.

An hour later Michael pulled off what he laughingly told Aaron was the reservation's main road and started onto a hard-packed dirt road that led southeast toward a high range of mountains.

Looking around, Aaron experienced a sense of insignificance. The land stretched for miles in every direction. Random stands of cactus reflected darkly off the sun.

Ahead the mountains grew taller. A few minutes later Aaron made out the defining lines ringing the mountains' sides. Bands of rusty red bled into gray, before fading into brown, then green, and then evolving into sand-colored layers that rose skyward like a mad baker's wildest achievement.

The mountains were awesome in scope and in power. They held no softness, no gentleness, as did the green mountains of the northeast. Yet they were utterly magnificent in their stark beauty.

This had always been a hard land, Aaron thought, and it had bred a hard people. He glanced at Michael. Michael's people were a shadow of what they once were, but even today Aaron saw the proud strength of Michael's Navajo blood.

"Almost there," Michael said.

"Almost where?"

For an answer, Michael pointed to a dot on the landscape. Squinting, Aaron saw a small adobe house.

"Grandfather lives there."

"Your grandfather?" Aaron asked, puzzled. Michael had told him that he had no living relatives.

"Grandfather is the wise man of our tribe. He is the oldest living member of the council and knows things that we can only imagine. And Aaron," Michael said after a moment, "you are

51

Belagana—a white man. Speak to him only if he speaks directly to you."

Aaron detected a tone that he thought bordered on the reverential. He had never heard that tone in Michael's voice before. He remained silent until Michael stopped in front of the house and, motioning to Aaron, stepped down.

Michael took out a shopping bag from the back of the jeep and started toward the house. Before he reached the door, it swung open to reveal one of the oldest men Aaron had ever seen. The old man smiled toothlessly at them.

"*Ya-tah*, Grandfather," Michael said in greeting.

"*Ya-ta-hey*, Seedling," he replied. He gazed into Michael's eyes for a moment before glancing at the bag in Michael's hand. "You have brought a bribe."

"A large one," Michael said, reaching into the bag and retrieving a three liter bottle of Paul Masson Chablis.

"Why is it," the old man asked when his gaze shifted to Aaron, his deep-set eyes staring openly at him, "that it was left to the *Belagana* to discover wine?"

Aaron tried to ignore the intensity coming from the old man's eyes. "So that Michael would be able to bring it to you as a gift," Aaron said as lightly as he could manage.

"He is the one I saw," the old man stated before stepping inside and motioning them to follow.

The Others

"You saw me?" Aaron asked, forgetting Michael's warning against speaking unless spoken to.

The old man went to the far wall and placed the bottle of wine on a shelf. "In my casting," Grandfather said when he turned back to them.

Aaron glanced about. The house was a large single room. There were underlying scents of mustiness and animals, but the dwelling was clean, almost fastidiously so. The walls were painted with hieroglyphics. The only furniture was an old table and two chairs near the stove. In the corner, on the ground, was a sleeping pallet with a single neatly folded blanket. Hanging from the ceiling were a dozen petrified birds. In a jar on a shelf in the middle of the far wall was a rattlesnake. In the center of the room was a circle of stones eight feet in diameter; within the circle were several paintings.

Staring at the circle, Aaron realized that what he was looking at were not paintings but images made of colored sand.

"Then you know why I am here, Grandfather," Michael said.

"I know. I am saddened that you seek that which may destroy you," the old man said, his dark eyes riveted to Michael's face.

"You deny me permission?"

"I deny you nothing. You, Seedling, are all that I have left. No other comes to me. None believe in the old ways. Only you seek my knowledge, only you seek to learn more about

53

The Way of our people, about *Yo'zho*. You are a man now, responsible for yourself. As such, I can deny you nothing. I can only warn you."

"Then we may go into the mountain?" Michael asked.

The old man studied Michael for several moments before settling his stare on Aaron. "He has been called upon. You must help him. That is what is decreed by the spirits."

"You said you saw Aaron?" Michael prompted.

The old man went to the circle, and Michael followed. Aaron stayed a short distance behind them, still unsure of what he was feeling.

"There," Grandfather said, pointing a gnarled finger at one of the sand paintings. There were several stick figures in it—some like humans, some like animals, and one like a bird.

Although Aaron was puzzled, Michael seemed to understand the painting. "Those?" Michael asked, pointing to the strange looking animals.

The old man said something in Navajo.

"Shapeshifters," Michael whispered loud enough for Aaron to hear. "I will be careful, Grandfather."

"You understand it all?" asked the old man. His eyes were alive as they searched Michael's face.

"Most of it, but I'm not sure of the last drawing."

"No man can look at such and be sure. You have learned well, Seedling. I am proud of you."

Watching the interplay between the two, Aaron realized that Michael did look at the old man as though he were his grandfather. The emotions flickering on Michael's face matched those on the old man's. Aaron sensed the two were a family.

"I will be careful," Michael repeated. "Thank you, Grandfather."

The old man looked at Aaron again. His face hardened into a mask carved from stone and lined with cracks of age and weather. "Michael is your brother, in spirit if not in flesh. Care for him. His life is in your hands."

Something crawled along Aaron's flesh. Fear, he realized, fear of the intensity of the words. "I will."

"There is great evil loose upon the world. You will either succumb to it or stop it." The old man gave a disparaging shake of his head before turning to Michael.

"Be careful, Seedling, but hold not back of yourself. You will need all." Then the old man reached into his medicine pouch and withdrew several objects. "You will need these tonight."

Michael put them in his pocket. "Good-bye, Grandfather." Stepping back, Michael turned and signaled Aaron to follow.

When the adobe house was far behind them and Aaron spoke, he found his voice shaky.

"What the hell was that all about?"

"Grandfather is the last *Yataalii*. He is the last shaman of our tribe," Michael said in a sad voice.

"Your last medicine man. Why?"

"He is more than just a medicine man. He is a wise man, a healer and a leader, but he is also the last of his sort. My people are losing themselves. They follow the ways of the white man, accepting blindly whatever they're given while turning their backs on their heritage in the hopes of finding something better."

"Which means that the Indian is human also. It's human nature to want what others have."

"I know. So does Grandfather."

"What's his name?"

"I don't know. He was called Grandfather long before I was born. He's well over a hundred."

"Jesus."

"Not quite," Michael said tersely.

"He said no others come to him, that you are his last. You're his student?"

"Apprentice. I'm learning the old ways."

"To keep the traditions alive?" Aaron's interest was genuine now that the creepy sensations he'd undergone in the house were passing.

"That too," Michael said with a grin. "He has knowledge of medicines that doctors have only recently discovered. They've been a part of our history for hundreds of years. In many ways Grandfather is more knowledgeable than most doctors."

The Others

"Grandfather said that no one comes to him anymore."

"Not the young. Only the few very old, and they will be gone much too soon. The rest go to the government clinics."

"Do you want to become a medicine man?" This time Aaron couldn't quite hide his humor.

"No," Michael replied seriously. "I just want to learn about it."

Aaron gazed at his friend for a moment. "How did Grandfather know I was coming? You told him, didn't you?"

Michael shook his head once. "He saw you. He drew you inside the circle. He is *Yataalii*, Aaron. He is one with The Way. He has visions. He can see things that are denied to most people. He saw you, Aaron. He saw you long before you even thought about coming to Arizona."

Silence fell, lasting until they reached the end of the road and entered the foothills. Ten minutes later, Michael stopped the jeep. "We go in on foot from here."

Aaron joined Michael at the back of the jeep and helped adjust Michael's backpack. When Michael did the same for him, Aaron said, "What did he mean that your life was in my hands?"

Michael looked at the high-rising mountain near them. When he spoke, his voice was low and strained. "Grandfather cast the sands last night. He saw the future in it. Our future."

Chapter Six

Orange flames licked skyward, the only light in a dark and moonless night. They were camped at the base of a tall mountain with a sheer side. In every direction, mountains loomed high and powerful.

Aaron lay on his sleeping roll, warm and content from the meal they'd finished an hour ago. He was more relaxed than he'd been in months and appreciative of Michael's silent company.

"It's been too long since I've done something like this. It's beautiful here. It's like an oasis where nothing can bother me."

"It's a good feeling," Michael agreed.

"You were right; this is a special place. I feel as if we're the first people to be here to feel its peacefulness."

The Others

"It is special, but not in the way you think. We are on sacred grounds."

Aaron sat up. Michael's face shone with the reflected light from the fire. "I can see why."

"No, Aaron, not that way. Not even today, with the millions of people clogging this country, do any come here. Very few white men have ever been on this spot. And I personally know only one who has gone where you will go tomorrow."

The seriousness in Michael's voice made Aaron pay very close attention.

"For hundreds of years this mountain has been part of our tribe. It is here where we honor our dead. It is here where we bury them."

"Oh, shit, Michael, are we camping in a cemetery?"

"Within this mountain," he said, pointing to the sheer wall behind him, "is our burial grounds."

"Why didn't you wait until tomorrow to tell me?" Aaron asked, only half in jest.

"Because we must start tonight."

"Start what? Are you going to tell me Indian ghost stories?"

Michael's smile grew. "No. You're going to tell me one."

"Michael . . ." Aaron began, but Michael waved away his protest.

"Do you think we started so early this morning for no purpose? We've been on the go for fourteen hours. We've driven for three and walked another two. We set up camp, and then we climbed. We're tired, but only physically tired. True?"

Aaron thought about it and realized Michael was right. They had been so active all afternoon that he'd hardly thought about her at all. "True. What story do you want to hear?"

"I want you to tell me about the woman again, from the very first instant you saw her on the road."

Aaron nodded, but before he could speak, Michael raised his hand again. "Wait."

The word was not a request; it was an order. Aaron waited while Michael extracted a piece of whatever the old man had given him from his shirt pocket.

Michael put the leathery thing on a rock, drew his knife and quartered it. Then he cut a quarter in two and handed the smallest piece to Aaron.

"Chew it. Don't swallow it—just your saliva."

Aaron took it. "More games?"

"Do you trust me?"

Aaron put it in his mouth. Ignoring the bitter dry taste, he chewed, working up saliva and swallowing.

"It's peyote. It will help to ease some of the subconscious inhibitions inside your mind. It will also make your thoughts clearer."

"My thoughts have never been clouded about her."

"We'll see. Close your eyes, and listen to my voice."

Aaron closed his eyes. A short time later a weightlessness eased through his body. It felt good.

"Think about that night. Not the accident, but the woman. You're driving, coming out of the turn when you see her. Tell me what you see."

Michael's words had a strange effect on Aaron. One moment he was in Arizona; in the next he was behind the wheel again, feeling the power of the Corvette. He spoke slowly, enunciating his words carefully as he described his first sight of her. Every detail of that night returned with an expanded clarity that filled him with wonder. And then, following Michael's gentle urging, Aaron retold his tale.

When he finished, he opened his eyes. His mind was clear, and although he knew he had ingested only a small amount of the drug, he was soothed by its tranquil effect.

"Think again. When you first saw her, what did she look like?"

"That's what bothers me. When my headlights first caught her, I thought it was an animal in the road. A large dog, maybe a wolf. But when she stood, I realized it was a woman. She must have fallen and was just getting to her feet when I came around the curve."

"Close your eyes. Picture that shape again, just as your headlights hit it."

Aaron did. He saw the wolf, and he saw something else. His mouth turned dry. "It's almost like two forms—one coming out from the other."

"Did she look frightened when she turned toward you?" Michael asked.

"No. Resigned. Her arms were open, as if she were going to . . ."

"To what?"

Aaron opened his eyes. "This is crazy."

"Tell me!"

"Embrace me. Embrace my car." Aaron took a deep breath. "Like I said, crazy."

"Maybe, maybe not. In your dreams you've said you can sense another force, an evil force."

"I never said evil. Dark, bad."

"Same thing. Aaron, have you read any of the books that deal with the experience you underwent? The case histories of people who died and came back?"

"All of them. That's when Richard thought I had gone around the bend. I ordered every book on the subject, and then went on to books about reincarnation."

"What did you think of them?"

"The reincarnation books were supposedly documented experiences of former lives. I can't accept that. But the other books—the ones about people dying, leaving their body, and then returning—they described what I went through."

"All of it?"

"Only the parts about leaving the body and rising to the pure light. Which is what happened."

"To a degree," Michael said. "Aaron, I've read those books, too, but I've never heard of an experience like yours. No one has ever reported an entity of some kind stopping them from reaching the light. What they've all said was that they were drawn back to their bodies. You say you were forced back, taken back almost physically."

Aaron watched his friend, wondering where he was leading.

"I've worked with a few people who have experienced death," Michael continued. "They don't have the dreams that you do. And they are usually peaceful afterward, not obsessed by searching for the answer to what happened to them."

"And?" Aaron asked, feeling a rush of excitement at his friend's words.

"I'm not sure. I may be able to help you, but . . ." Michael's words trailed off. Aaron saw his friend's gaze harden. "A month ago I would never have considered talking to you about any of this. You've always been the logical one, the person who sought and found solid answers to problems. You were the one who always had to find the realistic cause behind anything. You never looked past the planes of the physical, and you've never been able to accept my theories on the paranormal."

"You think I've changed?" Aaron asked.

"Have you?"

Aaron continued to hold Michael's penetrating stare. Although he was still affected by the peyote, he knew he was in control of himself. He took his time thinking about Michael's question. He understood that somehow this question was of enormous importance to Michael as well as himself. He searched inside himself before saying, "Have I changed? I think so."

"I sure as hell hope so, White Man."

"Try me."

Michael nodded. "All right. But you're going to have to suspend your inflexibility concerning your perception of the world."

Their eyes locked. The only sound was the crackling of the fire. Carried within the silence was the certainty that Aaron had to make a choice. Whatever his decision, it was one he would have to live with for the rest of his life.

He'd been alone for the last five months, feeling and experiencing things that no one believed or accepted. Now he had someone who would listen to him and who might be able to help him. Still, his whole life had been structured around the acceptance of concrete facts, not in the beliefs of illusionary metaphysical phenomena.

Suddenly, Aaron understood that his decision already had been made that night in Virginia. "She was real. She was there, and I have to find her," he said, speaking as much to himself as to Michael. "Whatever it takes, I'll do it."

Michael's breath hissed outward. "The occult, the paranormal, the metaphysical and the parapsychological are names used to explain away those things which go beyond normal comprehension.

"Ghosts, demons, vampires and evil spirits are considered to be the occult. Telepathy, telekineses, pyrokineses and precognition fall under the classification of parapsychology. Werewolves, shapechangers and shapeshifters are what we call the metaphysical.

"But generally," Michael said, "unexplained happenings have a tendency to be called the supernatural."

Aaron watched the animation in Michael's face. He felt himself flowing with his friends words, not necessarily agreeing or disagreeing.

"Aaron, you're more than aware that I've been doing a lot of studying on these subjects. I've seen—" Michael paused and shook his head. "What I'm trying to say is that through my research, I may have come across something important. While my discoveries aren't unique, there are very few people in the field of parapsychology who have explored this particular avenue."

"Which is?" Aaron asked, impatience suddenly getting the better of him.

"Parallel worlds."

Aaron bit back a nervous chuckle. "I thought we were talking about the supernatural, not about science fiction."

"Does it matter what label you use?"

It wasn't the words, but the way they were spoken that made Aaron realize he had no argument for Michael's logic. "Go ahead."

"The most popular of parallel world theories is that there are an infinite number of worlds, all coexisting with our own. On each of these worlds, life has evolved differently from our own. Some in only slight ways, others in more startling ways.

"For example, on one world the Germans won World War Two. On another, England still rules the American colonies. On another, Rome dominates its world, and the pagan gods rule supreme."

"Which has nothing to do with my situation."

Michael sighed loudly. "I don't know how your people ever defeated my ancestors. You don't have a damned bit of patience."

"Michael . . ."

"I said I was going to help you. Have the courtesy to listen to me." Aaron nodded apologetically. "The theory that I find the most kinship with is one that espouses the idea that if we evolved on a physical/scientific level, why couldn't one of the parallel worlds evolve along metaphysical lines? Why couldn't these beings communicate via telepathy in the same way that we use a telephone? What about were-wolves and shapeshifters? Couldn't this be a replacement for a gun in hunting? Since we invented cars to travel long distances, could these people not change into another form to cover the distances? How about becoming a bird to go from here to Phoenix? Think about the possibilities."

Aaron shook his head slowly. "I agreed to listen to you, to try and accept your theories, but, Michael, you're sounding more like a fiction writer than a psychologist."

"Pretend you understand me, just for another minute."

"Understand what? That on some freaked out parallel world, people become birds and talk with their minds instead of their mouths?"

"Yes, damn it! That's exactly what I want you to believe. Aaron, I think your woman is trying to communicate with you, using telepathy."

Aaron fought the swift rise of his temper. "I didn't come here for you to make fun of me."

"Damn it, Aaron! You're the one who told me that you think she's trying to talk to you in your dreams. You said it, not me. That's called telepathy. When you saw her that first time on the road, she appeared animallike. That's shapeshifting!"

"So now she's a werewolf?" Aaron shouted, sarcastically. "She fell down on the road!"

"Bullshit!" Michael said, his eyes narrowing.

Aaron tried to shake away the power of his friend's glare but could not. He reminded himself that he had come to Michael for help. His anger lessened, and he exhaled slowly. "All right, even if what you're saying is possible, and she's from another world, how the hell did she get here in the first place? Better yet, why did she even come?"

"Both questions have the same answer. Theoretically—"

Aaron cut him off sharply. "Theories, Michael. What about facts?"

"Theoretically," Michael continued, "it's believed that occasionally a doorway between worlds comes into existence. A doorway that opens into our world."

"If this theory of yours is viable, how do the doorways work—and why?"

"I don't know. If I did, I would have gone through one by now."

Aaron believed him, totally. "How about one of your theories to explain it?"

"I have two. One is that some physical force, perhaps an electromagnetic energy or possibly a spatial warp, causes a doorway. The other is that there are certain stress points between the worlds, and at those junctures a doorway exists. It could be a combination of the two. I don't know."

Trying hard to curb his distaste of the subject matter, Aaron said, "How does this tie in with me?"

"I'll get to that. Let me finish what I started." When Aaron nodded, Michael picked up his narrative. "When a doorway opens, and if there is someone in the vicinity, they may fall into this world. The common theory is that these people are from a plane—a world—that evolved similar to ours, except in one aspect. Where we went through a physical-scientific form of evolution, they evolved along a metaphysical level. This would explain the supernatural."

"But are they human like us?"

"As far as their normal body shape is concerned. But what makes us human—our bodies or our minds?"

"And thereby the legends of werewolves and vampires are born," Aaron said, this time unable to curb his sarcasm. "But if they're like us physically, why do we fear them? Why are the legends always evil?"

"I have theories on that, too."

"Naturally."

"But until I find someone from another world to study, they'll just stay theories."

About to make another acerbic comment, the implication of Michael's words hit him like a hammer. Michael's face twisted out of focus. "You son-of-a-bitch."

Michael smiled.

"You believe me. You damn well believe me. You want to use me. You hope she's from a parallel world, don't you?"

"You got that one right, White Man."

Aaron felt the perfection of his friend's trap. Michael had outmaneuvered him all the way. "Okay, tell me about your theory."

Michael continued to grin as he spoke. "My first theory is that, perhaps like us, these people are both good and bad. Their bad people or their criminals might be considered evil in our world. But are they evil or just insane?

"Think about it. If you suddenly found yourself on a world that was the total opposite of your own, how would you react? These people arrive here without warning, without knowing what's happened to them. Wouldn't they view us with fear? Wouldn't they be frightened and become defensive?"

Aaron's thoughts whirled. Michael's theory frightened him because the germ had been planted and he was starting to believe. "You said that there were other theories?"

"Sure, but if you're having trouble with that one, the next may put you around the bend."

"Not any more than I already am," Aaron said, shifting self-consciously and drawing his sweaty shirt from his skin without realizing that there should be no reason for him to sweat. The temperature of the mountain air had dropped 20 degrees in the last hour.

"Aaron, I've spent my life steeped in the legends and history of my people, especially the history that Grandfather taught me. I used that as a base when I started researching the paranormal. I've found some very strong correlations between my people's legends and the paranormal.

"I've seen the likeness of a man considered to be a werewolf. I saw the same likeness in its animal form. They were both twelfth century woodcarvings from Germany, which matched almost exactly a drawing from seventeenth century Rumania and another from eighteenth century America. The American drawing was of a Sioux Sachem, a medicine man."

"Which means?" Aaron asked.

"That maybe there aren't a whole lot of these people. It could also mean that these people are as close to immortal as we could ever imagine. Which also brings to mind the possibility that living for untold centuries could make a person insane, turn them evil. They could be the reality behind the legends."

Aaron shivered. His friend's words and the last of the peyote had joined forces to form a mental image of irrepressible horror. "And?"

"And I want to know all about them."

"You really believe that she's one of them?" Aaron asked, hoping suddenly that she was not what Michael theorized.

"Do you want to find out?" Michael said in a very low voice.

Aaron closed his eyes. He had known that it would come down to this. "I have to find her first."

"I know how."

Aaron opened his eyes and stared silently.

"If she's from a parallel world and she's trying to contact you, I think we can accomplish that by using astral plane projection."

"Astrology?"

He shook his head. "It's a method used to project your consciousness onto another plane, a purely mental plane."

"What would I do there?"

Michael gazed at Aaron for so long that Aaron became uncomfortable. And then Michael said, "Find her, of course."

Chapter Seven

"Find her, of course." Michael's words kept echoing within Aaron's mind, building in power and stirring his own need to find her. It was his obsession, his compulsion. Yet doubt and logic were still strong in him.

"And how would I get to this astral plane?"

"I'll take you there," Michael said casually, stretching out his arm toward Aaron.

In the center of Michael's open palm rested another piece of peyote. "Michael . . ."

"Do you want to find her, or do you want to keep playing head games with yourself?"

"Nothing seems real anymore."

"Take it, Aaron."

"Why?"

"There are experienced people who can put

themselves into a trance in order to reach another plane. You're not one of them. We have to overcome certain inhibitions," Michael said, his voice devoid of condescension.

Aaron took the peyote. "Have you ever done it? Gone to the astral plane?"

Michael looked up toward the stars. "Once."

Aaron heard both longing and fear in the answer. It was enough to stop any more questions. "I don't want to trip."

"You won't. Take it and trust me, Aaron. I'm your guide. I'll watch over you. It will be similar to hypnosis. Just listen to my voice. Do what I say and don't fight me."

Logically, Aaron knew he should put an end to this. Then the haunting vision of the unknown woman arose, and he knew he was too far involved to back out.

He put the peyote in his mouth and chewed, letting his saliva build before swallowing. He did this for several minutes, until his mind began to react.

The surrounding world faded. The fire rose in random silhouettes of unearthly images. He stared into the fire, trying to see through the flames.

"Aaron," Michael said softly.

It took Aaron a moment to focus on his friend. When he looked at him, Michael said, "Lie back."

When Aaron was lying down, Michael said, "Close your eyes."

The Others

Aaron tried, but each time he did, the world spun like during a drinking binge. "I can't." He felt Michael take his hand and clasp it tightly.

"Try again."

The warmth and strength of Michael's hand became his anchor. With it, the world steadied, and he closed his eyes.

"Good," Michael said. "Concentrate on yourself. Feel your body, your entire body. Feel your heart pumping. Feel your blood flowing."

Suddenly, Aaron could almost see his body stretched out on the bedroll. He felt his heart contract and expand. He envisioned the blood drawn sluggishly into one chamber, being revitalized, and then pushed out again to race through his veins and arteries. He traced the flow of his life's fluid, flowing within its infinite energy. He had never felt more alive, more attuned to his body.

"Good," he heard Michael say from a distance. "Look outward, look into the universe, Aaron. There's a rainbow there, a rainbow with every color of the spectrum. See it. Go to it."

It appeared in the distance, hazy and light-years away. As he concentrated on the rainbow, it grew bolder, raced closer. The colors melted across his eyelids, electrifying in their brilliance. A multifarious shower of color rode the highway of his mind.

"Pick one," Michael commanded. "Pick her color!"

Following Michael's command, Aaron

reached out to the rainbow. He didn't know how he did it, but he did. The universal rainbow was made of a hundred colors in thousands of shades, but there was only one color that called to him—a narrow band of amber-gold. He stared at it, wondering how he could see the rainbow with his eyes closed.

"Are you there? Do you see it?" Michael asked, his hand tightening on Aaron's.

"See it," Aaron mumbled without breaking his concentration.

"Don't just look at it. Feel it. Touch it. Blend with it. Become a part of it. It feels good, doesn't it?"

Aaron wasn't aware of his grunt of pleasure as he merged with the amber-gold band. It was like a heated bath, surrounding him with soothing, pleasant waves of warmth. Then everything turned golden.

"You are one with the color, Aaron. It is a part of you. You control it. It does not control you. Remember, Aaron, you control your plane. Go now. Project your mind, and explore this new universe."

He felt Michael release his hand. And then Aaron floated within his universal matrix. His need to become one with the rainbow grew stronger. He remembered Virginia and that strange, wrenching sensation. He imagined it again and willed it to happen. The sensation of floating grew more pronounced. There was a tentative pressure within his mind that held him back. He thought himself free of it—and he was!

And then he was adrift in the golden universe.

Looking down, he saw the ground was far beneath him. He gazed upon his body lit by the campfire. Michael was still sitting next to him, talking to him.

"Go, Aaron, and find her with your mind. Search for her with your thoughts."

He experienced another shifting sensation, and he was standing on a golden plateau. He was surrounded by the whispering trees of his dreams. Above him lazed clouds of platinum and silver in a lavender sky. When he took a step forward, he glided on a sward of amber grass.

He stood still, unable to believe he was in a bodiless state. He thought about her, pictured her long black hair floating behind her. He made himself see her eyes, luminescent and warm, set within the alabaster confines of her face.

Where are you? He sent the question outward, using his mind to push it as he searched for her.

Sometime later came a gentle caress within the center of his mind. He had never before felt its like, but instinctively he knew it to be the caress of someone who knew another intimately. Within it was the feel of love.

I am here.

As the thought reached him, he knew her name. It was Kali. *Kali*, he said, using his thoughts.

Aaron, came the returning thought.

Aaron pictured himself with the ability to see her. He turned on the soft golden grass and saw her walking toward him.

She stopped before him. Once more he felt her sweet caress within his mind. He reached for her with his hands, but nothing happened.

Use your mind.

He sent his thoughts to her, reaching for her mentally and caressing Kali as she had caressed him in his dreams. *We have been here before.*

Many times, Kali agreed.

But this is different.

Before, when I spoke to you, you did not hear me.

But now I do. I have learned the way.

You have always known it. It was a part of your heritage that your people chose to ignore. You had but to open your mind. Now you will have no need to use the drug again.

Never having experienced this intimate a level of communication with anyone, he did not know what to expect. But while he spoke with Kali, he learned. Her thoughts reached him as distinctly as words. There was other information that he gained without trying, as though it were wrapped within the covering of her silent thoughts.

78

The Others

Although Aaron reveled within Kali's thoughts, he knew he must learn more about her. *Who are you?* he asked, hating the analytical part of his mind for compelling him to ask the question. Her thoughts changed. She grew distant but did not withdraw from his mind.

Must you know?

If I am to come for you, I must know. He sensed her draw further away. Within his mind was a sensation of loss. *No! Stay with me.*

When you learn what I am, you will hate me.

No! My mind is open to you. I cannot hate you.

For now. But later you will.

Why?

Because of what I am.

I will not hate you! he told her, his thoughts strong and determined. Bound within those thoughts were his emotions, emotions he was only beginning to understand.

Her thoughts came, shaded with sadness. *Aaron, I was wrong that night in asking what I did. You must forget me. Forget that night. That is why I tried to contact you.*

No! You gave me my life. And you gave me your love.

It cannot be.

Why were you on the road that night? Why did you tell me to find you?

Her thoughts turned cold, but she withdrew no further from his mind. *I was trying to die.*

I wanted my life to be over. But when I stood before you, waiting to be struck, you tried to sacrifice yourself for me. I could not allow that to be.

Why?

I am not from your world. I cannot go back to mine. I wanted to end my imprisonment. I did not know I would fall in love with you, but when I touched your mind, something happened. I asked you to find me in a moment of weakness. I should not have let that happen.

But it did! He heard her laugh then. It was a bittersweet refrain that eased his tension.

You do not question what I have told you.

Aaron looked around the golden plateau, a place he would not have believed in ten minutes ago. *I question nothing you tell me.*

Why?

Aaron did not reply immediately. Why? he asked himself. When the answer came, he knew it for the truth. His obsession with her was more than just a dream of some sort of afterlife. It was deeper and more basic. He looked at her and opened his mind.

No, Kali told him. *It is wrong. I put this compulsion upon you.*

And I accepted it.

Is it so easy to love? Kali asked.

Not easy at all. But I will not let you go now that I've found you again.

You cannot come for me. I want nothing to happen to you.

The Others

It has already happened. Kali, trust me.
I do.
Where are you from?
Here—but not here.
A parallel world?
That is what they say, came her gentle thought. Then Aaron felt something change. *No!*

Kali's word was like an explosion in his mind, shattering the warmth they shared. And as it had happened in his dreams, Aaron smelled that putrid odor, a rankness that reviled his senses.

What? he asked as the air around them changed. Aaron felt that other presence from his dream, but this time he also felt the deep evil that corrupted the other presence. And with this taint of evil came the first stirrings of fear.

He has returned. I scent blood. Something has happened—something terrible. He knows I am projecting. He's seeking me. Aaron, do not come for me. Do not!

Who is seeking you? he asked, trying to draw her thoughts closer and protect her from whatever it was.

Too late, came her cry. Aaron felt her recede from his mind. *I will find you,* he called after her.

Do not come. It is too dangerous.

And then she was gone, and he was tumbling through the universe, falling back toward the earth and his body.

"Aaron . . . Aaron . . . Aaron . . ." came a far-away voice. Aaron focused on the sound of Michael's voice and felt the pressure of his friend's hand on his.

He opened his eyes. "Jesus," was all he could say.

"Sit up," Michael said, pulling Aaron up by his hand.

A moment later, Aaron took a deep breath. "Kali."

"Kali?" Michael asked, repeating the strange word.

"Her name is Kali."

"You found her. I—"

"Give me a minute." Aaron checked himself, looking inwardly to see if any traces of the drug were still in his mind. He found all his senses surprisingly clear.

"I found her. Her name is Kali. Michael, you're right."

"Right?"

"She is from a parallel world." After saying this, he looked at his friend. What he saw made him pause. Michael's eyes were wide, his mouth hung half-open. He stayed that way for several seconds.

"Tell me what happened."

Aaron wanted to tell Michael, and he would—but not at this moment. He needed time to think about what had happened.

"In the morning. Before I can talk about it, I have to figure it out myself."

Michael clasped Aaron's head between his hands and bent closer. "Your eyes," he said. "The pupils should be dilated by the peyote. They're not. They're completely normal. How do you feel?"

"I'm fine," he said, unaware of how distant his voice sounded.

"We'll talk in the morning," Michael said.

"In the morning," Aaron agreed in a faraway voice.

Chapter Eight

Frannie Coltrain waved good night to her boss, pushed a strand of red hair out of her face and stepped into the parking lot. Behind her, the lights winked off in orderly fashion, leaving only the always glowing, graphic sign of the golden arches.

Adjusting her top, which accented her full breasts, she looked around the parking lot. There was only one car in sight—her boss's. She shook her head.

He had promised. And because of that promise, Frannie had not driven to work today. She had also lied to her boyfriend.

Where was he?

She started toward the street. A half-dozen steps later, a car turned into the parking lot and the flare of headlights washed over her.

Smiling, Frannie waited for the car to stop next to her.

"I thought ya'll forgot about me." She opened the door and slipped into the plush bucket seat.

"How could I forget you," the driver said, staring into her eyes. His gaze stayed there for only a moment before he glanced down at the swell of her breasts.

"Well, jest the same, I sure am glad ya'll didn't." She leaned over and kissed him. Her hand lingered warmly on his thigh. "I just love these cars."

"Is that why you're here?" he asked with a teasing half-smile.

"Partly," she admitted, "but ya'll are the real reason. I love your eyes even more than your car. I never saw eyes as green as yours."

With a quick racing of the engine, the driver pulled out of the parking lot.

"Where are we goin'?" Frannie asked, completely unconcerned as she stroked the driver's leg with her long fingernails.

"To a special place," he said.

"I just love special places," Frannie said, her fingers trailing higher on his thigh. Then she leaned back in the seat and closed her eyes.

From the moment she'd met him, she'd constantly been thinking about him. It had been like a compulsion. She couldn't get him out of her head. She knew he worked at the government installation near town—that in itself made him attractive—but his handsome face and fabulous green eyes had added even more appeal. The car had been the topper. She loved fancy cars; they excited her enough to lie to Bobby.

Frannie was almost 19, and she was neither a stranger to men, nor even remotely faithful to her boyfriend. Although she told herself that she loved Bobby, he could never satisfy her physically or mentally. She craved the excitement of newness almost as much as she needed the constant reaffirmation that she was pretty.

"You smell good," the driver said, breaking into Frannie's thoughts.

"It's musk," she said without opening her eyes. "I kinda thought ya'll'd like that."

"I do." He slowed down the car and turned off the main road onto a dirt track. In the headlights, Frannie saw a small stand of trees. The driver maneuvered between several, coming to a stop deep within their center. Then he turned to her and smiled.

The reflection from the dashboard gave his face an eerie glow. Anxious, Frannie stared at him for a moment, but when he bent and kissed her, she forgot about everything else.

When the kiss ended, her breath was ragged, and she could feel the wetness beginning inside her. "Outside," she whispered.

They got out of the car. As Frannie walked toward a tree, the driver took a blanket from the back seat. He spread it on the ground as

The Others

Frannie unbuttoned her blouse.

When the man turned back, he stood still, watching her. Frannie liked the way he stared at her. She liked men's eyes to show their appreciation of her body.

She undressed slowly, taking off the blouse first and then the bra. When her breasts were free, she stretched her arms up, letting him see their lushness.

She took off her jeans, kicking off her shoes as she slid down the pants. When she was finished, she stood wearing only dark bikini panties and a smile. "Like?"

Without answering, the man pulled off his shirt and, as Frannie walked toward him, took off his pants. Frannie smiled. He wore no underwear.

"That's nice," she whispered when she reached him. "Very nice."

He pulled her to him, crushing her breasts to his chest and kissing her roughly. Frannie groaned at the ferocity of the kiss, matching his strength with her own. A moment later they were lying on the blanket, his mouth racing across her body.

"Easy," she cried out when he bit her nipple. He did not listen, and she didn't care. Passion ripped through her body, brought on by his none-too-gentle ministrations.

His hand slid under her panties and caressed her. Her hips bucked. He slid a finger inside her, and she cried out again, unintelligibly. Then there was a pressure around her hips. She was too late to stop him from tearing the bikini off. When his hand came back to her skin, she no longer cared about the ruined panties.

His mouth replaced his hand, and pleasure coursed through her body. "Yes, oh, yes, I like that!" But when she reached for him, he pushed her hands away. Frannie didn't mind. Most of the guys she went with wanted her to do all the work. This was better.

Then he pulled her legs apart and fitted himself between them. She opened her eyes to look at him and froze. Her breath caught in her chest. For just a split second, she'd thought his eyes had been glowing like a cat's eyes do when light hits them at night. It was an exciting thought, and Frannie's blood burned hotter. An instant later that strange idea was chased from her mind by the force of his entrance.

She adjusted herself, wrapping her legs around him and eagerly meeting his thrusts.

So intense was their lovemaking that they did not hear the footsteps until it was too late.

"Bitch!" came Bobby Framton's angry, whining voice. "You rotten goddamned bitch!"

Frannie and the man froze. The fear that grew in the pit of her stomach raced through her mind. She knew Bobby was capable of hurting her—of hurting them both. Opening her eyes, she saw him pointing a gun at them.

"Bobby, no," she pleaded, fighting to get out from beneath the man.

The Others

The man pulled out of Frannie, rolled off her and crouched feline-like on all fours. His green eyes bored into Bobby's face.

"You're a liar, Frannie! You tol' me ya'll were going out with Pammie after work. I didn't believe you, bitch, so I followed you. You're both gonna be sorry!" he shouted.

Still on all fours, the man backed away. Bobby shifted the pistol toward him. Frannie tried to stand, but fear stopped her from moving.

"You first," Bobby told the man.

"Bobby!" Frannie cried.

For a moment she thought she had stopped him. Bobby had frozen. But then his eyes got wider than she'd ever seen them before.

Frannie looked at her lover, and her mouth opened in a silent scream.

The man was changing. He was turning black, changing into—"Oh, my God!" Frannie screamed.

Bobby jerked the trigger. The loud echo of the gunfire bounced in the trees. He missed. The black shape took form.

His face elongated. His eyes turned evil, green and glowing. He screamed. The sound turned into a wild howl that sent Frannie's skin crawling. Moonlight reflected on ivory fangs. His body gleamed in the night, sleek and black.

He raised his head and gave vent to another keening scream. Then he leapt forward. His no-longer-human body hurtled through the air toward Bobby.

The night was irrevocably shattered by human screams and the hunting cry of a black leopard as it leapt toward the man with the gun.

Frannie's hand covered her mouth. She could not believe what was happening, but the sound of Bobby's screams made her believe.

The leopard snarled when he struck Bobby. Its rear legs were pulled under him. The deadly claws came out from their sheaths. With its front paws wrapped around Bobby's shoulders, the leopard ripped downward with its rear paws, tearing Bobby open from chest to groin.

Bobby's screams tore through the night. Frannie, her stomach spasming, managed to stand up.

Bobby's wailing cry turned to a bubbling groan before it died completely.

Then she was facing the animal. She tried to back away but could not. The leopard's luminescent green eyes stared at her, the vertical black pupils drilling into her head. The cat's eyes were the same color as the man's. "This cain't be," she said as if in prayer. She looked around frantically. "Where are you? Help me!" she cried to the man she'd come with.

The leopard growled, and it sounded like a death knell.

The sexual heat of moments ago had turned to an icy knot of fear. Terror reigned within her. She stared at Bobby's torn body and screamed again. Then the leopard moved closer to her.

Screaming again, she charged blindly through the trees. Behind her came the padding of the large cat's paws. She hit a tree and tumbled to the ground, her breasts scratched and bleeding. She scrambled to her feet and started off in another direction. The soles of her feet were cut apart by small, sharp rocks.

Through her fear, she could hear the breathing of the animal. She ran until she couldn't catch her breath. Stopping to hold onto the bole of a tree, she looked around. She heard nothing. She saw nothing.

After several shuddering breaths, Frannie stood straighter. Listening intensely, she heard no sounds. "I got away," she said. She waited another minute. Still nothing. Then the reaction set in.

"My God, my God, my God," she cried, over and over in a monosyllabic litany of fear, as Bobby's death hit her again.

Marshaling whatever strength she still possessed, she battled to keep her wits about her. Carefully, she started walking in the direction of the road. She reached another tree and stopped to listen.

There was no sound.

She took a step forward and stopped. Suddenly she smelled the cat. Where was it?

Frannie heard the low growl before she realized it came from above. Terrified, but unable to stop herself, she looked up.

Above her, on a thick limb, crouched the large black shape. Its luminous eyes were locked on hers. The blood drained from Frannie's face. Turning, she lunged away.

The cat snarled and jumped. It struck her before she could scream. She felt it turn her, its front paws raking her back and shoulders. Through the incredible pain she smelled its fetid breath and stared into the green depths of hell that were its eyes.

Slowly, its eyes locked on her, the cat reared back on its haunches.

"Please," Frannie cried. "Please, no."

The cat struck then, ripping Frannie's body open.

Chapter Nine

The night passed slowly. Aaron's thoughts were both tortured and happy. He had found her. He had proven, to himself at least, that she was not a fantasy created on the highway and in the operating room. He remembered the gentle and loving touch that was the entrance of her mind into his.

During the long hours of darkness, Aaron made himself remember everything that had happened on this special night. He could still see and feel her absolute beauty—not just the visual perfection, but the vast beauty of her inner self.

A tremor tainted his thoughts with the fear of Michael's earlier words. Werewolves? Vampires? Was that the world she was from?

No. He had been in her mind. He would
have sensed something perverted, something
evil. What he had sensed in Kali was gentleness, love, and—dread.

Of what? Aaron went back to the heavy
undercurrent of fear that had been so much a
part of their last few moments together. He had
sensed that Kali's fear wasn't normal fright. It
was rather a deep-seated dread that had forced
her to flee from him. Who was the he she had
spoken of? Who was the man she feared so
much? And did Aaron's fear draw from Kali
or from the man himself?

The night dwindled. Gray fingers of dawn
pushed away the darkness. Suddenly, Aaron
realized that the compulsion he'd been under
for these past five months was gone. Last night
Kali had wiped it away.

Aaron watched the sky. The gray slowly gave
way to bands of corral and pink. Turning, he
glanced at Michael. His friend's eyes were
open.

"How are you feeling?" Michael asked.

Aaron shrugged. "Different. Not different."

"Did you sleep?"

"No."

"That's just the aftereffect of the peyote."

Aaron shook his head. "No, it was out of my
system hours ago."

"Are you ready to talk about it?"

Aaron nodded. He stood, stretched and began
to pace. "It was wonderful the way we talked."

"Telepathy."

"Whatever you call it, we talked."

"And?"

Aaron inhaled slowly. "That night on the road, she was trying to kill herself. She told me that she could no longer stand her eternal prison."

"Eternal? What did she mean?"

Aaron glanced sharply at him. "You're the expert, not me. She also said that she had no way to go home."

"That may be true. Tell me everything," Michael said.

"She said we've always had the ability for telepathy but chose to ignore it. She also said I won't ever need a drug again to talk with her.

"There's something else. Something . . ." He struggled, looking for the right words. "Your people," she'd said. Aaron tried to sort out his feelings about what he had learned. "And you were right, Michael. Kali says she's from another world."

"I knew it," Michael whispered. "Go on."

Aaron spoke for another half hour, detailing everything that had happened on the golden plateau. When he finished, he shrugged. "Last night is so damned hard to believe."

"Is it hard to believe, or is it that you're afraid to believe?" Michael asked.

"Oh, I believe it. It was too real, too physically real not to believe. I touched her and felt her hand on me. Felt, not just thought."

"That's what you wanted."

Aaron nodded. "She told me not to come after her. She said it was dangerous. And I could feel her fear as if it were coming from within me. What the hell is going on?"

Michael stood. "Do you really want to find out?"

Aaron stared at him for several seconds, unable to reply.

Michael stepped up to Aaron and put a hand on his shoulder. "It's your decision, Aaron. I won't press you either way."

"Is it?" he said, doubt rising in his mind.

"Yes. You can quit now. We can go back to the jeep. I'll drive you to the airport, and you can go back to Dallas. Or you can finish what was started. Which one, Aaron?"

"I can't stop, not after last night."

"Good." Turning from Aaron, he went to the fire and put up a pot of coffee.

Later, when they'd finished their coffee, Aaron said, "I'm in love with her, you know."

"I know."

"There was something when she warned me not to come after her. She wasn't afraid for herself. It was for me."

"Are you afraid?"

Aaron studied his friend's face. "Yes."

"Grandfather has always maintained that fear makes the mind more alert. Without it, he says, a brave man is only a fool. And you'll need a little fear today."

"What's happening today?"

Michael smiled, and Aaron thought he looked like a giant cat astride a mountaintop. "We're going to check out a doorway, maybe."

"What kind of doorway?"

"One to Kali's world, perhaps." Lowering his cup, Michael tossed what was left into the fire. The dark liquid hissed loudly, a tendril of white smoke and ash rising skyward.

Michael pointed to the mountain. "Inside is the ceremonial burial ground. Very sacred. Big medicine, if you believe in those things."

"Do you?"

"Sometimes. But rather than burial grounds, it's something else. It's been there since before my people came to this land, before the tribes ended their nomadic wanderings and settled. Grandfather says it has been here since our sacred spirits created this world."

"And you believe him?"

Michael smiled secretly. "And you will, too." In the silence following Michael's statement, both men watched the stark Arizona sunrise.

"It's time," Michael said when the trailing edge of the sun cleared the mountains on the eastern horizon.

They put out the fire and stowed their gear. Michael gave Aaron an industrial torchlight before leading him to a narrow path chiseled in the mountain.

Without a word to Aaron, Michael started up. The path was not as steep as it first appeared, and Aaron realized that the rocky surface had been worn smooth by years of feet traveling on it.

As they worked their way up the mountain side, Aaron saw symbols carved into the mountain's face.

The higher they went, the more Aaron could see of the land around them. The desert stretched for miles in every direction. From his vantage point, Aaron saw one thin, black band in the distance. Heat shimmered from it in waves as the sun baked the asphalt of the poorly maintained reservation road.

An hour after they'd begun their ascent, Michael stopped. "We're here." Sweat beaded his brow, but he was not sweating anywhere near as much as Aaron. "You're out of shape," he commented.

Aaron smiled. "You, too. I thought Indians didn't sweat."

"That's an old myth. We just don't show it as much."

"Where are we exactly?"

"At the entrance to my ancestor's burial ground. It is a sacred place, one not to be entered without reason. Be careful when we go inside, and stay close to me."

"Ghosts?" Aaron asked, trying to keep his voice light.

"Snakes. Bats. Spiders."

"Wonderful."

Michael smiled. "Nature is wonderful." Then,

stepping into the darkness, Michael flipped on his torchlight.

Aaron did the same.

When Michael pointed his light toward the cave's ceiling, the beam of light cut through the darkness. The darkness was so complete that the outline of light was a perfectly defined, two-dimensional line, showing nothing outside its edges.

The circle of light on the ceiling moved in slow arcs. Aaron saw dark forms clinging to the cave's ceiling. "Bats," Michael advised.

"So I see."

With both their lights on, they started forward, sweeping the beams from side to side. An occasional spider skittered aside when the light washed across it, but Aaron thankfully saw no snakes.

While Aaron followed Michael, an eeriness edged into his mind. Although he knew he had nothing to fear, he could not push the disquiet from his thoughts.

Ten minutes into the cave, they reached a fork divided by a wedge-shaped wall with several painted Indian symbols. Aaron had only an instant to glance at the petroglyphs before Michael turned left and continued on. The instant they entered the new tunnel, a rank odor hit.

"What?" Aaron whispered. Michael played his light back and forth, until it illuminated the carcass of a decaying animal.

"Mule deer," Michael stated. "Dead about ten days."

"Jesus," Aaron said, following Michael around it. Eventually the air grew cooler, and Aaron's skin goose bumped. Rather than dwell on the chill, he moved his light over the walls. There he discovered more petroglyphs. Most of the painted symbols were faded by time, however there were others that had been etched into the walls and looked as if they might have been done recently.

When Michael paused, Aaron studied the drawings on the wall. Most of it was of stick figures depicting a man involved in some form of activity. Fighting was one; the most common was hunting.

"Aaron," Michael called.

Turning, Aaron saw that his friend was shining his torch on the far wall. As the beam of light moved, Aaron saw several openings in the wall. The light finally held steady at the opening furthest to the left.

"This opening leads to the burial cavern."

Aaron started forward, but Michael stopped him. "You can't go in there."

"Bad medicine?" Aaron said, pointing his light into the cavern. Then the stench of ammonia hit him. More bats. A lot more.

"You're a visitor, Aaron. I brought you here, and I've given my word that you would not enter the burial cavern."

Aaron contemplated his friend's features, but

there was no sign of humor on Michael's face. "All right. Can I look from here?"

When Michael nodded, Aaron moved his light slowly. From where he stood in the narrow opening, he could see nothing. But, as he followed the light, he saw that inside the entrance was a mammoth cavern. Looking up, he could not find the ceiling; the torchlight just faded into the darkness. He looked down and saw nothing either.

"How big is it?" he asked.

"The mountain is a shell around it. In the old days, the entire tribe would come to lay the dead to rest. Legend has it that the first tribe carved stairs from this entrance to the floor of the cavern."

While Michael spoke, Aaron moved the light to the floor near his feet. He saw the pathway and, leaning in, the first few steps.

"Let's go."

Aaron turned to Michael. "Go where?"

Michael moved to the right. He went about 50 feet past the burial cavern and stopped in front of an entrance to yet another shaft of the tunnel. This one made a sharp right turn. "Here."

Michael went inside and flashed his light along the wall. Aaron stood next to him, staring at the paintings.

"Look at them carefully. Tell me what you see."

Aaron studied the first line of paintings. It

took him a few moments to adjust to the pattern, but when he had, he was able to make sense of the figures.

The first one looked like a man either being struck by a dozen bolts of lightning or discharging the bolts of lightning from his body. In the second picture, the man was running with the lightning in the background. The third picture showed the man still running, but in the background were several warriors with bows. The fourth picture was of the same figure, but it looked strange, as if the runner were dissolving though the armed Indians were still there. When Aaron's eyes fell on the fifth picture, the hackles on the back of his neck rose. The fifth picture was an animal, a dog or wolf, with the warriors shooting arrows at it.

The sixth picture was of the warriors watching the animal run away. "What the hell is this supposed to mean?" he asked Michael.

Instead of answering, Michael moved to another set of paintings. The first one showed the same lightning bolts, but there were three figures in the middle of the lightning—two large people and a small one. Again, the series followed, except this time the people changed their shapes into large birds and flew over the heads of the waiting Indians.

"Talk to me, Michael," Aaron asked, his nerves jumping wildly the more he looked at the petroglyphs.

Michael still said nothing as he led them deeper into the cave.

Then Aaron caught the first traces of the scent. It wasn't a dead animal, and it wasn't the ammonia residue of bat excretion. It was ozone. It smelled like a thunderstorm about to happen, only heavier.

The hair on his arms stood out in reaction to the electricity permeating the air. The cool and stale air turned heavy. When he focused his light ahead of him, he saw the cavern walls glow iridescently.

"Michael," he said, focusing the light on his friend. Michael was staring at him, a half-smile on his face.

"Grandfather says that a race of people came through here hundreds of years ago. They entered the world through a storm of lightning and fell to the ground here," he said, pointing to the spot on the cave floor, five feet in front of Aaron.

"When they arrive, they are naked. When those few who have come are seen, they change their shape and escape. Not once in all the records, all the stories, is there anything about these people having harmed anyone." To accent his words, Michael moved his light across the cavern wall where a different group of stone paintings detailed another story.

"It did not happen often, but if this phenomenon was seen seven times, how many more times was it not seen?"

103

"Why here?" Aaron asked, intrigued yet doubtful.

"Because this is where the doorway is. Can't you feel it?"

Aaron's muscles knotted. "I feel something. Show me." He tried to ignore the way his body was reacting to the forces at play within this cave.

"Turn around," Michael said, handing Aaron a penny. "Copper is a good conductor. Throw it straight ahead."

Aaron tossed the coin. Three feet from him, a bright flash lit the cave.

"What the hell was that?"

"The doorway. Damn it, Aaron, it's a doorway from another world."

Aaron looked on the floor for the penny. When he found it, he looked back at Michael. "It's still here," he said, his voice showing his doubt.

"I know. Nothing gets through whatever field that is."

"But if it's a doorway . . ." Aaron let the rest go unsaid.

"A one-way doorway. Only in," Michael stated.

Aaron stared at the spot where the coin had flashed, his mind vacillating between his desire to believe Michael and his own deep-rooted need to find a logical reason for what had happened.

"Try it yourself. Touch it," Michael suggested.

Aaron picked up the penny and looked at it. There wasn't a mark on it. It should have been charred at the very least, but it wasn't.

Aaron reached forward, his stomach tightening as his fingers inched tentatively toward whatever might be there. A second later his hand was stopped by an invisible barrier. A crawling sensation spiraled along his spine. A tingling, not unlike a low voltage current, raced across his fingertips. He pushed harder, but all that happened was that the tingling grew stronger and spread up his arm.

When he dropped his arm, the tingling stopped.

"I've spent a lot of hours in here. I've done everything I could to break past that force." Michael laughed sadly. "I've run headfirst into it, but I never made it. I wanted to; I still do. I want to know what's on the other side."

"If it is a doorway."

"It is, Aaron. Grandfather says it is. Grandfather knows."

"And you believe him."

"So do you, Aaron. It's on your face."

Aaron's breath rushed out, and in that moment he knew Michael was right "And you think Kali came through this doorway?"

"Or one like it."

Aaron looked closer at the other petroglyphs. When he was finished, he turned to Michael. "I guess the only way we're going to find out is by finding Kali."

"That's right," Michael said.

Moving his light across the cavern walls, Aaron looked at the drawings that covered its surfaces. The logical part of his mind told him that what he was looking at was superstition. Yet that special place in his mind, where Kali had first touched him, told him that what he saw was truth.

"Any ideas on where to start looking?"

Michael nodded. "You found something in the Department of Defense computer before you were discovered—the project you'd tried to break into in Sperry. What was its name?"

"Doorway," Aaron replied. He stiffened and looked toward the electrical force in the cavern.

Michael's smile widened. "When you told me the name, it struck a chord. I spoke to someone a while ago. We were discussing parallel worlds. He's a leading authority on them."

"On their theory, Michael. There's no proof."

"You found my proof last night," Michael said before continuing. "This man is an expert on the theory of transworld survivors. In one of our conversations he mentioned something about a government project called Doorway."

Aaron shook his head. "It seems a bit convenient."

"Whatever it seems, be grateful if it helps us."

The Others

"Who's your expert?"

"Herman Gable."

"Oh, shit! Michael, old man Gable's crazy."

Michael smiled strangely. "That's what the shrink in Dallas said about you."

Chapter Ten

Sperry Hollow, Virginia.

The office was soundproof, which suited Amos Aldredge's purposes. The walls were off-white. No pictures broke the sterile plainness. The room's single window was covered by closed, white vertical blinds. The overhead light was fluorescent. Two chairs were sitting before the desk. Only one was occupied.

Aldredge sat behind the large desk. His salt-and-pepper hair made a striking counterpoint to his parchment-colored face, the color of a man who spends all his hours indoors. Moist and pale eyes, watery blue, gazed over the rims of silver, wire-framed glasses set low on a narrow nose. His lips were thinned into an angry slash.

"It was you, wasn't it?" he asked the man sitting across from him. The man's face was expressionless, his age indeterminable. He could have been 20 or 40. Only his green eyes showed any animation.

"Me?" Charles Langst replied. His gaze never wavered, his stoic expression remaining the same.

"Don't play games with me. We have an agreement. I've stuck by mine. You broke yours. It has to stop!"

"Amos," Langst began, his voice soothing, "I gave you my word, and I intended to abide by it. However, being shot wasn't part of our agreement."

"What the hell were you doing out of the compound?"

Charles Langst stared openly at him. "Having fun. I've been cooped up here for a long time. I needed a change, and I took it. As you know, I have many needs. At times, those needs must be fulfilled."

"You might have endangered the project."

"But I did not. And I will not have you calling me down for this. You know how to cover those things up. And," he added, cocking his head to the side, "I'm sure it's already been taken care of. After all, your government is very powerful."

"It can't happen again," Aldredge warned.

"They won't keep on cleaning up after you."

"Then keep your promise and get us home," Langst said. He stood, towering above the seated scientist. Looking malevolently down at the smaller man, he added, "Do it soon, or I won't be able to hold the others."

Amos Aldredge refused to be faced down. He stood and shook his head. "Don't threaten me, Charles. Don't ever threaten me."

Langst smiled. Within his soul, Amos Aldredge shivered, for he could almost see the canines growing.

"I don't threaten, Amos. I just do what is necessary. By the way," Langst said offhandedly, "keep your eye on Kali. She's made contact with someone."

"Contact? Impossible."

"Oh, she has. And nothing is impossible. You should know that by now."

"With whom? Another of your people?"

"No, he's not one of us."

"She hasn't been out of her room since her escape attempt. She couldn't contact anyone. How could she?"

Langst tapped an index finger against his temple. "We don't need phones. And, Amos, the one she's been in contact with is the man who was on the road the night Kali tried to . . . ah, escape."

Langst turned then, leaving Aldredge to stare after him. Once outside, Langst walked toward the building that housed him and his people.

The Others

He breathed deeply of the night air, drawing in a profusion of scents, many of which were undetectable to a normal person.

Pausing halfway to his destination, Langst looked up at the sky. He knew the sky and its stars well. In fact, there was no one alive on the face of this earth who knew it better than he. He was, he believed, the oldest survivor of his people.

He heard a truck in the distance. Turning, he gazed toward the sound. Headlights cut through the night, reflecting off the chain link fence. Seeing the metal barriers so illuminated made Langst feel confined.

He needed to be free. He needed to range. He thought about Aldredge's pathetic warning and almost laughed. He needed the man, and the man needed him. But no one ever told him what he could or could not do. No one!

He started forward again, but instead of going to the building, he skirted it. When he was out of sight, he disrobed; then he inhaled deeply and shifted.

Seconds later, using the shape of a hawk, Langst rose high above the compound. He moved fast, riding the air currents to gain height. Below him the earth spread out in dark night contours. He leaned into the wind and let the currents take him with them.

To his left, Sperry Hollow glittered in the night. He fought his impulse to go there to hunt. Instead, he ranged on, looking for game that was not part of the area.

A half hour later he spotted a man walking along the darkened interstate. He was young, bearded and husky, and he was alone.

Langst looped above him and gave vent to the cry of a hawk hunting.

When the man looked up, Langst dove. He swooped over the man, missing him by less than three feet. He felt pleasure at seeing the man duck even before he halted his swift dive.

Then he flew to a branch not 20 feet away. The man stared at him for a full minute before headlights broke the night.

The man turned to the road and held out his right hand, his thumb sticking almost straight up. Langst dropped to the ground. He stared at the man and slowly shifted again, almost casually as the scent of the man filled his nostrils.

The car didn't slow down for the hitchhiker. When the man turned back to the tree, his face registered relief at the vanished hawk.

Then Langst rose on all four legs and started toward the man. He'd chosen the form of a mastiff. He moved slowly, watching for the instant that the man would spot him. He halved the distance before the man's face tensed with recognition of the dog. The wind blew toward Langst. Not three seconds after the man spotted him, Langst smelled the fear seeping from the man's mind. He inhaled deeply and picked up his pace.

The hitchhiker turned and started to run.

Langst followed at a lope.

The man ran faster, looking over his shoulder frequently to check on Langst's progress.

Langst could feel the panic beginning to set into the man's mind. He was in no hurry and reveled in the smell of fear.

Langst increased his pace, and the man ran faster. He could hear the man's tortured and gasping breaths. The sound and the fear fed Langst's mind and made his body tingle with expectation.

Langst did not rush but rather paced himself carefully. A quarter of a mile later, he was within a dozen feet of the man. He was teasing him, waiting for the man to reach that rare point when the pulsing fear that powered his feet would paralyze him and hold him in readiness for Langst to take him.

The growing fear fed Langst. It was fear that nourished him. It was fear that gave him his power over others. Fear was his drug—his heroin, his crack.

And it was in that last moment of consciousness, as his victims breathed their last gulps of air, that Charles Langst achieved a release so far above the sexual that he could only think of it as spiritual.

It was for that precise moment that he lived. The sensation of ultimate power—the knowledge that he had total control over the life and death of any living thing—was so intense and so important that he needed to have it more and more often. And he knew that nothing could stop him, ever, for he was truly the most superior being that this world had ever known.

The hitchhiker stumbled, fell and started up.

Langst stopped two feet from him. His dark green eyes locked onto the man's frightened blue eyes. Langst growled, saliva dripping from the corners of his mouth.

Langst's muscles bunched tightly. His rear legs coiled like a steel spring awaiting release. The man's fear was palpable. Langst breathed it in, sucking it deep down into his very being as he prepared to spring.

Before he could launch himself, a new set of headlights broke the darkness and pinned the fallen man. The man scrambled to his feet, waving frantically at the oncoming car.

The car slowed down, and Langst growled deep in his throat. When the car came to a stop, Langst howled once before running off into the trees that lined the side of the road.

An instant later his form coalesced into the human shape that was his from birth. He stood next to a tree and watched the man who he had been hunting get into the car. As the vehicle drove off, Langst saw the man stare back to where he stood.

Langst laughed, loud and harsh, until the sound grated in his ears. His temper was roiling. He needed release, and it had been taken from him. He had been thwarted, and he was angry. He still needed to hunt.

And then, before he could change and fly off, he sensed something.

Him again, Langst thought. He concentrated but could not reach them. He was too far away from Kali to interfere.

He did not like this outsider knowing about them. He could not let it continue.

Chapter Eleven

"I'm sure about it, Herman," Michael said after giving his mentor a brief summation of Aaron's story and problem. "She had set a compulsion in his mind, a compulsion to find her. They spoke telepathically, and she admitted her origins."

The older man's voice lost its tiredness and became excited. "Bring him to me, Michael. Quickly."

"Tomorrow," he promised.

"I'll wait at my office in the lab," Gable told him before hanging up.

Michael looked out the glass door and saw Aaron staring up at the starry sky. He sensed the tension and need radiating from Aaron and wished he could help him to relax.

Before joining Aaron outside, Michael called the airlines. He changed their reservations to an earlier flight to Dallas, arranged for a layover so that Aaron could get his computer, and confirmed their connecting flight to D.C. The operator assured him that they would arrive in Washington tomorrow night.

When that was done, Michael went out to the patio. "Gable expects us tomorrow night. I changed our flight to an earlier one."

"I still don't know how Gable can help us," Aaron said. "People think he went around the bend twenty years ago. The only name anyone used when they talked about him was Ghostchaser."

"None of that matters. Herman Gable has his finger on the pulse of the paranormal world. What I mean by that is that if anything is happening, anywhere in this country, Herman knows about it."

"What makes you so certain?"

"Trust me, White Man. Just remember, our first step is to see him, tell him what we know, and hope that he has information that will help us."

"Unless he thinks we're crazy."

Michael shook his head. "He won't, Aaron. He's been waiting for this all his life."

"Waiting for what?" he asked.

"For Kali. For you. His research has always leaned toward parallel world theories. He believes in their existence, as I do. Aaron, with

Gable's help, we can find her."

Aaron stared at his friend for several moments. "I'm not trying to find her so that she can be turned into a lab experiment for Gable."

"He wouldn't do that, Aaron."

"We don't need him."

"If I'm right, and I'm sure I am, you need him and his knowledge."

Aaron closed his eyes. "The man's senile. He's eighty."

"Eighty-four," Michael responded. "And he's far from senile. Besides, who else do we have?"

"You're crazy," Aaron stated.

"I'm crazy, am I?" Michael asked, raising a single eyebrow. "Am I the one who came to you to look for a telepath from a parallel world who brought me back from death?"

Aaron had no argument for that.

"Aaron, you haven't slept for two days. You're tired, and you're not thinking straight. Get some sleep. We're leaving at three."

"All right," Aaron whispered. "Have I thanked you yet?"

"For what?"

Aaron gazed at his friend and placed his hand on Michael's shoulder. "For believing me. For helping me."

"No."

"Thank you."

"Go to sleep, White Man."

Aaron left the patio and went into Michael's guest bedroom. He didn't bother to get undressed; he just lay on top of the covers and closed his eyes. Although he was physically tired his mind was still speeding. He thought back to the cavern, to the drawings, and to the strange electrical barrier within the cave.

Doorway, he thought. Is it possible? Am I crazy? His body tensed and his muscles trembled. Slowly, he willed himself to relax, and as he did, he thought of Kali. He pictured her as he had seen her on the golden plateau. He felt again the familiar, warm caress of her mind within his. And he knew he had to try and reach her again.

You won't need the drug anymore. You can do it by yourself, Kali had told him.

Carefully, he erased all thoughts from his mind. Slowly, he began to project and push his thoughts skyward. This time the wrenching sensation came quicker and was less violent. In an instant, he was moving through the starstrewn universe and focusing upon the infinite rainbow colors of the astral plane.

Just as suddenly, he was at the golden plateau, walking upon its soft grass. He thought of Kali and pictured her walking toward him, but when he looked for her, she was not there. Instead, he felt an alien force. He smelled the putrescent odor of that other being and, in the distance, saw a speck moving toward him. When it was closer, it looked like a man. He watched, fascinated and not a little fearful, as it grew larger. When the man got close enough to be seen, the man began to waver and then coalesce into another form. Aaron found himself staring at the glowing green eyes of a black leopard. The smell of its fetid breath was that of decaying flesh, the same scent that he had not been able to identify before.

Not real! he told himself as fear tried to hold his mind a prisoner. But he could smell and see the thing. It seemed as real as he, himself, was.

Facing the oncoming vileness that was projected at him from those evil green eyes, Aaron stood his ground and refused to be frightened away. Waves of energy hit him, thoughts so strong they were akin to a physical blow.

As the black leopard continued toward him, Aaron knew this was not happening in flesh and blood. But Aaron also knew it was real nonetheless.

His eyes locked with the panther's. He experienced the cold evil of the other's mind and shrank away.

The panther stopped moving and stared at Aaron. He fought to hold himself strong against this enemy, but he was unable to stop himself from being invaded. This being, whatever it might be, was violating his mind and thoughts. He reached within himself, searching for the power to push the intruder away.

He failed, and his mind was filled with scenes of death and torture that were so loathsome that they were almost beyond belief.

Suddenly, the cold invasion withdrew, leaving in its wake a haunting laughter that echoed in his mind. With that laughter, the fear he had been holding at bay flared.

Who are you? Aaron flung the thought at the animal with every ounce of his remaining strength.

The panther took another step forward. As it did, Aaron's mind erupted with pain as the panther gave vent to a horific howl that turned into a single word.

DEATH!

Then the black leopard rushed at him. When it was a dozen feet away, it left the ground. Its mouth opened to expose long glinting fangs that looked more like the gates of hell than teeth.

Battling the fear that held him immobile in the face of this oncoming death, Aaron shook himself free and instinctively withdrew from the astral plane. He catapulted his thoughts from the golden plateau and sent his mind back to his body. Through it all, the dark and evil laughter continued to vibrate within his mind.

A heartbeat later he opened his eyes and focused on the white painted ceiling of the bedroom.

His breathing was forced. His body was bathed in sweat. A chill spread across his skin. Forcing himself to breathe calmly, Aaron tried to figure out what had happened, but all he knew for certain was that someone, or something, was blocking Kali from him.

Then another disturbing thought intruded. Whoever the entity was that he'd met on the astral plane could already have Kali. Closing his eyes, Aaron willed his adrenaline-saturated body to calm down.

When his body and mind were relaxed, Aaron reasoned that if he could project himself to the astral plane, he might also be able to project his thoughts to Kali herself.

Slowly, carefully, Aaron built a picture of Kali within his mind. He thought back to the area where he had first seen her on the road outside of Sperry Hollow. Concentrating totally, Aaron launched his thoughts toward that area and to Kali.

His hands were balled into fists. The muscles in his neck knotted powerfully as he built up his thoughts of her. Then, using every once of energy he possessed, he sent out his thoughts of her laced with his need for her.

And then he touched her mind. He felt the gentle presence of her thoughts. *Kali.*

Go, Aaron. For your own good, get away! But even as she tried to send him away, he read the emanation of her own emotions for him.

I'm coming for you.

He will kill you. He knows you are trying to find me.

Who? The one I met on our plateau?

He was there? Langst was there?

The Others

A black leopard. Aaron sensed a new fear riding on Kali's thoughts.

Think about what happened so that I may see.

Aaron brought up the memory of the black leopard.

Langst. He was waiting for you. He blocked your thoughts from reaching me.

But not now. Why?

He plays his games. He is insane.

We are coming tomorrow.

Don't forfeit your life because of me.

We are coming for you.

Be careful, my love.

As soon as those last thoughts reached his mind, Aaron felt her presence dissolve.

"I will be careful," he promised her.

For a long time after his thoughts and Kali's had parted, Aaron's mind worked at a furious pace. Although he had wanted to believe Michael, when his friend had espoused his parallel world theory and his theory about the metaphysical beings that lived on that other world, he had not been able to really accept that.

But after encountering the black leopard, Aaron was no longer positive about anything, least of all his doubts about Michael's theory.

Finally, the lack of sleep caught up with him. Aaron's mind gave into his exhausted body's need for rest. He fell into a deep and dreamless sleep.

D.M. Wind

Washington, D.C.

The plane made its final circle and descended smoothly into National Airport. Twenty minutes later, Aaron and Michael drove the rental car to Georgetown University.

They entered the university grounds at 7:45 and headed toward the large, red brick building that housed Gable's laboratory.

A few minutes later they were at Herman Gable's office. When the door opened, it revealed an old man with a lined face that radiated energy.

"Michael," the professor exclaimed, a smile spreading across his weathered features as he reached out and gripped Michael's hand.

"And you must be Mr. Blaine."

"Yes, sir," Aaron said, extending his hand to the professor. He was surprised by the strength of the older man's grip. He looked quickly around and saw that the office had been kept simple. A few awards hung on the far wall. Several photographs of a younger, dark-haired Herman Gable, always with other people, dotted the wall above a couch. The professor's desk was littered with papers; his computer monitor was filled with numbers.

"Your call took me by surprise, Michael, but now that you're here I'm as impatient as always. Talk to me," he said as he guided the men to the small couch.

When they sat, Gable went to his desk. "You mentioned project Doorway and a woman from a parallel world," he said pointedly. Aaron immediately liked the man's crusty, no non-sense manner.

"It's a complicated story," Michael began.

"They all are," Gable replied quickly.

"I think it best if Aaron begins."

Aaron looked from Michael to Gable and took his time while he studied the older man. Gable's head was bald, except for a fringe of white hair barely a half inch wide. His gray eyes were calm, steady and alert. His face, although heavily lined by his years, emanated vitality. Disregarding everything he had heard about the man during his school years, Aaron intuitively sensed Herman Gable was a man whom he could trust.

"I'm a member of the Dallas Police Department—or I was until a few days ago. At present, I'm on medical leave. They think I'm crazy."

"Are you?"

"I don't think so."

"Very good. Michael mentioned something about an experience with a person from a parallel world," the professor prodded.

Aaron exhaled sharply. He looked at his hands and wove his fingers together. Then he separated them and looked at Gable again.

"I believe so." This time his story flowed out smoothly. His words were almost detached as he told of that long-ago night on the Virginia road, of his death, and of his resurrection. It wasn't until he described his experience on the golden plateau that he became hesitant. He stumbled a few times, debating upon the wisdom of opening himself completely to a man he'd just met, but rationalized that he had already said enough to condemn him anyway. When he finished, he sat back wearily.

"That was very interesting," Gable said, his gray eyes sparkling with some hidden secret. "You say you broke into the Department of Defense computer?"

"I got into it, but that's all. I couldn't get any information."

"Michael has told you about me, has he not?" Gable asked.

"He told me what you do, and I've known about you since my undergraduate years at G.W."

"You know about me or about the Ghost-chaser?" Gable responded with a smile.

Aaron flushed.

The professor waved a hand of dismissal. "I'm not offended." Then he sighed. "Amos Aldredge."

"Excuse me?" Aaron said, caught off guard by the name.

"Amos Aldredge is in charge of the Sperry Compound and Project Doorway."

Aaron tensed at Gable's words and stared silently at the man, his eyes commanding the professor to continue. Gable yielded to his unspoken plea.

"Fifteen years ago, Amos Aldredge became my assistant. He taught at the university and worked with me on several government funded projects, all dealing with the paranormal. I have always believed, although without a great degree of physical evidence, that parallel worlds exist."

As he spoke, Gable's face became animated. His old, arthritic hands moved quickly in the air before him. "Think of it as an infinite chain, one planet linked to another through a spatial dimension. Picture also, in the same way, interlocking universes connected to each world."

"Infinite?" Aaron asked.

"It's as good a theory as any other. If there is one parallel world, why not an infinite number? And wherever these worlds touch, possibly in only one area, possibly in more, a doorway is created between the worlds."

"Then travel between two parallel worlds should be possible?"

"We won't know that until we find a doorway," he said. Aaron caught the quick flicking of Gable's eyes toward Michael. "However, if the worlds are linked through a spatial field—an electromagnetic field, if you want—I am of the opinion that it would be a one-way field. Each portal would lead to a different world."

Aaron digested everything that Gable said, yet he could not fully accept it. "Your theory

would negate a possible return to this world if
you went to another world."

"Yes, and it's to that end that I've been working. When Amos first came to me, I learned that
we both shared a desire to discover the truth
about parallel worlds. Amos was an inquisitive
man, but also a man driven to find out about
the paranormal.

"We spent many hours theorizing about
supernatural occurrences. We ran a multitude
of experiments looking for some evidence of
parallel worlds."

"And you found none?"

"We found a multitude of possibilities," Gable
said.

For the first time since Gable had begun,
Aaron heard hesitation in his voice. But when
Gable's eyes again sought Michael for a split
second, Aaron knew what was happening. "He
knows about the cave?" he asked Michael.

Michael nodded. "He knows."

"Then it's more than just theory?" Aaron
queried.

Gable nodded. "Michael brought me to the
cave two years ago. I took readings, which confirmed my theory. The electromagnetic spatial
field is unidirectional."

"Can it be reversed?"

"Possibly. I'm getting close to success,
but . . ." His words faded slowly, and Aaron
understood what Gable had not voiced. Herman
Gable was old and half-crippled with arthritis.

He would not be able to continue for much longer.

"What about Amos Aldredge and Project Doorway?" Aaron pushed, trying to hold back his impatience.

"Ten years ago, Amos left me to ply his theories in the private sector. He ran the lecture circuit, wrote several books that did not fare well, and then returned to paranormal investigating. He was able to get a few minor government grants, and then he managed to convince someone in the Defense Department that he had a way to utilize his paranormal discoveries to help with the country's defenses. I know that he believes that once he reaches a parallel world, he can gain the knowledge to use their paranormal powers."

Aaron shook his head. "And the government accepted this? How is that possible?"

"It was seven or eight years ago, and the Soviets were very deep into paranormal research. Parapsychology is . . . was a legitimate science in the Soviet Union. Before the collapse and breakup of the Soviet Union, the Soviets had huge programs to develop paranormal powers. Telepathy and telekinesis were their primary goals. When Amos applied to the government, he made the people he talked with believe that our country couldn't afford to take the chance that our opponents might develop paranormal powers before we did.

"Therefore, young Mr. Blaine, it was quite

easy for Amos to get funding for what most people would consider to be futile endeavors." Gable's last words were heavily tinged with sarcasm.

"But the Soviet Union no longer exists. Its threats—at least in that aspect—are no longer valid. Why is the Doorway project still going on?"

"I must assume that it was continued because it took on a force of its own. Amos Aldredge must have found allies to convince the people in charge—the people in the D.O.D.—that he was on the right track and close to success. If that is what happened, and I'm sure it is, then he would not have to have the specter of an enemy having an advantage over us."

Aaron looked at Michael whose attention was fixed on Gable. "What is Project Doorway?" Aaron finally asked.

"A way of finding a portal into another world. A parallel Earth, if you will."

"Then he must have had proof of another world's existence to show the government? Perhaps he knows of Michael's cave?"

"No, to the last question. If he did know of Michael's cave, the government would have set up a quarantine," Gable stated confidently. "And you must also understand that when one deals with the theories of parapsychology, one doesn't always have or even need physical proof."

"But—"

"Patience," Gable advised. "First you must learn about the man you're going up against, if you want to find your woman."

Your woman. The two words bounced madly within Aaron's mind. "Kali," he whispered. "Then you do believe what I told you?"

"I trust Michael implicitly. If he believes you, than I do. And I've learned that almost anything is possible in this world, whether we understand it or not."

Aaron nodded. "I won't interrupt you any more."

"Good, because this is important. If Aldredge has the woman you call Kali, then she might conceivably be in a great deal of trouble. You see, Amos and I parted on rather bad terms." Gable paused to cough into the back of his hand. "I fired him, had him discharged from the university. Amos Aldredge is a man who will go to any lengths to get what he wants.

"He's dangerous because he wants respect in an area of endeavor that draws ridicule. He wants to prove his theories of the paranormal—his belief of parallel worlds and the metaphysical beings who dwell on them—to a world of doubters. He wants to be recognized as a discoverer of great scientific findings. But Amos Aldredge's theories are not well accepted even among his own peers in the parapsychology community, much less by other scientists."

"Why did you fire him?" Aaron asked, slipping into his policeman persona momentarily.

"For using proscribed drugs on students to heighten their senses during tests," Gable stated. "There was one boy in particular, a confirmed telepath . . . Aldredge had the idea that he could use a telepath to break into a parallel world." Gable's eyes became unfocused as he spoke. "It took the doctors three years of intensive psychiatric, inpatient therapy before the boy could step foot into the real world again; he was an emotional cripple."

The old man's eyes widened as the intensity of his emotions poured forth. "You see, and this is very important, Aldredge didn't give a damn about the people he tested. All he wanted was to find evidence of an 'otherworlder,' as Aldredge called them. He has an obsessive compulsive personality."

"Do you think he found what he was looking for?" Aaron asked, a feeling of disgust building within him.

"I never really did, not until today. Your story makes it sound possible."

This time it was Michael who spoke. "What's he doing at Sperry?"

"What do you think he's doing?" Gable snapped dryly, staring hard at his ex-pupil. A moment later, Michael nodded.

Aaron silently watched the interplay between the two, but when silence dragged on, he spoke. "What is he doing?"

Gable turned to him. "He's building a doorway to another world. Why else would he have an otherworlder with him? Why would the government go to such lengths to hide the woman who you said was on the road? Why were you being persecuted when you tried to gain information from the computers? Or," he said, his voice lower this time, "don't you think what happened to you in Dallas was persecution? Was it just government regulations?"

Aaron's breathing was shallow as he digested the older man's words. And then, all the pieces fit neatly together—the shrink's sudden ultimatum of therapy and lack of computer access or no job. The too quick tracing of his calls to the data bases was just a shade too unusual, and the total evasiveness of the people at Sperry when he tried to find out what had happened that night fit with the rest of the pattern.

Slowly, Aaron nodded his head.

"What are you going to do? No, let me amend that. What are you capable of doing?" Gable asked shrewdly.

Aaron's face turned hard. His eyes bored into Gable's. "Whatever I have to do to get Kali out of there."

"That will be dangerous."

"I know."

Gable looked from Aaron to Michael and back again. "I want to know everything you learn. Everything!"

Michael nodded. "Of course."

Gable focused his attention on Aaron, his eyes remaining on Aaron's face until Aaron grew uncomfortable. "Why haven't you tried to contact this woman again?" Gable asked.

Aaron stared at him, wondering if he should speak of last night's encounter. He looked quickly at Michael and then back at Gable.

"I did," he admitted.

"When?" Michael asked, caught off guard by Aaron's reply.

"Last night," Aaron replied, looking at Michael instead of Gable. "I projected myself to the astral plane. I went to look for Kali."

"And?" Michael prompted.

Aaron shifted uncomfortably. "I found a black leopard waiting for me."

"A what?" Michael asked.

"First it was a man; then it was a leopard. I ran and then willed myself back to my body. I think that if I hadn't, it would have killed me."

Aaron did not miss the look that passed between Michael and Gable.

"Why didn't you tell me about it?" Michael asked.

Aaron had no ready answer. But after facing the abomination on the golden plateau, he'd not wanted to speak to Michael about it.

"Then you didn't talk with her again," Gable said.

"Yes, I did. A short while later. She warned me that Langst, whoever or whatever he is, is trying to stop me. I think Langst is the leopard."

The Others

"Michael has explained his theory of other-world involvement to you, hasn't he? He's discussed his ideas about a metaphysical evolution in comparison to our physical evolution?"

Aaron nodded as he studied Gable. He waited silently, knowing the older man had more to say.

"I am of the same beliefs. I've spent forty years investigating the paranormal. Almost everything I know is in the data banks of the university computer. There is also a special file that I have maintained through the years. It concerns animal attacks in areas where those particular animals are never found. You're welcome to go through them."

"Thank you," Aaron said.

"Have you reservations at a hotel yet?" Gable asked Michael.

"At the Holiday Inn near here."

"Good. I'll expect both of you to be here at eight tomorrow morning. We have a lot to do if we're going to find out what Aldredge is up to."

Later that night, when Aaron and Michael finished their dinner, the conversation turned to Aaron's solo experience with Kali.

"Why didn't you tell me about it?"

Aaron shook his head, knowing the time for honesty was here. "I'm not sure. Partly because of the fear that I had felt. And I guess that if I had discussed it with you, I also would have had to admit that shapeshifters—your name—exist. And I would have had to concede that Kali is one of them."

"That bothers you?"

Aaron nodded; then he smiled wryly. "How would you feel if you were in love with a were-wolf?"

"Hey, good point, White Man. But no one is saying that Kali is a werewolf. And no more trips without someone in the room with you."

"Why?"

"Because it's dangerous with the new factors that have come into the picture."

"What new factors?"

"The black leopard, Aaron. If you hadn't got-ten away in time, he could have killed you."

Again, Aaron shook his head. "But I wasn't there, just my thoughts. He couldn't have hurt me."

"Aaron," Michael began in a low voice that was filled with emotion. "Your mind and your thoughts *are* you. Where your mind is, is your reality. If he'd struck you on the astral plane, it would have been the same as if he'd attacked you on the physical plane."

"But he didn't," Aaron countered.

"There's one other thing."

Aaron didn't speak; he just waited.

"He knows you're coming after Kali. He'll be ready for you."

"Us, Michael. If he knows about me, then he knows that *we're* coming. I told Kali that *we're* coming, not that *I* was coming."

Michael just stared at Aaron and said, "We're going to have to move fast, White Man, real fast.

Langst walked toward the wooded area behind the buildings. He was fuming at his latest argument with Aldredge and needed the release of something physical to expunge his mounting tensions.

Where are you? he called.

When he received no answer, Langst sent out a probe. It took him a few minutes, but he finally located her. He pushed, and he was in her head.

Join me, she said.

No. I'll watch.

She looked around, and he saw that she was at a huge amusement park. People were everywhere. He smelled them.

She walked slowly along. Her tall and slender body, clad in skintight clothing and capped with tawny blonde hair, attracted attention from any man she passed.

Still, she held herself back, not settling for whatever came at her but looking for exactly what she wanted. It took a while to choose, but when she did, a small push from her mind was all that was necessary to make her target interested.

He was as tall as she. He had long hair that was tied back into a pony tail. He wore tight

jeans and a black tee shirt that showed a muscular expanse of chest.

Within minutes, the man was at her side.
"Alone?" he asked.

She looked at him. Her dark eyes locked on
his. "Not anymore."

He smiled. "Come on," he said, putting his
arm around her narrow waist and guiding her
toward the roller coaster.

No sooner had they reached the coaster than
the park's loudspeaker system announced that
the park would close in 15 minutes.

They stood in the line, and behind them an
attendant closed the barrier. They were the last
ones.

They looked at each other, not talking. She
leaned against him, rubbing him, making him
excited and keeping him that way so that when
they were finally granted admittance onto the
coaster, his mind was a jumbled knot of desire.

She guided him into the last car, and as they
waited for the coaster to start, she kissed him
deep and hard. She bit his lip, drawing blood
even as her hand squeezed him and made him
grind his hips in anticipation.

Then the coaster took off. His arm was
around her shoulders, and his hand squeezed
her breast. They went up slowly. At the first
crest, he leaned against her. "Here it comes,"
he said.

She smiled. "Not yet."

The car sped downward with the sound of

a runaway locomotive. The people in the front seats screamed and raised their hands.

They went high again, crawling up to the second crest. She turned to him, put her hand on top of his and pressed it against herself. "You want me."

"Bad, baby, I want you real bad. And when we leave here, I'm going to have you!"

She smiled broadly and leaned toward him as the coaster reached the tip of the second crest. She pulled his face to hers and kissed him. Then she slid her mouth to his neck and bit.

The car went down, moving crazily fast. He tried to pull away from her, but she was too strong for him. Her teeth changed, elongated and became sharp. She bit harder, drawing blood and severing veins.

The salty taste of his coppery blood sent her mind reeling with pleasure. She held him fast, her strength 20 times his. She sucked on him and drew in more than just his blood. She drew in the very essence that made him alive.

He screamed, but his scream was lost as everyone else cried out at the sudden drop of the coaster. Then she pushed at his mind and took control of his voice.

At the bottom, she drew away from his neck and stared into his shocked and pain-filled eyes.

He tried to speak, but she would not allow it. She watched him trying to fight her and

139

laughed loudly. She sniffed in the scent of his flowing blood. She leaned forward and licked at the blood that pulsed from his neck.

"You wanted me, and now you have me," she said as the coaster reach the highest point on the ride. As it climbed slowly to the peak, she shifted, just slightly.

Her face thinned, and she grew taller, almost skinny. Her canines elongated until she looked like a misshapen human bat.

She had used the form time and time again over the centuries, and it never failed to elicit the same response—pure and unadulterated fear, the type of fear that sent every hormone in a man's body into a frenzy that made his heart pump and his breathing come to a stop.

It was for that very moment that she waited. His fear and his very existence were wrapped together in those terrified few seconds.

The coaster began its mad downward plunge then. And in the very instant that it plummeted earthward, she tore his throat out with a single bite.

Before the coaster reached the bottom of the drop, she ripped his dead body from the seat and flung it back onto the tracks, where the maintenance men would find it later.

Thirty seconds before the end of the ride, she shifted again, assuming the shape of a black feathered hawk, and began her flight back to Sperry Hollow.

Later, in the wooded area at the rear of the

Sperry Enclave, the hawk settled on Charles Langst's bare shoulder.

Langst lifted her from his shoulder and held her before him. Then he released her. Before she hit the ground, the tall blonde woman replaced the bird. Her bare skin glowed beneath the stars. She leaned to him and kissed him, drawing his tongue slowly and deeply into her mouth. Then she bit his tongue, and they both tasted his blood.

Without releasing him, she drew him to the ground. He was as excited from her kill as she was.

Chapter Twelve

The next two days flew by in a blur of computer printouts and the correlation of the thousands of files Herman Gable had meticulously kept over the past four decades.

At first, Aaron had balked at Gable's insistence that he needed to learn everything he could about the otherworlders.

"What I need to know is what's happening at Sperry Hollow and what Aldredge is doing with Kali, so that we can get her out."

Gable was unperturbed by his heated words. "You can't go up against the unknown without preparation. Not if you want to get her out alive."

"What I have to do is get inside the government computer and learn about Sperry Hollow," Aaron countered.

"What would you learn? What would you look for? If you don't know anything to begin with, you won't find anything. And you can't go into the computer until you're ready to move, because as soon as you tap into their data banks, they'll be alerted."

"They already are, if Michael is correct," Aaron stated.

"They only know that someone is in contact with Kali. They don't know how near you are to learning about them."

In the long run, Aaron had no choice but to impatiently agree to begin his education on the paranormal.

As the men worked, they found the mass of information was so overwhelming that they were unable to put it together in any pattern, until Aaron began to collate it all by adapting a data base search program to weed out anything they determined to be unnecessary.

On the morning of their third day in Washington, Aaron and Michael, with Gable's help, had gathered enough information about parallel world research and metaphysical phenomena to be able to pinpoint several ongoing government research programs.

But by midafternoon, Aaron felt they were no closer than before. He knew he had no choice but to get into the Department of Defense computer.

"There's one other area we have to look at first," Gable stated. "Animal attacks."

Aaron looked from Gable to Michael and saw his friend nod. Again, Aaron conceded to the other two, and for another hour they went over Gable's animal files. In the files were many photostats of articles. After reading a third of the stories, Aaron saw that a pattern was forming. The earliest reports had been found in old newspaper accounts dating back to the turn of the century.

In each instance, an animal, be it a large cat, a wolf, or some other creature that was not indigenous to the area, killed a person. In each account, the person had been mauled or killed, but not eaten. That one fact showed that the attacks were not for food, as would be natural for most animal attacks.

Several documented cases were from Europe, but most were from this country. The two which fascinated Aaron the most were occurrences in California, described as leopard attacks by the experts who were interviewed. Both happened within a month of each other in Santa Barbara.

The animal experts had voiced their opinion that the cat must have been privately owned. They believed it had escaped and was recaptured by its owner, for it was never found. But as Aaron went over the files, he found other similar attacks in four other states.

"Do you think that this leopard is the same one?" he asked Gable.

Gable shrugged eloquently. "The same—or another of the otherworlders."

Aaron exhaled slowly. "It's hard to accept."

Gable laughed, taking Aaron by surprise. "I've felt that way for forty years, but I haven't given in to the rest of the world's idea of what is real and what isn't."

Aaron looked down at the file. "The last report of an animal attack is two years ago. There haven't been any recently?"

"There was one a few days ago. In fact, it was the day before you called, Michael. But they found the cat. It had escaped from an animal testing laboratory in Virginia," Gable told them.

The instant Gable finished speaking, Aaron and Michael looked at each other, both remembering the significance of the night Gable spoke of. It was the night of Aaron's first astral projection.

"The day before I called?" Michael asked in a hollow voice. "Do you still have the report?"

Gable nodded. "It was in the paper the day after it happened. I got excited about it, but there was a follow-up story describing the escaped cat." Gable paused, his face going tight. "It was a leopard."

Standing slowly, Gable went to a file cabinet. When he returned he had two neatly cut articles which he put on the desk.

Aaron picked up the first one and froze.

MAN-EATER CAT
KILLS TWO

SPERRY HOLLOW, VA—In the early morning hours police found the mutilated bodies of two local youths in a secluded section outside the town limits of Sperry Hollow.

Police experts are baffled by the deaths, which they attribute to an animal attack.

"I've never seen anything like it," said Sperry Hollow Police Chief Malcome Corning. "Their bodies were just ripped apart. That animal chased the girl for almost a quarter mile. It was like it was playing with her. It just doesn't make any sense. We don't have cats that big in these parts."

Chief Corning said that an investigation is being started, along with a manhunt for the animal.

Aaron looked thoughtfully at Michael. "Sperry Hollow. That seems a bit too coincidental."

"Perhaps," Gable said. "But they caught the

cat the next day." Gable pointed an arthritically swollen finger at the second clipping.

MAN-EATER CAT CAPTURED
ESCAPED LEOPARD RESPONSIBLE FOR SPERRY HOLLOW DEATHS

SPERRY HOLLOW, VA— Following a two day intensive manhunt by local and state police, aided by officials from a nearby government installation, a spotted leopard who had escaped from an animal testing laboratory was captured. It was confirmed by State Police Captain Clive Barrow that this cat was the one responsible for the mauling deaths of two local inhabitants of Sperry Hollow: Francis Mary Gregory and her fiancé Bobby Framton. Funeral services for the young couple will be held tomorrow at 10:00 a.m. at the Sperry Baptist Church. (Continued on page 7)

Beneath the article was a picture of the man and woman. When Aaron looked at the woman's likeness, his stomach twisted.

"I knew her."

Both Gable and Michael stared at him. "Her?" Michael repeated.

"The girl. Oh, damn, she was just a kid." Closing his eyes, Aaron pictured her as he'd seen her on the night of his accident. She had been a sensuous woman/child, filled with life and looking for excitement.

"Who is she?"

Aaron opened his eyes and looked at his friend. "On the night of the accident, I was in Sperry Hollow."

"I know."

"She worked at the McDonald's where I stopped for some food. We'd talked. She . . . she seemed like a nice kid. She liked my car."

"So?"

Aaron shrugged. "I don't know. A hunch? Something isn't right," he said, continuing to read the article. As Aaron read on, he experienced a darkening in his mind, and a moment later he realized what it was. Looking up, he stared directly into Michael's eyes. "It happened the same night I met Kali on the plateau. She told me about it. She said, 'He has returned. Something has happened. Something terrible.' "

"But they caught the animal," Gable said.

"The whole story stinks. Since when does a secret government installation aid police in a search for an animal? And what kind of testing laboratory has a man-eater cat that could escape? It was him. It was Langst!"

The laboratory was deathly silent as the three

men looked at each other. Finally, Herman Gable shook himself free of Aaron's haunted stare. "It's time," he stated.

"Not yet," Aaron said, once again going against the wisdom of the older man. "We can't just hop into the government computer and expect not to be caught, especially if they're aware of me. No, we do that tonight after midnight."

Gable nodded solemnly. "You're right."

"Now what?" Michael asked.

Aaron looked at Gable again. He had been waiting for this ever since Gable had first mentioned his research. "I want to know about your research into Michael's doorway."

Gable smiled knowingly and said, "Of course you do."

Standing, Gable went over to a computer terminal and pressed several keys. With Aaron and Michael peering over his shoulder, a revolving schematic appeared on the monitor.

"This is the spatial formation of the doorway—its matrix. Notice the unusual curvature of the electrical field. It emanates from within the rock of the cave's ceiling and burrows into the floor. It is a negatively charged field. I have duplicated this field in the lab, and I believe I might have found a way to reverse it."

Gable turned to Michael. "But I haven't figured out where it goes when it's reversed. What I planned on doing is to return to the cave and reverse your doorway. That's the only way I can think of to open a way into a world we already know exists."

"Why haven't you done this already?" Aaron asked as the possibilities of Gable's words filled his mind.

"For several very good reasons, my impatient young friend. Firstly, without someone from that world, there is no proof of its existence. Secondly, if no physical proof exists, would you go through an interdimensional opening? For all we know, the other side of my artificial doorway might be deep space or even open into the center of a sun. No," Gable said, his voice impassioned, "with someone from a parallel world, we not only have proof of its existence, but we would also have a guide and hopefully a friend."

"That's what Aldredge is planning?"

"God only knows what Aldredge is planning, but if I'm right about him, he wants into the other world to gain power to use here. And," Gable whispered, looking from Michael to Aaron, "he must not be allowed to get there."

At midnight the university parapsychology laboratory was silent; the only sounds were of three men breathing and the low hum of the computer fans and drives. Aaron had set his own portable computer up and had linked it to Gable's. All they were waiting for now was for Aaron to call the government computer at the Department of Defense.

With a sigh, Aaron keyed in a telephone

number. As he had explained to Gable and Michael, he was not worried about being caught tonight. When he'd been put under suspension, he'd gathered his equipment together in his Dallas office, and while he did, he'd reset their mainframe computer and given himself an authorization code that was hidden from any casual observer. Between the hours of midnight and 7:00 a.m., no one was in the computer room of the forensic lab—unless they changed the routine, which he doubted.

He picked up the phone and dialed the Dallas police computer's number. When he heard the electronic signal, he switched the telephone wire from the receiver to the back of the computer and plugged it in. A moment later he was in full communication with his old office.

Aaron explained that they would only have tonight to get the information he needed. By tomorrow the Dallas P.D. and the entire forensic department would be swarming with Feds.

After a slight initial hesitation, Aaron began to issue commands to the computer. His main objective for tonight was the Department of Defense, where he'd first gotten an inkling of Sperry.

Once in the D.O.D. computer's memory banks, he used the password he'd discovered on his last abortive attempt; it was the first of the double password entry. For the next 15 minutes, his very altered communication program talked with the D.O.D. computer, until he broke the secondary security password code and found himself staring at the user menu.

"We're in," he half-shouted, his words loud in the quiet lab.

Michael was on one side, Gable on the other. "I'm going to pull some files. Give me some idea as to what we should look for."

"Experiments in parapsychology. Anything with Aldredge's name on it," Gable commanded.

"Try telepathy, telekinesis and shapechanging," Michael added.

Aaron's fingers flew over the keyboard, making request after request. Whenever he found a file that had anything to do with Sperry or the paranormal, he used a dumpfile program to transfer the information to his own computer.

Two hours after he began, he broke the connection, leaned back and rubbed his eyes. Exhaustion was setting in.

"What did we get?" Michael asked.

"A lot, maybe nothing. There was a coded entry file about Aldredge and the Sperry installation."

"Let's look at it," Gable said.

Aaron brought the file up on the screen and, as the three men looked at it, the tension grew thick. The first lines were the Department of Defense warning that the material in the file was top secret and could be viewed only by those with proper authorization. A 30 second voluntary cut off warning followed that. Aaron hit two keys. The screen flickered and the file appeared.

CODE: RED TOP / HIGHEST AUTHORITY ONLY
PROJECT: DOORWAY
INCEPTION: 3 MAY 1987
PROJECT DIRECTOR: ALDREDGE, AMOS / Ph.D.
INSTALLATION COMMANDER: LOWELL, THOMAS / CAPTAIN, UNITED STATES ARMY, INTELLIGENCE.
TELEPHONE: 555-9890. ACCESS CODE: BLUE 3700221 - 119977.3
COMPUTER TYPE: IBM 4381 (ENGINEERING/SCIENTIFIC)
PRIMARY OBJECTIVE: PENETRATION OF PARALLEL WORLD AND RECOVERY OF PARAPSYCHOLOGICAL METHODS TO INTEGRATE WITH DEFENSE PROGRAMS.
OBJECT: USE OF TEST SUBJECTS TO CONFIRM EXISTENCE OF ALTERNATE WORLD EVOLUTION. SECONDARY OBJECTIVE: COVERT INTELLIGENCE GATHERING
PRIORITY AGENCY: NATIONAL SECURITY AGENCY
SECONDARY AGENCY: CENTRAL INTELLIGENCE AGENCY
INSTALLATION: SPERRY COMPOUND. SHENANDOAH COUNTY, VIRGINIA.

29,423 ACRES. ONE MAIN ACCESS ROAD. DEDICATED TRUNK LINE TO MAIN D.O.D. DATA BANK ARLINGTON MODEL -IBM 3081
SECURITY: INFRARED INTERNAL/ EXTERNAL. CLOSED CIRCUIT MONITORS.
MILITARY POLICE, ARMY INTELLIGENCE, NATIONAL SECURITY AGENCY.
TEST SUBJECTS: BOULE, HENRY
                          BURKE, AMELIA
                          LANGST, CHARLES
                          MOSS, KALI
                          RICHTER, ADOLPH
                          WARREN, EVAN

Aaron took a deep breath and pushed himself away from the screen. The sight of Kali's name had shaken him, but at the same time it had given him a small sense of accomplishment.

While he tried to adjust the information he had gained to fit in with what he'd already known, Gable and Michael continued to look the data over.

"They have a platoon of soldiers stationed at the compound, not including the MPs. They're not taking any chances," Michael said darkly.

"Six of them. Aldredge has six of them!" Gable shouted excitedly. "My Lord, the power he has at his command!"

Aaron looked at Gable and at the animation in his face. The old man's words could be taken in two different ways. Aaron didn't want to think of the second. And a moment later he was proven correct.

"We must stop him before he can open a doorway. Michael," Gable said, turning to face his student, "I know Aldredge. He'll use these people. Others will be harmed. If he succeeds in gaining their powers, he can wreak havoc on this world. What he is capable of will make your worst nightmare seem like a child's fantasy of good."

Gable turned to Aaron. The old man's eyes were wide, and his hands trembled visibly. Intensity and need radiated from the man. "Can you get into the Sperry computer banks?"

Aaron nodded.

"Do it now."

"No." The single word hung acridly in the room. Gable stared at him, his body stiff, while he waited for Aaron to go on. "We can't go in there yet. When we're discovered—not if but when, because they'll know—we have to be ready to move. We're a hundred and fifty miles away. I want to be closer."

Michael shook his head. "They'll trace the call and come after us if we're that close."

"No, they won't. I've worked out a way around that. They'll find where the call will originate from, but it won't be where we are."

"The police department computer again?"

"No. That's finished as of right now," Aaron said as he broke the connection between his computer and Dallas. "My apartment phone has call forwarding. They'll be able to trace the call to there, but no further until they set up a tracing sector for incoming calls to my phone. That should give us one full day, perhaps two.

"Professor," Aaron said, turning to Gable, "will you help us after we get Kali out?"

Gable clasped his hands before him, wringing his arthritic fingers together like a master chef about to concoct his most favorite dish. "Don't ask foolish questions. Just get her."

Homicide detective Sergeant Richard Blaine sat across from his boss, a puzzled expression on his face as he waited for the chief's tirade to end.

"He's in Arizona. He's not here," the elder Blaine brother explained.

"Then who in the hell used our computer last night? I've just spent four hours with the Feds. They woke me at five-thirty this morning. Our computer, that fucking forensic monstrosity, was plugged into the Department of Defense computer and was going through a hell of a lot of top secret documents. They want some answers. So do I!"

"What makes you so sure it was my brother?" Blaine asked. "He's been in Arizona for almost a week."

The chief of detective's stubby finger rose toward the ceiling, wagging in absurd warning. "Because he did it once already. Because he went into the same computer and used the same codes."

"Did anyone see him here?" Blaine asked quickly.

"Not a damned soul."

"Then it wasn't him."

"It was. The Feds are sure. They said that their trace came to here. Their computer expert says he has evidence that our computer was manipulated by another computer."

"That sounds like the usual government high tech paranoia. Did they trace that supposed call to our computer?"

"By the time they'd worked out the first trace, your brother was off the line."

Richard Blaine's eyes narrowed dangerously. "Don't forget that he is my brother. And don't make an accusation you can't back up."

"Not me, Sergeant, the F.B.I. They told me that they were issuing a warrant for him."

"What kind of warrant?"

"Whatever they want. They'll use a national security blanket warrant."

"Shit!" said the older Blaine.

"Call him, Richard. Tell him to clear the air before it's too late."

A somewhat shaken Richard Blaine nodded his head and stood up. After leaving the chief's office, he went to the forensic lab and spoke to Aaron's replacement and to the F.B.I technician who was still going over the computer. When he was finished, his worst fears were realized. Aaron had set up some sort of a password code in the computer. They had hard proof of that.

When he returned to his desk, he called his wife and got Michael Noriss's phone number. He dialed Arizona, only to get an answering machine that informed him that Dr. Michael Noriss was on vacation and would return in another week.

"Damn it!" he shouted as he slammed the receiver down.

Chapter Thirteen

The afternoon's late summer sun illuminated the blacktopped road. In the distance was a group of buildings, their shingled roofs shimmering under the heat of the day. When he was closer, Aaron saw that the buildings behind the main office were in two clusters. To the right were three barn-style buildings, while to the left were a dozen smaller barrack-type structures.

According to the information in the D.O.D. computer, the dozen smaller buildings housed the army personnel, while the three larger buildings were research facilities. One of the research buildings also housed Kali and her people.

The grounds were well-maintained. The parking area was organized with rows of neatly striped, angled parking spaces. Aaron pulled into a visitor's spot, which was designated by white painted and stenciled letters. His nerves were taut. His mind raced with the anticipation of facing Captain Lowell, the one witness to his accident.

Before he got out of the car, he leaned back and closed his eyes. The day had been a long one, starting when he and Michael had left Washington before dawn and driven to Harrisonburg, some 30 miles outside of Sperry Hollow. They'd taken a room in the Sheraton, registering under Michael's name, and slept for five hours.

After eating, Aaron had called the Sperry compound and arranged for a meeting with Captain Lowell for later that afternoon. Then Michael had rented a second car, for that day only, and while Aaron had driven to the research enclave, Michael had gone to Sperry Hollow to do some investigating of his own.

Shaking his head, Aaron pulled the keys out of the ignition and left the car. He knocked at the front entrance. When his knock went unanswered, he opened it and found himself inside a large reception area. At the far end, a young, uniformed woman looked up at him.

"Can I help you?" she asked when he reached her desk.

"Aaron Blaine to see Captain Lowell."

The Others

The woman picked up her phone. "Through that door," she said, pointing to a door across from them. "Captain Lowell's office is the third on the right."

Aaron thanked her and followed her directions. Alone in the hallway, he paused to look around carefully. The outside of the building and the reception room had looked civilian normal, but the inner hallway was painted standard army gray-green. He sensed a vastly different atmosphere than what the exterior had projected.

Reaching the third door, he knocked. When the door opened, it revealed a pleasant looking uniformed man in his mid-forties. Captain Lowell's hair was short, and his eyes were brown. The man's jawline sprouted a prominent five o'clock shadow. The dark circles under his eyes told Aaron that the captain was either overworked or worried about something.

"Mr. Blaine. I'm Thomas Lowell," he said, offering his hand to Aaron. "What do I owe this meeting to?"

Accepting the hand, Aaron returned the firm, even pressure. "I never thanked you for calling the ambulance. You saved my life."

"Come in," Lowell said, stepping aside to let Aaron enter. "I only did what was needed. Have a seat," he added, pointing to a nearby chair as he went around his desk and seated himself.

Aaron sat. "Nevertheless, what you did saved my life," he told Lowell, picking up the conversation at the point they'd left it. While he spoke, he studied Lowell intently. His field experience in the Dallas P.D. came to the forefront as he watched the man's reactions.

When Lowell spoke again, a telltale flutter of his left eyelid told Aaron that he'd struck a sore spot. "I was glad I happened to be driving in the same area."

"Happened to be?" Aaron asked. Then he smiled easily. "Do you often go for drives at two in the morning?"

"As a matter of fact, I do," Lowell responded, his voice and face now equally under control. "Why are you here?"

"To find out what happened that night," Aaron stated.

"You lost control of your car," Lowell told him.

"So I've been told. But I didn't lose control, Captain. I purposely ran off the road."

"Purposely? Were you trying to kill yourself?" Lowell asked, working his features into a surprised mask.

Aaron didn't buy it. His smile was without humor. "You know, as well as I do, what happened that night. You know about the woman on the road, don't you?"

"No, Mr. Blaine, I don't." Again Lowell's face was stoical.

Aaron changed the subject immediately. "Exactly what kind of a government installation is this?"

Lowell sighed. "A research facility, Mr. Blaine."

"What type of research do you do, Captain Lowell?"

"I don't do any. I'm the military commander of the base."

"Excuse my semantics. What kind of research is done here?"

"I'm afraid that topic is not open for discussion. Our work here is classified secret."

"I see. So secret, perhaps, that you lied about what happened to me?" Aaron probed, his voice as level as possible, with only a tinge of his real anger showing through.

"I resent that charge," Lowell replied, his shoulders stiffening.

"And I resent being lied to. There was a woman on the road, and there were a hell of a lot of vehicles chasing her. Vehicles with spotlights, Captain. Army vehicles!"

"I'm sorry, Mr. Blaine, but you're mistaken."

Aaron rose and leaned over the desk, resting his weight on his knuckles. "Am I, Captain? What about Project Doorway? What about Kali Moss?"

"Kali Moss?" Lowell asked.

When a betraying muscle ticked just below the surface of Lowell's cheek, Aaron knew he had the man. "The woman on the road, Captain. Kali Moss."

Reacting sharply, Lowell stood. "You don't know what you're saying, Blaine. And I'll pretend you didn't say anything, other than to thank me for saving your life. And now, get out of my office, get off this post, and go back to Dallas. Do it now, Blaine. Don't wait until tonight or tomorrow."

"Why, Captain?" Aaron asked, his voice level, his eyes flickering over Lowell's face.

"For your own good, man, for your own good!"

"All right, Captain, I'll think about what you said."

"Don't think about it, Blaine. Do it!"

Their eyes locked. There could be no mistake about the warning message that showed on the captain's face. Finally, Aaron nodded and started toward the door. When he opened it, he turned back to Lowell. "I did mean it—thanking you for calling the ambulance."

"I know," Lowell said, his voice softer and lower. "And Blaine . . ." Aaron raised his eyebrows. "No more tricks like last night. They're on to you."

"Last night?" Aaron asked innocently.

"Forget what happened last spring. Go on with your life."

"I fully intend to go on with my life, Captain Lowell. You have my word on it."

Stepping into the hallway, Aaron closed the door behind him. He stood still for several seconds, breathing calmly and sorting out what he'd learned from Lowell. Uppermost in his thoughts was the belief that Lowell seemed to be a basically decent man. Aaron was certain that Lowell was only doing what he felt was his duty.

"So am I," Aaron whispered.

Once outside the building, Aaron did not go to his car; instead, he veered toward the side of the building. Walking casually, as if he belonged there, he headed toward the first research building. With each step he took, he glanced around to make sure that no eyes were following him.

When he was within 20 feet of the first lab building, he gave a little push with his mind. He inwardly called Kali, letting her know he was near.

Then he crossed the remaining distance to the door. Carefully, Aaron reached for the knob, his eyes moving everywhere, watching everything. But just as his fingers touched the sun-warmed steel, he felt as though a needle had pierced his head.

Go! Get away! Now! Reacting immediately to Kali's warning, he released the doorknob and walked away from the building. Just as he stepped onto the blacktop, he glanced backward over his shoulder and saw a figure emerge from the building.

Aaron looked away and went to his car. As he opened the door and started to get in, he glanced back and froze. The man was closer now, but he had stopped walking. The distance between them was no more than 100 feet. Aaron saw the man clearly, and he knew who the man was. He had seen him on the golden plateau.

Langst!

Suppressing a shudder at the hatred reflected on the man's face, Aaron got into the car, started it and drove away. He felt a searching finger of alien thought start to reach into his mind. From somewhere inside him, he found an instinctive inner strength that enabled him to build a shield around his mind and stop the unwanted probing.

But even as he drove, it took him a long time to push aside the feeling that the other man was still watching him.

Instead of going back to Harrisonburg, Aaron pulled into a small truck stop off the interstate. He sat in a back booth and ordered a cup of coffee. A red-haired, short and heavyset waitress brought the steaming cup to him and left a check at the same time. While he drank the dark brew, he sorted out his impressions about what had happened at the compound.

He had accomplished his main goal. He knew which building Kali was in, as well as the basic layout of the compound. But he was not pleased about the strange and sudden rush of fear that had gripped him when he'd recognized Langst.

The Others

He needed to control that fear with the same kind of strength he'd found that had enabled him to block Langst's attempt to penetrate his thoughts.

Langst snarled when the man deflected his probe. He glared angrily as Blaine drove away and continued to stare at the car until it was out of sight. Then he returned to the building and to his quarters.

Inside and alone, he opened a window, undressed and shifted into the form of a sparrow.

Seven minutes later and from 100 feet up in the air, Langst watched Blaine leave his car and go into the restaurant.

Then, as Langst landed, he shifted again. Where the small sparrow had touched the ground, a large mastiff walked. He went to a spot where he could watch Blaine's rental car.

Later, as Blaine came through the door, the mastiff rose and started forward. When Blaine put his keys into the car, the mastiff growled.

Aaron's hand froze on the door handle when a low and dangerous growl reached his ears. He looked over his shoulder and saw the huge dog that had made the sound. The brown and black mastiff sat on its haunches, a half dozen feet from the car.

Not wanting to provoke the dog, Aaron held

still. When the animal did not start forward, Aaron carefully pulled the door handle and began to open the door.

When the dog still didn't move, Aaron relaxed. But as he started to ease himself into the car, the dog growled again. Aaron looked at the dog. Its canines were bared in a fierce grimace.

The air around the giant dog crackled with danger. Holding himself perfectly still, so as not to provoke the animal, Aaron looked at the mastiff's eyes.

Shockingly he recognized the green and evil eyes. He felt a tentative probe push against his mind. His stomach churned with revulsion, and he swallowed hard. "No," he whispered. The word seemed to have been pulled forcefully from between his lips.

He sensed the dog move even before it rose onto all fours. The air changed around them. The ozone scent of a thunderstorm flooded his nostrils. He half-fell, half-leapt into the car, slamming the door an instant before the giant of a dog crashed against it, snarling and snapping at Aaron's face.

Watching the dog's frenzied attack, Aaron knew that if Langst wanted him right then, the otherworlder could shatter the glass and tear him apart.

As he thought this, the mastiff stopped its onslaught and sat back down on its haunches. When Aaron again stared into those malevolent green eyes, a chill settled over him.

The Others

Aaron turned on the ignition, jammed the gear shift into reverse and stepped on the accelerator.

Michael returned to the Sheraton shortly after 6:00 and called up to their room. A half hour later, while they were seated in the dining room, Aaron ended his story about his visit at the Sperry compound.

"I can't get rid of one thought," he said.

Michael remained silent, waiting.

"Before today, Langst was chasing me on the astral level. But now he's chasing me here as well. He's after me on two levels, Michael."

"Which you're unable to do anything about. However, you did learn a few things of your own today. I just wish you hadn't pushed that hard. Now they'll be more on guard."

"They already were. Didn't it strike you as strange that Lowell agreed to see me so quickly?" Then Aaron changed the subject. "Did you learn anything in Sperry Hollow?"

Michael shrugged. "They wouldn't talk to me."

"Did you try any of the girl's friends?"

"Yeah. Two of them wouldn't talk to me. Another one was spouting foolishness."

"What foolishness?" Aaron asked as he pushed away his plate.

"She said that it was probably some guy who Frannie was sneaking out with. Someone with a fancy car. This girl also said that she thinks that Bobby—that's Frannie's boyfriend—caught them, and that the guy with Frannie killed them both and made it look like an animal attack."

"Sound a little farfetched to you?" Aaron asked with a smile.

"Doesn't it to you?"

"You can't ask me a question like that. After all, I'm the guy who's in love with a werewolf."

"Aaron," Michael grumbled.

Aaron laughed. "A week ago, I would only believe in concrete facts, and you believed in the impossible. Why not in that girl's story? The story does makes sense, at least to me. Think about it. When I met Frannie that night, she tried to pick me up. All she could do was talk about my car. What if this Langst played her game? What if they went out, and the boyfriend followed them? He caught them in the act, so to speak, and went after Langst who changed, shapeshifted and killed the boyfriend. Then he had to finish Frannie. She was found a quarter mile away. She was running from him, Michael. She had to be."

Michael nodded. "That makes sense."

"A sick kind of sense."

"What now, White Man?"

"Hey, I thought you were the one with all the ideas." When Michael remained silent, Aaron said, "Okay. We need to check out the names of the six subjects. Let's find out about them and try to correlate them to the animal attacks."

"You're going into the computers again?" Michael asked.

"No, not this time. I'd have to use the F.B.I. data banks, and they'd get wise. They're already on to us."

"What then?" Michael asked.

"Richard," Aaron said simply.

"Your brother thinks you're crazy."

"Yeah, but he's still my brother."

"I think you're crazy."

"You're still my friend.

After finishing a second cup of coffee, Aaron and Michael went up to their room where Aaron called his brother's house. Kay Blaine, Richard's wife, answered the phone. After a few worried and tense questions, she turned the phone over to Richard, whose first words were, "Where the hell are you?"

"With Michael."

"In Arizona?" Richard asked.

Aaron ignored his brother's question. "I need a favor."

"Do you know how much trouble you're in? The Feds have a blanket warrant out for you. National Security. Aaron, what the hell have you gotten yourself into?"

"Richard, since you wouldn't believe me when I told you the truth before, you won't believe me now. But I still need a favor."

"Let me speak to Michael."

Aaron handed Michael the phone. "I think he wants an analysis of my mental health."

"Richard, this is Michael."

Aaron leaned his head against Michael's to hear his brother's words. "I thought you were going to help him to get better, not help him go to jail. Or are you as insane as he is?"

"He's as sane as I am," Michael told Richard. "He's not crazy, Richard."

"The shrink here thinks so."

"Richard, we don't have a lot of time. Aaron needs your help. He is in trouble, but he's not insane. There was a woman on the road the night of the accident. She is part of a government experimental program, and I can't say anything more about it. You'll have to trust me—and trust Aaron."

"Tell him to come back. Tell him it's not too late to clear himself with the Feds. He's a cop. They'll go easier with him."

"No, they won't, Richard. Didn't you hear what I said? With what we've learned, they'll put us both away—forever."

"What the hell is going on?" Richard demanded.

"You don't want to know, not yet."

Then Aaron took the phone. "You're the only one I can trust, Richard. You're my brother. Help me, Richard. It's important."

There was a moment's silence before Richard spoke again. "What do you need?"

"Get a pencil. I'm going to give you a list of names. I need them traced. I need to know everything about them."

"And how will I find out about them?"

"Make them part of a homicide investigation. You do have one or two of those going on, don't you? Use the F.B.I. criminal investigation procedure. Let them do the work."

"All right, Aaron. But when this is over . . ."

"You'll be the first to get the story." Five minutes later, Aaron finished with his brother, after learning that his condo building was being watched for his return.

"At least they haven't put a tap on my phone."

"How do you know?" Michael asked.

"Procedure. You don't waste time when it's pointless. They're pretty sure I'm not in Dallas. They've already tossed my apartment and found my portable computer was missing."

"So?"

"So I can still use my home phone." Smiling, he picked up the telephone and called Dallas again. The call was answered on the third ring, and Aaron spoke briefly to his neighbor, Carolyn Parks. Carolyn had a key to the apartment and had always taken care of his plants when he was out of town. He asked her to set up his telephone for call forwarding and gave her the Sperry computer number. When he hung up, he smiled again.

Michael's face was still blank.

"When we call the computer at Sperry, I don't think it would be wise to do it from this phone. It would be too easy to trace."

Michael's face was still a blank. "So?"

"Call forwarding."

"Fancy white man's extravagance. On the reservation, all we get are the basics. Sometimes we even get a dial tone."

Ignoring Michael's denigration, Aaron went on. "Baby Bell will throw off the call tracing, at least at the beginning. I'll call my home phone, which will be set to dial the Sperry computer. The call will go through my lines and will then be shuttled over to Sperry."

"In other words, you're going to make a twenty-five hundred mile phone call to a place thirty miles from here."

"Yup."

"But eventually they'll get wise."

"Eventually, but not right away."

"It's the eventually that worries me."

"That's why we make reservations in another motel for each time we call Sperry. We'll go there, use that phone, and as soon as we're off line, we get out.

"When do we start?"

"Not until Richard gets us the information."

"What do we do until then?"

Aaron shrugged. He didn't have an answer. There was only his sense of underlying impatience and the knowledge that something was going to happen soon.

The next day, and with his impatience growing out of hand, Aaron called Richard's house every hour, starting at noon. At four, Kay had some information for him.

"Richard says that only three of those names checked out as of a half hour ago. Those three were under suspicion in connection with a double death on their property. It happened ten years ago."

"Which three?"

"Charles Langst, Kali Moss, and Amelia Burke."

Aaron closed his eyes for a moment. When he opened them, he exhaled slowly. "Thank you, Kay. Thank Richard for me."

"Take care, Aaron. And Aaron . . . I . . . we miss you."

"I miss you, too, Kay." Aaron hung up.

Turning to Michael, Aaron shook his head. "Three names checked out. Langst, Amelia Burke, and Kali."

"Check out how?"

Aaron told him what Richard had learned and waited for Michael's reaction. But there was none.

"Well?" he asked.

"Well what? We already know what Langst is. We already know about Kali. All this does is confirm our own information."

"Why was Kali part of the investigation with Langst?"

Michael shook his head. "You'll have to ask her."

Aaron stared at Michael for several moments. "All right. I'll do that."

"When?"

"Tonight. Later. Before we go into the Sperry computer."

"This is it then?"

"This is it."

Chapter Fourteen

"This may be dangerous. Remember the last time."

"I remember," Aaron said, his eyes locked on Michael's. "If I can't reach Kali immediately, I'll withdraw."

"Okay. Do you need any help in projecting?"

Aaron shook his head. Aaron lay back on the bed and closed his eyes. His body was rife with tension, but he slowly willed himself to relax. His mind was jumbled with a myriad of thoughts. One by one, he put them aside. Even the knowledge that Kali had been a suspect in a murder investigation was shunted away.

When he was totally relaxed, he began to breathe evenly, not deeply but shallow. His breaths were short, but he was not aware of that.

One moment he was lying on the hotel bed; the next he was floating in the heavens, rising toward the rainbow levels of the astral plane. When he reached the golden band, he stepped onto the golden plateau.

Carefully, willing control over his mind, he pushed out a single thought. *Kali.*

He waited tensely, looking everywhere, watching for Kali or for anything else that might appear. A moment later he felt Kali's caress-like greeting within his mind. He inhaled her special scent.

She coalesced before him, and he drank in the beauty radiating from her astral embodiment and communicated with her. *He did not stop you this time.*

Not this time. He is away.

For how long?

I don't know.

Aaron reached out with his thoughts, using them as he would his hand to caress her cheek. They gazed at each other for several seconds.

He will be waiting for you when you come for me. He knows what you plan to do, Kali told him.

No, Aaron replied, *he only knows that I am coming. He doesn't know about Michael. He doesn't know when or how.*

If I ask you again to go away, will you?

Will I? he asked, opening his mind fully to her.

The Others

I am sorry, Aaron.

Aaron felt what he could only describe as tears within her thoughts. *But I am not. We will survive this, Kali.*

And if we do, what then?

We'll have to find out, won't we?

Aaron reached out, and as he did, it seemed as if his real body had risen to this upper plane of existence. When he touched her, he felt her. When he drew her to him, he could feel the heat from her breasts pressing on his chest. And when he lowered his mouth to hers, he tasted the sweet warmth of her lips.

Time halted. Their kiss deepened, and passion burst forth. Aaron did not once wonder about the reality of what was happening, or of the fact that it was only his mind that was with Kali on this plateau.

All he knew was that they were together. They sank slowly to the golden carpet of grass, and without willing it to happen, they were making love. As they joined together, giving to each other rather than taking, their love and passions burst forth to seal their fate and consummate what had begun that long-ago night outside of Sperry Hollow.

Later, after their passions abated and Kali lay within the crook of Aaron's arm, Aaron gazed down upon her. *I don't know how this was possible*, he said, *but it did happen.*

It's possible because we wanted it to be. Making love is not done with just the body. The mind is

179

just as important. What we have done tonight is more than make love. Aaron, we have become one. My mind is yours. There is nothing that we can hide from each other. Where I come from—my world—when two people are certain of their love for each other, they join not only physically, but mentally. Their minds are open, and they are locked together until death. This mating of body and mind is not a step lightly undertaken, for one's life is forever linked with the other's.

Marriage, Aaron said to her.

It is more than marriage, Aaron, much more.

And that is what we've done?

It is what I've done. I have committed myself to you. We are different. You do not yet know your mind. The option is still open for you.

No, Kali, there is no option.

But you have doubts still.

Aaron gave himself a mental shake. *My doubts will ease. My love will stay.*

As will mine, for as long as you live.

Aaron sensed sadness within her thoughts and asked her why. *On your world, I am what is called immortal.*

Aaron tried to understand what she was saying. *You never die?*

No, I can die, but not like you. When we are pulled into this world, something happens. I do not know what. Our bodies never age. We remain the same age physically, as when we arrived here. We are immune to your diseases. Death can come

from a physical object, but not disease or age.
  How long have you been here?
  A long time.

Aaron felt her sadness again, but the sadness was taken from him as he felt Kali's warm caress within the very center of his being. Her visual image shifted, and she sat up across from him. She took his hands in hers, drew him to a sitting position, and then looked directly into his eyes. *Come inside, Aaron, come into my mind. There is much you must learn.*

Aaron gripped her hands tightly, even though he was aware they did not exist, and let his thoughts reach out toward where she had already opened her mind.

Her gentle touch covered his thoughts and brought him within her mind. She traveled with him, guided him even, as she completely opened herself up to him.

Aaron did not know how long he was within her mind. Time no longer held any value for him as he learned about Kali and Kali's world.

Her world was a place just like his Earth. It had the same continents, mountains and oceans. And he soon discovered that both Gable and Michael had been right about the evolution of Kali's species. They had evolved into metaphysical beings. They were a race of people who could change their bodies into those of other forms to accomplish whatever

181

they needed to do. Yet they were not an evil species, but the same kind of people as were those of his own world.

They grew up, worked, lived, loved, raised families and died, just as the people of Aaron's world did. Yet there was a peacefulness to this parallel Earth that was alien to him. The people of this world lived in harmony with the planet, utilizing it but not destroying it.

Aaron saw one other thing with a clarity of sight that left him shaken. Kali's world was a gentle world, a peaceful world that was almost like a fairy tale. This scared him more than anything else could have, for he remembered Herman Gable's warning about Amos Aldredge. On an innocent world like Kali's, Amos Aldredge could gain control of the unsuspecting people, and before they realized what had happened, Aldredge, with his knowledge of physics, science and psychology, could do things that were never done on that world before. He would be able to take over that world. Kali's people were too vulnerable, because they were too good.

With his newfound knowledge, Aaron withdrew slowly from Kali's mind. *Your world is beautiful. The people also. Why is Langst so different?*

He was once like the others. He is very old, Aaron. At first, living in fear of the people who inhabited this world made him become a hermit. But as the years passed, and he learned that he had become immortal on this world, he ventured out. Whenever he thought himself endangered, he would revert to his animal shape. Over the centuries he killed many people and became insane. I think his insanity was caused by a combination of killing and living for so long.

And you? Aaron asked, daring to bring out his thoughts at this time. *Why did the same fate not happen to you?*

Can you be sure it did not?

Aaron stared at her ethereal body, his mind going cold for a second. *Ten years ago, two people were killed in Santa Barbara. They were killed in animal attacks. You lived with Charles Langst and Amelia Burke then, didn't you?*

Yes.

Why?

Find your answer within my mind, she told him, her thoughts calm and gentle.

No, Aaron replied, refusing her offer and pulling back from the warmth of her mental touch. He wanted her to tell him; he did not want to look for the answer. It was important for him that she tell him.

Several years ago, Charles Langst went all over the world looking for my people, people who survived the separation from our world. He was gathering them because he had found someone who told him that he could make a doorway back to our world.

Aldredge.

Yes. I was the first he found. I was living in Canada in a sparsely populated area, content to spend my time away from people. It is best that way. When you do not grow old the people around you become frightened; then you must move again and start over. It is a lonely life with nothing stable.

What happened in Santa Barbara?

Kali mentally turned from him when he asked the question. For a brief moment, Aaron thought the worst. Then he tossed that thought away, remembering the beauty and innocence of Kali's mind from when they made love.

You are not capable of those things, he told her.

Kali turned to face him. *Can you be so certain?*

I have to be.

You are a special person, Aaron. I knew that when you drove off the road rather than hit me. When your spirit was leaving, I felt it then, too. I fell in love with you, Aaron, with the essence that makes you who you are. No, she went on, *I did not know that Langst killed anyone at that time. It was only when the police came to question us that I found out.*

Did he keep you a prisoner?

No. His mate—his wife—Amelia pleaded with me not to leave. She said he couldn't help it, and that once we were able to return to our world, he would be better. She promised she wouldn't let it happen again.

184

The Others

And you believed her?

I did, but I didn't stay with them. One day when I was alone, I left without telling them where I was going. I moved to New Mexico. I stayed there for the next nine years, until Langst found me again. When he did, he told me that we would be going home soon. I went with him after he'd told me that he'd found three more of our people. I wanted to go home, Aaron. Is that so wrong?

No. The thought was but a whisper.

Now even that hope is gone. Aldredge will find a way to get to my world, but I won't be going. Only Langst and Amelia will go at first. The rest of us are to be used for some sort of spy work. Only after we've done what they want will they send us home. But I don't believe them, Aaron. I don't trust them. I've already told them I won't be a part of it. Aldredge will destroy my world, Aaron. He and Langst will do it together. Aldredge believes he can join with my people, become one of them while using his knowledge of the sciences of this world.

Do you think Aldredge is capable of doing that?

I don't know. Aldredge thinks so.

What about your other people? Will they help to stop him?

No, they believe what they're told. They want to believe because they want to go home. They're all against me in this. I have no allies among my own.

The rest want to go home. What about you?
I am not from this world. Have I a choice?

Aaron gazed at her for several minutes, his eyes caressing the lines of her face, his thoughts gently moving over her mind with their own caress. *You have a choice.*

Once again Aaron felt Kali's sadness. *Do I?*
I will get you away from them.
Why? We are too different.

Why did you ask me to find you? Why did you make love with me now? Because you love me. Because I love you. And, Kali, I will get you away from them.

You are the first, Aaron. You are the only man I have let into my mind. There were other men over the years, men who I lived with, who I shared my body with. But never did I open my mind to any but you. Aaron, I have waited so long for you. And now I must lose you.

You will not lose me, Kali, not the way you think. Be ready when I come, Aaron told her as he let his thoughts entwine with hers and embrace her, showing her his love.

Come soon, was the whispered reply within his own mind.

"Damn it, Aaron, wake up!" Michael shouted, frantically shaking his friend's almost lifeless body. Finally, just when he thought he'd have to use CPR, Aaron's body spasmed, and Michael was staring into Aaron's deep blue eyes.

His audible sigh was followed by heated words of relief. "Jesus, are you trying to scare me to death? I've been trying to get you back for ten minutes."

"I'm fine," Aaron said matter-of-factly as he sat up. He felt good, relaxed, as if he'd slept for a full night.

"Are you? Your pulse was nonexistent. You weren't breathing, or at least you didn't seem to be."

"I don't know. I wasn't here. But I'm fine, Michael."

"Yeah? Tell me about it."

"I intend to."

For the next hour, Aaron spoke and Michael listened. When Aaron finished, Michael was silent for several minutes. When he did speak, his voice was heavy with emotion.

"We have to get her out. And we have to try and stop Aldredge."

"We have to find out just how close Aldredge is to making a doorway if we're to stop him. But," Aaron added fervently, "no matter what, I'm going to get Kali out."

An hour and a half later, Aaron had his computer set up in a dingy room of a third rate motel a half mile off the interstate. He had registered under a false name, paying cash for the room. He had just finished hooking up the telephone coupler and dialed his home phone number, which transferred him automatically to the Sperry number.

D.M. Wind

Michael stood behind him, watching Aaron's fingers race over the keyboard. A few seconds later, the computer's green screen came alive as the connection with the Sperry enclave was made.

Michael handed Aaron the printout of the D.O.D. file on Project Doorway, and Aaron entered the access number. The screen flashed briefly, and a listing that was the Sperry computer's directory appeared on the monitor.

Aaron looked over the listings, choosing one at random. But when he pressed the enter key for the selection, the screen changed, and he was asked for a password.

Aaron glanced up at Michael. "I didn't expect that."

"What?"

"A secondary in-house security system. This might take a while," he added, turning back to the screen. Before he could try out a coding sequence, the request for the password flickered off, and a blinking ACCESS DENIED appeared. Then the screen went blank.

"What happened?" Michael asked, puzzled.

"Timed password response. If the password isn't entered within preset time specifications, the computer automatically disconnects the call. It prevents someone from playing with code sequences to break into the program."

"Now what?"

Aaron shrugged and redialed. When he was connected with Sperry again, he brought up the user menu. This time he studied the list more carefully. Five minutes later, he tried another file. He got the same results as before.

"Dead end?"

"Maybe not," Aaron said, leaning back to stare at the screen. "We can't use a phone, but I don't think we'd have the same problem if we were inside, at a terminal."

"Inside? Aaron, that's lunacy!"

Ignoring Michael's tirade, Aaron shrugged. "We have to find out how far Aldredge has gotten."

"No, White Man, what we have to do is help Kali, remember?"

Aaron's eyes locked with Michael's. "I never forgot." He picked up the phone and realized that the line was still open. Holding the receiver to his ear, he listened to the high-pitched sounds of a computer generated signal.

"Damn!" he swore. Standing, Aaron disconnecting the computer. "We have to get out of here. The line is still open. They have a lock on it. I was wrong," Aaron admitted. "They are using an automatic trace through my phone in Dallas. Stupid!"

Working together, they gathered their things and left. Just as they turned onto the ramp of the interstate, they saw three cars speeding toward the motel. Aaron recognized the uniformed man in the lead car. It was Thomas Lowell.

"That was close," Michael whispered.

Aaron held the car at 55 and stared straight ahead. "Tomorrow. We have to do it tomorrow."

Behind him loomed the Capitol Building. Ahead of him was his concrete veldt. Langst walked with determination. Eyes tracked him but quickly left him. They knew instinctively that he was not prey, not a weak man, not a lost soul wandering along the slum street.

The night smells assaulted him. Filth and decay overrode most other scents, but he could still detect food and fear and—blood. He smelled it. He could almost taste it. Somewhere nearby, someone was dying, violently.

He began to shake, just a little, as his need swelled within him. The need and the hunger had to be satisfied. He had to have his draught of death fear. He had been denied the other night on the road. Amelia's little hunt had helped to assuage his hunger, but it had not satisfied him fully. Tonight he would not be denied!

But as he sent his senses out to range for prey, he was struck with a wave of disgust. He had always scorned those of his kind who had hunted this way. He was a hunter who liked to run beneath the open sky. He abhorred invading the warrens of a rat-infested city, choosing his prey by where they lived and in what conditions. But he had no choice. Aldredge held too much power over him. And until Aldredge could open a doorway back, he had to bow to that egotistical fool's will.

He growled, deep in his throat, and felt his body start to flow into another shape. He stopped himself before it happened.

He walked slowly along the sidewalk, his senses reaching outward. He went another two blocks before stopping at the mouth of an alley. He looked into the alley and saw halfway down its length.

The darkness was no obstacle for Langst. His eyes pieced through the night, and he saw a man trying to build a bed out of cardboard and old newspaper. He studied the homeless man for several seconds. The man was tall, and from the way he moved, Langst could tell that he had once been a strong man. But now he was thin and weak. He wore old stained pants and a floppy, flannel checked shirt that was drenched in sweat.

There was no one else in the alley.

Langst started forward. By his second step, he flowed, and the giant mastiff emerged. The homeless man didn't even glance at the dog as it pretended to sniff at the piles of refuse lining the building walls.

But when the green-eyed dog edged closer to the man, the man picked up a piece of wood. "Watch it," he warned the dog. "This is my house for tonight."

Langst stood still. He stared at the man through the dog's eyes, watching him, waiting for the fear to begin.

"Git!" the man shouted.

The dog growled. The man held his small club in one hand and picked up something from the ground. "Git!" he shouted and flung an empty can at the dog.

The can hit the dog on the shoulder. The dog didn't move.

"What the—"

The dog's growls deepened. The folds of skin over the dog's mouth drew back, and it bared large white canines. The man tensed. He gripped the club in both hands and scooted to his feet.

The dog moved forward as Langst's need burned hard inside him. The man stepped back until he was against the wall. He held the club defensively.

The man's fear began to leak out and Langst sucked it in avidly. His head began to buzz, and his need cried out for more. He moved closer, growling low.

The man was shaking now. His fear vibrated through the alley in undulating waves that cascaded through Langst's mind until Langst could no longer hold himself back.

192

The Others

He charged. The man swung his club and caught Langst on the shoulder. The dog ignored the pain as he landed high against the man's chest.

And then Langst shifted. He flowed from the shape of the huge mastiff into a sleek and slithering, wide-bodied constrictor.

The man began to scream as the terror overwhelmed him. The club fell from his hands, and his eyes locked with the evil green eyes of the giant snake. An eternal instant later, Langst struck.

The boa constrictor bit into the man's shoulder and then threw its first coil around the man's legs.

A half minute later, the man fell to the ground, screaming and kicking at the living rope that bound him.

Langst drew his snake's head back and stared into the man's eyes. Then he slowly crushed the life out of his victim. During every second of the man's slow and agonizing death, Langst sucked into himself the fear and the pain and that one special moment of final release—the instant the man died.

When the man breathed his last breath, and there was no more left for Langst to feed upon, he shifted back into his real body.

He knelt at the man's side, touched his chest and felt the broken mass of bones and crushed organs. No one would connect him to this death. They would find the man in the morning and think he'd fallen from the roof.

Langst laughed, loud and long. A moment later he shifted. Using the shape of a bird, he rose high above the nation's capital. He wheeled in the sky, cried out once and headed back to Sperry Hollow.

At exactly 2:30, Aaron, using a pay phone, called Thomas Lowell at Sperry. All he had to do was say his name and the captain was on the phone.

"That wasn't a brilliant move. I'd expected better from you," Lowell said. "Didn't you think we'd have a trace set up?"

"I don't know what you're talking about," Aaron replied, "and I don't think I want to. But I do want to talk to you."

"Why?" Lowell's voice was guarded, edgy.

"Privately. Off the installation."

"Why?" Lowell repeated.

"That's what you'll have to find out. And Lowell, only you. No Feds, no army intelligence."

"If you had come today, instead of yesterday, you wouldn't have left."

Rather than reply to Lowell's statement, Aaron told him to drive into Sperry Hollow at 4:00 o'clock. Then he hung up.

Turning to Michael, Aaron shrugged. "Strange . . . He was trying to warn me that the Feds know I'm here. Why?"

"Will he meet us?"

"I don't know. We'll have to wait and find out."

At 3:30, Aaron and Michael were parked on Sperry Hollow's main street, 100 feet from the town's only traffic light. Both men were alert, watching everything and everyone that passed. They waited patiently for the full half hour, Michael in the back seat, Aaron at the wheel.

At exactly 4:00 o'clock, Aaron spotted Lowell's army green sedan. He cut in front of it and slowed at the intersection. In the back seat, Michael turned to stare at Lowell. Then he motioned Lowell to follow them.

Aaron turned the corner, went one block, turned again, then stopped. When Lowell made the second turn and stopped behind Aaron's car, Michael was at Lowell's door.

"Out. Give me your hat. Now!"

Lowell stared at the stone-faced Indian and then opened the door. He handed Michael his hat and went to the passenger side of Aaron's car.

When Aaron started off, Michael U-turned and drove out of Sperry Hollow, leaving Aaron and Lowell together. If anyone was tailing Lowell, they would be following Michael now.

"What's the point of this?" Lowell asked.

"Call it caution. I don't like the view from inside a cage."

"Then give it up, Blaine. You're going against something you have no idea about."

D.M. Wind

"Don't I?" Aaron asked, turning back onto the main road. He drove silently for a half mile, checking his rearview mirror to make sure he wasn't being followed. When he was certain, he U-turned and drove to the McDonald's.

Parking the car, he shut off the ignition and faced Lowell.

"Talk to me, Lowell. Tell me about Sperry. Tell me why you came alone today."

Lowell stared at him before he slowly shook his head and sighed with frustration. "You're in a lot of trouble, Blaine. You're putting your nose into a place that is best left alone. I came because I felt you've had enough trouble and grief. I don't think you're a bad person, Blaine, just someone who's acting under a misconception."

"I can't accept that. Tell me about Project Doorway."

Again, Lowell exhaled loudly and shook his head. "Mr. Blaine, I've made allowances for you because of what you've been through. But your action last night and your insistence that something is being covered up can no longer be tolerated. Our work at Sperry is very delicate. We can't have people barging around. Go home, Mr. Blaine. Go back to Dallas and cover your tail. Face the warrant. You're a smart man. Concoct a good enough story to get you off the hook. If you do it now, I'll use all my influence to help you get out of the charges. Let me help you. Please."

Aaron smiled. "That's very generous. Exactly what charges are being brought against me?"

"You're a member of the Dallas police department. Surely you know that we can use any charge we feel like, under the blanket of national security."

"And when I come to trial, I'll expose Sperry."

"You'll never get to trial, Mr. Blaine. They'll never let you." Lowell's tone carried a sense of something that was already accomplished. It had a feel of regret to it, also.

In that very moment, Aaron knew that Lowell was telling the truth. His breath hissed out; his hands knotted into fists. "If I don't give up?"

Lowell shrugged.

"I think you are a decent man, Captain. I felt that yesterday, and I feel it even more today. I don't think you like what's happening at the research facility any more than I do. I believe that's why you met me today, and why you're warning me off instead of arresting me. If you had wanted to, you could have arrested me when I was in your office."

Aaron pointed toward the entrance of the fast food restaurant. "That is where Frannie Coltrain worked."

"Who?" Lowell asked, refusing to meet Aaron's eyes.

"The woman who was killed last week by that, ah, escaped leopard."

"So?"

"I know what killed her."

"You already said it was a leopard."

"I said what killed her—not who. If I stay around here, will you send one of your pets after me, too? Dear God, she was only nineteen years old. Lowell, she was a child. Why was she murdered? Why, damn you?"

Lowell turned pale, but he refused to back down. "You don't know what you're talking about. Get out, Blaine, get out now!"

"Aldredge is playing with something very dangerous. He's involved in something that he has no real conception of. If he succeeds in opening a doorway, it may very well end our world as we know it. Think about that, Lowell. Think about having to wonder if every person you meet might not be what they appear to be. Think about someone you love, Captain, and then remember what Charles Langst did to Frannie Coltrain and her boyfriend."

Staring at Lowell, he saw that the man was in the midst of an inner struggle. But Aaron also knew that Lowell was loyal to himself and his country.

Finally, Lowell shook his head. "If you come near Sperry again, you'll leave me no choice."

"If . . ." Aaron replied as a dark form approached the car.

"Out," Michael ordered as he opened the passenger door.

Lowell spun at his unexpected appearance.

"Your car is on the shoulder, a hundred yards toward town."

The Others

Lowell got out of the car and said, "Leave it be, Blaine. You're in over your head."

"Captain," Michael called. When Lowell was looking straight at him, Michael smiled. "It's not Aaron. It's you and your people who are in over your heads."

"I don't know who you are, but tell your friend to leave this area if he wants to live to his biblical age."

"As opposed to the people in your lab?"

Lowell stiffened. But instead of leaving, he bent and spoke to Aaron once again. "If you're willing to leave, I'll get you out of Virginia and make sure that all federal charges are dropped. You'll have to sign the standard National Security Act agreement never to divulge what you know about Project Doorway, but I'll get you out of this, and you'll be clean."

"I'll think about it," Aaron promised.

"I'll do the same for your friend." Then he turned and walked away.

Michael got in the car, glanced at Aaron and sat back. "When do we get Kali?"

Aaron watched Lowell's retreating back for several moments before he answered Michael.

"Tonight."

Chapter Fifteen

Humidity clung to the night air like vines to a trellis. Overhead, clouds gathered in angry swirls to hide the moon. The scent of rain was accented by flashes of lightning that illuminated the far-flung mountains of the Shenandoah Valley. It was a perfect night for Aaron and Michael.

The two friends, standing at the tall chain link fence, were dressed in black. Five feet from them was a no trespass warning.

Twenty-five feet further away was their rental car. It looked as though the car had a flat. The jack was set up on the side of the car, facing away from the road. A flat tire lay in plain sight on the ground near the jack. But there was no flat, and although the car appeared to be jacked up, it was ready to be driven away.

"You're sure these suits will work?" Michael asked as he readjusted his shirt and pulled his collar high over the material of the exercise/sauna suits they had purchased earlier at a sporting goods and hunting equipment store.

"They'll work. The infrared sensors' sensitivity have to be set high enough so that a small animal's body heat won't be detected. Our faces and hands are all that's exposed. These exercise suits are thermal suits that seal our body heat inside. When we're closer, we'll put the masks on."

"And sweat to death."

"Not if we move fast enough. Ready?" Aaron asked.

"Almost." Michael reached to the small of his back. His hand dipped into his waistband, and when it reappeared, he held a Smith and Wesson .38. The pistol's blue barrel was almost invisible in the darkness.

"Where the hell did you get that?" Aaron asked.

"The same place you got yours, White Man—from my suitcase. I put it there before we left Phoenix."

"Michael . . ." Aaron began but stopped himself. Since Michael was exposing himself to danger because of him, he wasn't about to tell

him to leave the gun in the car. "Be careful."
Then he touched the butt of his own pistol to
reassure himself it was there.

"Hey, you too. Now, hand me the clippers."

It took them four and a half minutes to get
through the fence, and after using garbage ties
to reseal it from any casual inspection, they
headed toward the research buildings a half
mile away.

"How much time before Lowell gets wise and
comes back?"

"Another hour, if we're lucky," Aaron replied
as he continued working his way forward. "And
if I read the man right," he added.

Captain Thomas Lowell drove the lead car,
his thoughts centered on the two men he was
going to meet. He felt just as betrayed as he
knew Blaine and Noriss would be. They had
trusted him, and he was about to show them
how misplaced their trust was.

When he'd returned from his meeting with
Blaine, he'd found two senior National Security
Agency men waiting for him. The agents—who
had been had assigned to the Sperry Compound
when Lowell had reported Blaine's first contact—had demanded a full report of his meeting
with Blaine.

"They switched cars. I had to go with Blaine
in his car."

"We heard that on the bug in your car. What
happened?"

"He drove me around."

"What does he know?" The N.S.A. agent who asked the question was a mocha-skinned Afro-American.

"Yes, what does he know?" Lowell turned to find Amos Aldredge staring at him.

"Nothing much. He knows that Kali Moss is here; he referred to her by name. He also knows that it was one of your people who killed the local girl."

"He must be silenced." The agent's statement had been spoken as an unemotional fact while his half-hooded eyes had locked with the darker N.S.A. man's in emphasis.

"They may come to us," Lowell told the other three men, although he himself didn't believe Blaine would quit. "I made them an offer. I told them that if they dropped their foolish investigation and left, and if they sign a secrecy act statement, I'd clear them and wipe their records."

"Good," the caucasian N.S.A. agent had said. "Where are they staying?"

"I don't know where they're staying."

"We're starting a check of all motels in a fifty mile radius. We'll find them, unless they call you first."

Even as the machinery to locate Aaron was put into motion, Blaine had called. He had told Lowell that he and Noriss would accept the captain's offer. The N.S.A. man who had been monitoring the call had nodded and motioned for Lowell to make the arrangements. But before he could give Blaine instructions, Blaine had cut him off.

"I'll call you later. I'll tell you where to meet us. And be alone, Lowell."

"Not alone. I'll have three other men. This has to be done legally. There must be witnesses to your signatures on the secrecy statements. After the papers are signed, we'll take you to the airport and send you back home."

"Do I have your word?" Blaine had asked. Lowell had stared at the two N.S.A. men for several pregnant seconds before making Blaine the promise.

When he'd hung up, he'd favored the N.S.A. agents with an angry glare. But all they'd done was to smile and say, "Good work."

And as he shifted his thoughts from the last phone call, Lowell realized in 15 or so minutes he would have the two men in custody and would have successfully betrayed them.

Yet, as he drove, a gnawing feeling that something was wrong grew within him. After talking with Blaine earlier that afternoon, he had not expected Blaine to give up.

Shrugging, Lowell looked at the country road they'd turned onto a moment before. The spot Blaine had chosen for the meeting was 40 miles from Sperry and ten miles outside of Harrisonburg. It was a desolate section of an old highway that had been replaced by the interstate, six miles away.

The Others

When he'd gotten Blaine's call, less than an hour earlier, he'd jotted down Aaron's instructions. With the two N.S.A. men in one car and one of his own security men in his car, they'd started out. But as he pulled the car to a stop next to a deserted and extinct Esso station and looked around, his uneasiness increased. It took a moment of staring into the dark night for his subconscious to sort through things and allow him to understand that his anger at what the N.S.A. men and Aldredge wanted to do to Blaine and Noriss had made him not think everything through in a logical way.

As he looked around the meeting place, Lowell intuitively knew that Blaine had sent him on a wild goose chase. He was now positive that Blaine and Noriss would not show up. He also knew that the N.S.A. men would not accept his instinctive judgment.

"Keep your eyes open," he told the soldier sitting next to him.

They made good time, covering the half mile in under eight minutes. Now Aaron and Michael were hidden by the cover of three large oaks, 50 feet from the research building entrance.

Lifting the infrared glasses he'd purchased that afternoon, Aaron looked carefully around. "Two cameras and sensors on the lab, one over the door. Two more on the administration building's roof."

"Is that all?"

Aaron swept the binoculars in every direction. "I think so."

"Tell her we're coming," Michael said as he drew the homemade thermal mask over his face.

Aaron did the same and then closed his eyes. He formed the thought and projected it to Kali. He waited, trying to feel her response, but a fuzzy interference formed within his mind. He shook his head but did not try to project his thoughts again. Instead he reached into his pocket and withdrew a thin double metal tube.

"Let's go."

Bending low, the two men moved stealthily across the open area. Aaron paused halfway to the door, turned a t-valve on the small cylinder and tossed it away.

The tube hit the ground with a light metallic clink, rolled a few inches and stopped. Aaron pushed Michael ahead, while the cameras and infrared sensors tracked toward the metal tube. Inside the cylinder, a magnesium fire burned, fed by the two and a half inch long oxygen tank strapped to the casing. The steel cylinder would contain the flames which the oxygen gave birth to, and it was strong enough not to explode. The tremendous amount of heat generated within the metal tube was enough to attract every sensor within 25 yards.

They opened the door and slipped inside. Resting their backs against the closed door, they breathed deeply. Aaron's nerves were humming; Michael's muscles were knotted with tension.

Aaron looked around. He had the impression of standing in a hospital corridor. The walls and floor were gleaming white. Four different color lines ran along the floor and ceiling, guideposts to other destinations.

"Where?" Michael asked.

Across from them and a few feet down the hall was a sign. Aaron motioned to Michael. The sign was the color legend for the building—blue for the lab, yellow for offices, red for the living facilities, and green for medical.

"It's too quiet," Michael whispered.

"It's three in the morning," Aaron countered, feeling the onset of a cloudy, not quite right sensation that permeated the air of the building.

The red and green lines went off in one direction, the blue and yellow in another. Aaron and Michael, following the red line, headed toward the living facilities. At the juncture where the lines divided, they flattened themselves against the wall.

Peering cautiously around the corner, Aaron saw two uniformed men barring the entrance to the living area. He drew his head back quickly. "Guards," he whispered. He started back in the direction they had come from.

He passed by the entrance, then followed the blue line to the lab. There were no guards at the door. Aaron slipped inside, drawing Michael with him. When the door was closed, Aaron took off the thermal mask. Moving slowly, he turned on one light. The sight that greeted his eyes made his hopes soar.

Michael watched uneasily when his friend moved toward the banks of computers filling the room and asked, "What the hell are you doing?"

"We're in the main computer room. Michael, we have a chance to find out what Aldredge has learned."

"I don't believe you! Man, do you have your priorities screwed up. We're here for Kali, not this!"

"Five minutes, Michael. Gable needs this, and I need five minutes." Without waiting for Michael's permission, Aaron went to a computer console and turned it on. Working quickly, he brought up the directory. When he found the file he wanted, he called it up and was proven correct in not having to have a secondary password in the lab itself.

With Michael looking over his shoulder, Aaron began to read and, true to his word, five minutes later he shut down the console. "He still hasn't completely figured out the spatial matrix. He's moving in the right direction, but he's off course. He's way behind Gable."

"Let's go," Michael suggested.

"Not yet." Aaron held up his hand to stop Michael. He closed his eyes and sent out a tentative probing thought. It went nowhere.

Aaron suddenly understood what had happened before. His thoughts were being blocked by someone.

"They know we're here," he told Michael.

"Who?" Michael asked, drawing his pistol.

"Kali's people. Maybe Langst. They're stopping me from reaching her."

"You want to pull out? Try again another night?"

"We can't. We'll never get back in." Shutting off the light, Aaron opened the door. "We'll take out the guards. We have to do it quickly."

Michael nodded. They went down the hall, following the red line once again. When they neared the spot where the guards were, Aaron took a deep breath and whispered, "Follow my lead."

When he started to move, a jolt of adrenaline surged through his system, twisting his stomach and making his heart pump hard. His nerves screamed as he reached the juncture and spoke.

"Doctor Aldredge wants that equipment now! He's crazy! It's three in the morning," Aaron spat disgustedly.

"I'm getting fed up with this crap!" Michael half-shouted as they turned the corner. The two guards stared at them, taken by surprise because they had expected to see familiar faces.

Before either guard could recover enough to pull a weapon, Michael and Aaron were on them. Michael's arm blurred in the air; a low thump sounded in the quiet hallway. An instant later came a second dull thud, followed by the moan of the man Aaron had struck.

Moving quickly and efficiently, Michael pulled out a roll of plastic tape from his pocket and bound each guard's wrists, while Aaron taped their mouths. After dragging the guards to the side, Aaron and Michael opened the door and entered the living quarters.

The instant Aaron crossed the threshold he found himself reacting strongly to some over-bearing presence. The sensation made his skin crawl, made him want to turn and run. Refusing to yield to the force, he drew on his inner strength and fought the feeling within his mind. At the same time, he looked at Michael and saw his friend's face twisted with his own private agony.

Reaching out, he grasped Michael's hand and squeezed hard while he continued to fight the tentacles burrowing within his mind.

Michael's eyes opened, and he exhaled slowly. He nodded to Aaron and exerted pressure on his friend's hand to show he was okay. An instant later the force disappeared, as if it had never been there.

"What?" Michael whispered.

"Who is more like it," Aaron replied. Then he started forward.

As Aaron and Michael went deeper into the living facilities, Aaron kept trying to reach Kali but received no response. The first two doors they passed revealed darkened, empty rooms. When Aaron looked in through the opening in the door, shock rippled through his mind. The room was no more than a cell. There was a toilet in one corner, a sink next to it, and a cot against the wall. The third room held one person. The low fluorescent light showed a pale man with blond hair. He was sleeping.

Aaron motioned Michael on, but he grasped Aaron's arm and leaned close to his ear.

"Have you reached her yet?" Michael whispered. Aaron shook his head. "Find her, quickly."

Again Aaron projected his thoughts. This time his head reeled as the thought was not only blocked but pushed back at him with tremendous force. Aaron leaned against the wall and gulped in air. Bile rose in the back of his throat. He was afraid he might throw up. He fought the sensations down and pushed himself away from the wall.

"Kali!" he yelled, the single shout breaking the suffocating silence of the hallway.

He started forward again. A sense of urgency added speed to his legs as he willed himself to ignore the force that was being thrown against him. He looked through two more door openings as he went past them. In the first, he saw a sleeping form. In the second was a man who sat on the bed staring listlessly at the ceiling.

"Kali!" Aaron shouted again. A moment later he froze at the faraway sound of her voice.

3# D.M. Wind

Instantly, Aaron and Michael were running toward the sound. They turned another corner and reached yet another door. Aaron was at it. When he looked through the small opening in the door's center, he saw Kali standing in the middle of the cell, and his breathing eased.

He tried the knob, but it wouldn't open. Then he looked at the digital readout of the special lock.

"They locked it two days ago and haven't opened it since. It's electrical. I can't manipulate it," Kali said when she reached the door and looked through the small opening at Aaron.

Aaron reached into the opening and met Kali's hand in its center. Her skin was vibrant, warm and alive.

"Can you open it?" Michael asked.

Aaron shook his head. "Not quietly, not without a digital analyzer."

"Damn it!"

"Stand back, Kali. Stand against the wall." Aaron drew his gun.

"Will it work?" Michael asked.

"It'll work, but it will also alert the people outside this building."

"Do it, man. Now!"

Aaron stepped back and fired directly into the electronic locking mechanism. Before the sound died, he pulled the door open and stepped inside.

Kali flew into his arms. As they physically held each other, their lips met for the first time. When they drew apart, Aaron gazed at her, drinking in the face he had only seen in his mind. "I love you."

Kali caressed his cheek. "I've waited so long for you," she whispered.

"There won't be any more waiting if we don't move," Michael stated bluntly.

Kali looked at Michael. "Yes, Michael Noriss, you are right." She turned back to Aaron. "I felt you come in. I heard you call me, but my thoughts were being blocked."

"Mine, too. Let's go."

They were not more then ten feet from Kali's cell when a door opened to reveal a tall and strikingly beautiful woman. She had tawny gold hair that reached to her waist and a lithe, muscular body. Narrowed black eyes, like two dark slits, fastened onto Kali. The woman raised her arms, her palms facing the three who would escape.

Kali froze. Aaron tried to step forward but could not. It was as though a metal band had been placed around his chest and was being closed slowly.

Kali's arms rose, her palms outward, her fingers spread wide. Electricity crackled in the air even as the atmosphere thickened further with tension.

Aaron glanced at Michael and saw his friend looking at him. "Help us," he called through suddenly parched lips. He didn't know whether Michael heard him or would know what to do, as he turned back to the stranger and projected his mind, not at her, but at Kali.

His mind and thoughts blended into Kali's with a swiftness that threw him off balance. Steadying himself, Aaron quickly settled himself within the familiar and comfortable contours of her mind. But once again, he was staggered by the intensity of the mental battle he had so lately joined.

Within his mind and Kali's, he felt the vileness of the other's thoughts. Coiled among those thoughts were the dark lusts and twisted desires that drove this strange woman at them. But he and Kali were united as one, and he was secure. *Take what you need*, he told Kali. *Use my strength.*

And mine, came a weaker thought, but one that was friendly. Instinctively, Aaron knew that Michael was with them.

The hallway shimmered and wavered as the power of the three minds combined to fight the long-haired woman. The battle grew frightening, and its toll was hard upon all combatants.

Realizing that the woman's strength came from her insanity, Aaron instinctively wrapped his thoughts protectively around Kali's and Michael's. The trio then formed a mental phalanx which they propelled at the other woman like a lance.

It struck the other woman's mental defenses and spread out along its surface. It erupted forcefully, smashing the woman's protective barriers apart and striking directly into her mind.

The woman staggered, her powerful mental link broken. The instant it fell, Michael detached himself from Aaron and Kali's minds and launched himself at their common enemy.

He left the floor five feet from the woman and slammed into her with the full weight of his body as Aaron and Kali ran past them. Rolling free, Michael gained his feet and followed the others.

They ran silently to the door and then burst through it. Aaron didn't toss another heat stick. There wasn't time. Lights were flashing on all over the compound. A high decibel siren brought forth the hue and cry of alarm.

They ran across the open space and entered the woods. They did not pause in their wild flight through the trees, and by the time they cleared the woods, the sound of their forced breathing was loud in the air.

Three minutes later Aaron was at the fence, kicking at the opening and breaking the ties that secured it. Relief washed through him when he saw that the car was still there. He separated the fence and pulled one side in. "Go through," he told Kali between tortured breaths.

She started forward, stiffened suddenly and stopped. "It's too late." She turned back to face the woods. Seconds later, as the clouds parted and allowed the moon's light to reach the ground, two forms emerged from the woods.

Michael, his eyes locked on the two people coming toward them, handed Kali the car keys. "Get the car started. I'll hold them back!"

Aaron stiffened. "No, Michael, not this time. Get Kali to safety. Get her away."

Michael turned to Aaron. "Back there," Michael said, "when we were fighting that woman, I joined your mind and Kali's. It was a good feeling. It was right. I knew then that your future and Kali's are linked. They are inseparable." Michael paused to look at the two forms coming at them.

"And I learned the truth about my destiny. My destiny is a far different one from yours, Aaron. My fate has led me here tonight for a reason. Remember the Grandfather, Aaron? This night was what he foresaw. I can't leave here now. I was meant to be here, meant to do what is necessary, so that you will be able to continue on. You must bring Kali to the Grandfather. He will know how to help you. And, Aaron, you must stop Aldredge. If he succeeds, everyone will lose."

Michael glanced over his shoulder at the oncoming forms. "You are as much my brother as my friend. Remember that, Aaron. Now, go!" he ordered. Before Aaron could react, Michael spun and ran toward the two who were tracking them.

Aaron watched, unable to move forward or step back, as Michael drew his gun. "Start the car!" he commanded Kali and took a step forward.

Not without you, came her voice in his mind. *Michael is doing what he must. Do not let his actions be wasted. Come, Aaron.*

Aaron couldn't leave his friend. As he stood still and watched, he was grateful for Kali's gentle and understanding thoughts within his head.

Then the two people changed in a shimmering coalescence that left him blinking and staring at two powerful, low-slung animals—a giant black leopard and a tawny lioness.

Their chilling cries echoed skyward, the hunting cry of nature's most powerful beasts.

"No!" Aaron shouted, drawing his gun and starting forward when the lioness broke toward Michael. The leopard moved also, but he veered toward Aaron and Kali.

"Aaron, we must go while we can."

Aaron's hand tightened on his pistol as he watched Michael face the lioness.

Michael fought to control the fear lacing his body and mind. He could feel the shapeshifter within his head, trying to paralyze him even as she charged.

Dark and blood-drenched thoughts flooded his senses, bringing up old childhood fears to terrorize him into submission. But when the lioness gave vent to a primeval scream, he pictured the Grandfather's serene face before him and remembered who Michael Noriss was. He was pure Navajo. Within his blood ran the quintessence of a proud, strong race. He was the descendant of great chiefs and warriors, and he had been given a strong destiny to fulfill.

Michael looked into the black eyes of death and raised his pistol.

The lioness sprang, her back legs drawing up in preparation for the kill.

Fighting against her mental control, Michael pulled the trigger. The night exploded. Within his mind, at the spot the lioness had been attacking, he heard her scream of agony. Then he was free of her mental dominance and threw himself sideways. The shapeshifter arched through the spot where he had been standing a half second before.

Her flight was erratic and uncontrolled. Her mind was empty.

Behind him came another sound. Turning, he found himself facing the black leopard's green eyes which spewed malevolent hatred at him. He tried to raise his pistol, but found he could not. His mind was no longer his to control.

He stared at the black cat and the glowing, green, evil eyes. Panic began to fill his soul. He fought it, commanding himself to keep his human strength and Navajo dignity even as the black cat leapt at him.

Time came to a standstill. He heard gunfire in the distance and knew it was Aaron firing at the black death that was almost upon him.

The Others

"Run!" Michael screamed to Kali and Aaron as he fought off the paralysis of mind control. "Run!" he cried again, a split second before the hurtling black death was upon him.

The burning entrance of the cat's razor-like claws tore through Michael's chest and stomach. When the giant cat's powerful jaws crushed Michael's head between them, darkness claimed him and soothed away the pain.

Aaron stared as the haunted and ethereal tableau unfolded. When he saw the lioness pass through the space where Michael had been a half second before, he gave vent to hope. But that hope was shattered when the black leopard came to a jarring halt and looked back at the dead lioness. The cat's raging howl vibrated madly, and he started after Michael.

Aaron stepped forward, raised his revolver and fired at the charging black shape. He watched helplessly when the leopard and his friend rolled on the ground. The eternal moment stretched on until the two figures became still.

When the leopard rose, he fired at it, aware that the distance and the night made an accurate shot impossible. Yet Aaron had no choice but to try. The leopard howled angrily and shapeshifted. Once again, the tall black haired man was staring at Aaron and Kali.

Turning slowly, Langst walked over to the fallen lioness. The tawny body of the animal had changed; in its place was the blonde, unmoving woman. Langst bent, drew her into his arms and started toward the trees. At their edge, he turned back to Aaron and Kali and projected his rage.

You will pay for this. You think you have won, but in the end you will fail. His next thought was to Kali, but Aaron heard it clearly. *Think well upon this act of yours. Will you damn us all to an eternal prison for your lover?* And then Charles Langst, with the limp body of his mate draped over his arms, turned and entered the woods.

Aaron looked at Kali. "We have to get out of here. Go through the fence," he said in a low but firm voice.

Kali slipped through the fence, but Aaron could not leave Michael's body to the others and started down the hill. He had taken only three steps when the night erupted with light. He saw army vehicles rising quickly on each side of the hill.

"No!" Kali screamed, her voice accenting the powerful thought she drove at Aaron. *Run!*

Aaron spun and dove for the opening. He hit it with his shoulder and rolled through. Gaining his feet, he ran to the car. Kali, already there, tossed him the keys and got in on the passenger side. Aaron got in and started the engine. Putting the car in gear, he backed off the jack and, with a squeal of tires, started onto the road.

The Others

Behind him were headlights. To his left the compound was brightly lighted; ahead, toward the interstate, was open highway.

When he reached the interstate, he turned north, blending in with the light traffic and holding his speed to the legal limit. Ten minutes later he pulled into a rest area.

In the rest area, nestled between two large trucks, he shut off the engine and stared through the windshield at the night sky.

"Why did Michael do it?" he asked, not to Kali, but to himself.

"It was his destiny. It was preordained, if you accept what he told you. And in part, it was because he knew that you would finish what you started, and because he loved you," she said, ignoring the tears that fell from her eyes.

"I know," Aaron whispered, his sadness and loss wrapped up within the two words.

Two thousand miles away, the Grandfather, his face painted in the traditional colors of mourning, ignored the tears streaking down his cheeks as the lighted torch illuminated the ancient burial cavern of his people.

He had laid out several of Michael's possessions on a stone pallet and, while the flames from the torch danced against the walls of the burial cave, he called upon the spirits of his ancestors to help his seedling and welcome Michael into their midst.

"He has done your bidding. He has proven himself worthy of his race and of the destiny that you have ordained," the old man intoned in the Navajo tongue. "Lift him to his rightful place at your side, wise spirits of the people."

Then the Grandfather became silent. Later, he climbed the 900 sacred steps up from the floor of the cavern. When he reached the outside, he drew himself straight and gazed at the rising sun before he began the long descent from the mountain.

He had much work to do. For he knew he must be ready when the time came, and his destiny, like Michael's, would be completed. He, too, would at last be allowed to join his ancestors.

Chapter Sixteen

Aaron stopped at a small motel, a mile and a half from the next exit on the interstate. He reasoned that Lowell and anyone else looking for him—and he was sure there would be many—would expect him to run as fast and far from Sperry Hollow as possible. Aaron had other plans.

On the short drive, he'd asked Kali if the others from her world could trace her telepathically. She'd said no; her people only could sense others from their world when one was close by. It was only mated people who could find their mate at long distances.

After registering in the General Lee Motel as Mr. and Mrs. Daniel Morgan, Aaron and Kali went into a small but clean room. Once the door was closed and Aaron put down the oval canvas bag he'd brought into the room, he turned to Kali and opened his arms. She came into them, her arms going around him, her hands pressing into the firm muscles of his back while her body leaned fully upon his.

Their kiss was deep and stirring.

When they drew apart, neither could hide their need or desire. "What now?" Kali asked, her ragged breathing making her words husky.

Aaron shook his head. "In the morning, we go to see Herman Gable. Then we have to leave this part of the country."

"And go where? They'll be looking everywhere for us," she said.

"Arizona."

"Why Arizona?"

"It's our only chance."

Kali's eyes, gold flecked and green, wandered across Aaron's face as if seeing him for the first time—which was true in its own way. "I am sorry to have done this to you," she whispered.

"Don't be." Aaron cupped her chin, cradling it within his palms. "Everyone, sometime in their life, hopes that there will be someone or something to come along and change that life, make it better or more exciting or just different. What happened to me was you. And Kali, I got all of that and more."

Kali's eyes grew moist. A single tear fell from the corner of her left eye. Aaron wiped the

The Others

tear away with a fingertip. "No sadness—not now."

Kali forced a smile, took his right hand in hers and brought it to her mouth. A tremor rippled through his stomach.

When Kali lowered his hand, she did not release it. Her eyes flickered across his face again, and she took a deep breath. "Make love with me, Aaron."

She released his hand and stepped back. Her eyes remained fixed on his as her fingers undid the buttons of the shapeless dress she had been forced to wear in the Sperry compound.

Aaron watched the dress fall to the floor. His breathing grew heavy, and his stomach tightened, but he did not move toward her. His eyes took in the perfection of her pale ivory skin. Her breasts were firm and full, tipped by peach-tinted circles the size of half dollars. Her narrow waist was complimented by finely etched lines which highlighted the muscles of her abdomen. Her hips flared smoothly; her legs were tapered and well-proportioned.

The sight of Kali's beautiful body was not new to Aaron; he had seen her this way before—not in the flesh but on the golden plateau. Looking at her face, he marveled at the way her silky black hair framed her ivory skin. Slowly, Aaron undressed and started toward her.

At last my love, Kali whispered within his mind when only an inch separated them and they could feel what they had never felt before—

the heat radiating from their bodies and washing across each other's skin.

They closed the small distance between them, and their mouths came together.

Aaron lifted her from the floor and carried her to the bed, where he laid her gently upon its cover. He joined her, and their bodies flowed together. Heat raced along the surface of their skin, and their passion and love grew electric.

Aaron drew slightly back to look into Kali's eyes. Within them he saw her belief, trust and love. Then he drew further away.

What is wrong? came Kali's thought.

What can be wrong? I've been in love with you for almost half a year. I've searched for you in ways I never imagined existed. I have learned of things that I never thought possible. I've been told I was insane. I lost my job, my credibility, and tonight I . . . Aaron's thought darkened under the weight of pain and mourning. Then he felt Kali's sympathetic and understanding reaction. A moment later, he willed himself to go on. *Tonight I lost my closest friend. I hold myself responsible. But I do not, I cannot resent anything else, because we are finally together.* Then his thoughts shifted.

On the plateau, after we had joined together and made love together in our minds, you told me that when our physical bodies joined, as well as our minds, that it would be a commitment that on your world would last for our lifetimes. Is that true?

Kali did not use either word or thought. She merely nodded.

Aaron smiled. "Are you sure that you want to do this?"

Kali rose, twisting slightly so that she was leaning on one arm while she looked at him. Her free hand went to his face. "I am sure. But I told you this already, just as I told you that it would be your choice when the time came. It is your decision."

Aaron's hand went to her hair. His fingers tightened, and he drew her close. His mouth covering hers was his answer.

They came together without another word. Yet their passionate joining was not the frenzied coupling of two people whose desires burst their containment; rather, it was as though they had been lovers all their lives and knew each other well.

There was no exploration for the sake of learning. They had already shared an intimacy few could ever imagine. Aaron moved gently, confidently, and Kali responded in the same way. When their bodies reached that special pitch, that one point where the world and everything in it becomes secondary, Aaron rose above Kali. She flowed beneath him, opening her body to his body, her mind to his mind.

When he entered her, the heat of her inner body encased him at the exact instant that his mind and Kali's blended. Their bodies froze together, and in a moment stolen from the mad universe they had become a part of, Aaron felt Kali's thoughts reach deep into his mind. Incredibly, while their bodies were locked together, Kali eased his hurt and soothed his heartache. And while she helped him to accept his loss, she also helped him to understand the real gift that Michael had given to both of them.

Then, and only then, did they become one—in their minds, in their bodies and in their hearts.

An hour after Kali had fallen asleep in his arms, Aaron was still awake. The music of her low and easy breathing was the only sound in the small room. His emotions were in flux, and he was doing his best to gain some control over them.

He had found Kali and freed her, and they had affirmed their love with their minds and sealed it with their bodies. But in order to have accomplished this impossible task, lives had been sacrificed.

With the compelling urgency of the last months finally put to rest by freeing Kali, Aaron realized that all his efforts had been merely warm-up exercises.

Aldredge must be stopped. If the man succeeded in reaching Kali's world, the potential for disaster there was unimaginable. He did not even want to think what Aldredge and Langst could do here, once they had conquered Kali's home world.

Aaron understood the gift of life Michael had given him and Kali. He also accepted the obligation that was set on his shoulders with the trust Michael had placed on him. That was why he had to get everything he could from Herman Gable, before leaving for Arizona. He must reverse the doorway in the ancient Indian burial grounds and send Kali back to her world to warn her people of Aldredge and Langst.

Is this what you meant by my destiny, Michael? Is it fate that, with Kali now free to be with me, I must give her up again?

Langst walked through the compound, holding the unmoving body of Amelia in his arms. When he reached the main building, the guards standing at the door stepped quickly aside.

A half dozen whirlwinds kicked up dirt motes between Langst and the door. Seconds later, the door flew open. Langst walked into the reception room, past the empty desk and over to the inner doorway. Again, the door flew open without the aid of human hands.

Langst continued down the long green corridor until he reached Amos Aldredge's office. Aldredge's door was already open. Three army officers were with Aldredge, each one shouting louder than the next, placing the blame of the infiltration on the other.

It took them all a few moments to realize that someone was in the room with them. As one, they turned to stare at Langst and the dead woman in his arms.

Blood covered her naked chest. The bullet wound was an open hole centered between her breasts. Her head lolled over his right arm. Her eyes were open. Her hair brushed the floor. Langst was as naked as his dead mate.

Aldredge rose, came around his desk and moved toward Langst. "Charles, I'm sorry. I don't know what to say, I—"

Langst cut him off. His voice was barely above a whisper, but it sounded to Aldredge and the others as loud as a cannon shot.

"No! She is dead. You are responsible for her death! You!" he said, his voice growing louder, turning almost into a growl.

"I want him! I want Blaine. And I want Kali. They must pay for what has happened. They will pay! I will have my vengeance. Do you hear me?"

"Charles, we will find him. We will make him pay for what he has done," Aldredge promised.

Langst stared at Aldredge. Then, slowly, he sent out a thought which filtered into Aldredge's mind.

He will pay. And Kali as well. But it will not be you or your people who will extract my retribution. I will make him pay. Me. Only me! Do you understand? As he fed his message into

Aldredge's head, he also emitted the putrescent and bloody images of what he would do to Blaine and Kali.

"Do you understand?" Langst repeated, aloud.

"Yes," Aldredge said, barely able to get the word through his suddenly dry mouth.

Captain Thomas Lowell waited patiently in his car. The sun had risen an hour before, just when he and the M.P. with him had pulled into the motel's parking lot to look at the license plates of the cars parked by each room's doorway.

The General Lee Motel had been the third motel Lowell had checked. He hadn't been overly surprised to find Aaron Blaine's rental car there. He had expected it.

Last night, after they'd left the deserted Esso station, they'd returned to the research compound within minutes of Blaine's successful abduction of Kali Moss.

He'd remained silent under Aldredge's angry tirade and said nothing to the two N.S.A. men who had fumed and threatened him with every sort of soldier's hell.

Then he'd listened to Aldredge's shouted orders that he was to find Blaine and the woman and bring them to him, no matter what!

But when Lowell had gone into the infirmary and had opened the body bag containing Michael Noriss's body, he'd been sickened beyond belief. He didn't give a damn that one of Aldredge's otherworlders had been killed by Noriss. He could only think back to Aaron Blaine's words, while they'd sat in Blaine's car that very afternoon. "Will you send one of your pets after us?"

Apparently, he thought, that's exactly what had happened. Lowell had not liked this assignment when he'd first received it, but because of the security level, he'd been unable to turn it down. He'd liked it even less when he'd met the six people who were supposed to be from a parallel world.

He had hated Charles Langst on sight and had realized that both Langst and his wife, Amelia Burke, were insane. He had not liked Kali Moss because of the alien quality he sensed in all the otherworlders and because of her escape attempt which had almost killed Aaron Blaine. Yet, in spite of that alien quality, Kali Moss had seemed the most normal of the six. The other three were always silent and seemed afraid of everything.

But after seeing Michael Noriss's mutilated body, he had begun to hope that Blaine and the Moss woman had gotten away.

For three hours, he had listened to the N.S.A. men call in other government agencies. The F.B.I. was already setting up a nationwide sweep for the two fugitives. The National Security Agency would do anything that was necessary, regardless of the consequences, to capture Blaine and Moss.

But Lowell believed he knew Blaine and the way Blaine thought. Last night had proved to be a perfect example of Blaine's reasoning processes. While he'd waited for Blaine and Noriss at the old gas station, he had been positive that they would not show up.

And in that moment, thinking of the time spent at the antiquated and dead gas station, Lowell had known how Blaine planned to make good his escape. He had listened to the N.S.A. men coordinate their search pattern, starting at a 100 mile radius away from Sperry Hollow. They were certain that Blaine was running fast.

Lowell had known he wasn't. Lowell knew that Blaine, a forensic police specialist, would think like a cop, not like a criminal. He would stay close by for the first night. Hide within sight, and by his obviousness, be out of sight.

With that in mind, Lowell had looked up all the motels within a 25 mile range and, with only one other man, had gone to look for Blaine and the woman.

When he'd found the rental car at the General Lee, his gut reaction was to forget he'd seen the license plate, but knowing where his obligations lay, he had checked with the manager to make sure that Aaron and the woman had indeed registered. Lowell took no satisfaction in having found them and was almost sorry he'd been right. At the same time, he

D.M. Wind

believed that Blaine and Moss would be better off under his custody—at least in the beginning—instead of the security agency's.

But before he took them in, he'd decided he would not take this one night from them. Blaine had worked too hard to get Kali Moss out of the research center. He would give them these last few hours.

Glancing at his watch, he saw that it was 8:15. He turned to the uniformed man next to him. "Soon."

Aaron woke slowly, feeling the warmth of Kali's bare body lying next to his. When he opened his eyes, he saw that she was already awake and looking at him with her large eyes. He kissed her gently, drawing her closer and enjoying the feel of her breasts on his skin.

She shifted and, using her fingernails, traced circles through the hair on his chest. "Do you believe we will be able to get away?"

"I have to believe that," he said honestly.

"But they know so much about you."

"What they don't know is how much I've learned or where we're going next."

"They will never stop looking for us."

"They? Your people or mine?"

"Both. Your people cannot afford to have this story become known. My people want to go home. If what's happening at Sperry becomes public knowledge . . ." She didn't bother to voice the obvious.

234

"It will be dangerous. We will never be safe. My people will eventually find us. We can sense the presence of another of our kind if we are close enough. They will know where I am."

"Then we'll have to stay ahead of them."

"Aaron . . ." she began, but he stopped her with his thoughts.

We will be safe. And we will stop Aldredge from destroying your world and mine.

I love you, Aaron.

Aaron's arm tightened, as his mouth sought hers. All thoughts of what might happen vanished as they reaffirmed their love one more time before starting on the next leg in their bid for freedom.

Later, after they had made love and showered, Aaron gave Kali a pair of jeans and a tee shirt he'd bought for her yesterday. When she was dressed, she pirouetted once. *Do you approve?*

"How can I not approve," he replied aloud as he gazed at her. The jeans were a little loose, but they did not conceal her shape. The pale blue tee shirt fit perfectly, outlining her breasts without overemphasizing their fullness. He unashamedly gazed at the way her nipples poked at their covering.

You approve? She smiled.

Absolutely!

Make your call, she reminded him.

Aaron paused for a second. *How did . . . ?*

Sorry, but it was on the tip of your mind.

It's all right, he told her. *I just have to get used to this.*

I can hold back, Kali offered.

No. Don't ever hold back, he told her and opened his mind fully.

Thank you. The thought was more than a thought. It was a caress, and even more—it was her love.

Aaron sighed. Pulling out his wallet, he withdrew Herman Gable's home phone number. He dialed the operator and the number, then told the operator that it was a collect call from Mr. Blaine.

A moment later Professor Herman Gable accepted the charges. "Is something wrong?"

"Very wrong, professor, but I can't speak on the phone. I'm near Sperry Hollow. We have to see you."

"Come to my house. I'll wait here. You know where I am?"

When Aaron answered in the negative, Gable gave him his Georgetown address. "Did you get her out?"

"Yes," Aaron said. He hung up and looked at Kali. "Let's go."

Aaron and Kali stepped through the doorway, and Aaron started to closed the door. Before it was closed, Kali shot a frantic thought at him. *They found us!*

Spinning, he saw Thomas Lowell and another uniformed man come to a stop five feet from them; the men already had their service .45s drawn and aimed. Aaron dropped the canvas bag and looked around for an escape route.

When I rush them, run! he commanded Kali.

Together, Aaron, always together.

"Blaine, you're under arrest," Lowell stated.

"Under arrest for what, Lowell?" Aaron bluffed, his muscles going taut, his body tensing, preparing itself for action.

Lowell's good-natured laugh caught him off guard. "Take your pick—espionage, interfering in a government project, violation of the National Security Act, trespassing, theft of government property."

"Theft?" Aaron echoed inanely. "What the hell did I steal?"

"Her," Lowell said simply.

Aaron's rage built. "Kali is a person, Lowell, a woman. She's not property." To Kali he thought, *When I say so, take a fast step sideways.*

"The government considers her property, and that's the way it is."

Move!

Kali moved. When she did, both pistols moved with her, which was what Aaron was waiting for. Aaron pulled his service revolver and, as he raised it, cocked it.

The click of the hammer setting into place was loud. Lowell turned to see the barrel of the .38 pointing at his head.

"There are two of us. You can't win, Blaine."

"In a manner of speaking, I've already won. You won't shoot Kali. You can't afford to. And you'll be dead before I will."

"Sorry," Lowell said, bringing his pistol to bear on Aaron.

Aaron knew that Lowell would use it, just as he knew the man didn't want to. Aaron accepted that while he tallied the odds on getting both men before he died.

"You know I can do it, Lowell. You know I can't allow this to end here."

"Perhaps. Perhaps not," Lowell admitted.

The tension became unbearable. Aaron refused to give in. There was too much at stake; Kali was too important. Even if he didn't make it, Kali would be able to go to Herman Gable and stop Aldredge. *You have to!* he told her, accenting what he knew she'd already heard within his mind.

Wait! Kali ordered.

Aaron held back. Behind Lowell, the soldier's face froze as he started to back away. In the next instant, both men threw their weapons away as if they were contaminated. Fascinated by this unexpected turn of events, Aaron watched as Lowell, hatred and fear written on his face, stared at Kali.

What Aaron didn't see, and didn't know about until later, was that Kali's golden flecked, green eyes had literally blazed like large emeralds exposed to brilliant sunlight. And then the soldiers' weapons had seemed to turn blistering hot.

"That's better," Aaron said, his pistol unwavering at Lowell's head. "Move slowly out of the way."

When Lowell did as he was instructed, Aaron nodded. "Do you really know what Aldredge is doing?" he asked.

Lowell didn't answer him.

"I think you know a little, but not all of it. I think that's why you went to meet us last night, even though you knew I wasn't going to show." Aaron smiled when he saw Lowell flinch slightly at his words.

"Aldredge is not doing what you think he is. Believe me, he's not doing Project Doorway for defense reasons. He's doing it for himself."

"I don't know what you're talking about," Lowell replied in a dead monotone.

"Bullshit! Did you see Michael's body? Did you see the way he was ripped apart?" Aaron shouted as rage filled his mind.

"Blaine, please," Lowell pleaded, "you have to give it up. The entire country is looking for you. Every government and municipal agency is on the alert. You haven't got a chance."

"You're wrong, Lowell. I have a chance, and you'd better hope, with every breath you take, that I make it—that I can stop Aldredge. Because if I don't, there won't be a world left, at least not the way we know it."

Lowell's eyes locked with Aaron's. "I don't know why you're doing this." He shook his head slowly and glanced at Kali. "Or maybe I just don't want to believe I do."

Turning to the M.P. who was now several feet away, Lowell told him to go to the car and wait there for him. Then he spoke to Aaron again. "Go quickly, Blaine. Make the most of whatever time you have left."

"Lowell," Aaron began, but Lowell cut him off.

"I don't want to hear any more. Just get the hell away from here and out of my life!"

"Watch out for Aldredge," he told Lowell. *Get into the car,* he told Kali as he bent and lifted the suitcase. He kept the gun pointed at Lowell while he sidestepped to the driver's door and threw the canvas bag into the back seat. Moving quickly, he got into the car, started it and sped out of the parking lot.

When they reached the interstate, he headed toward Washington. He stayed on the highway for only two exits. Then Aaron used the map from the rental agency to plot the route along the back roads toward Washington and to Professor Gable's home in the fashionably wealthy section known as Georgetown.

When they were driving on the lightly used highway, Aaron spoke to Kali. "What happened back there? What made them drop their weapons."

Kali's laugh was light and sounded wonderful in the confines of the car. She told him what she'd done.

"Michael called that . . ." he found himself searching for the word.

"Pyrokineses."

"You burned their hands?" he asked, somewhat surprised.

Kali laughed again. "No," she said. "It wasn't pyrokineses. I used my mind to project an image of my eyes glowing like a fire, and then I made them think I'd turned their guns into white hot metal."

"But they weren't hurt?"

"No," Kali replied. "They'll realize that when they think about what happened and then look at their hands for burns."

"I think Lowell will end up helping us in his own way."

"Why?"

"Because he's a decent man."

Chapter Seventeen

Aaron and Kali reached Georgetown at 1:00 o'clock. As they drove to Dr. Gable's house, they passed rows of elegant town houses, which were the homes of government officials, senators and congressmen, all mixed in with the older homes of the elite members of Washington's high society.

When they turned onto Silver Street, a magnificent block of old homes, Aaron slowed down the car. Halfway down the block, he pulled up to the curb.

Glancing at Kali, he saw that her face was drawn by tension. He covered her hand with his. *Gable is a good man. He will help us.*

How can you be sure?

He smiled. "Because we have no choice.

Without Gable and his knowledge . . ." Aaron shrugged his shoulders instead of finishing his statement.

"All right." Kali's words were more a sigh than an agreement.

Aaron drew her close and kissed her. The kiss was light and brushing, yet it carried with it his love for her and his promise to protect her.

Releasing her, they got out of the car and went to the front door of the house where Aaron used the brass door knocker. The door was opened a few seconds later by a middle-aged woman. "I'm Aaron Blaine. Professor Gable is expecting us."

"Yes, Mr. Blaine. He is in the study," she said as she admitted them.

Aaron, with Kali's hand tight in his, entered. Everything was neat and in place. The furniture was old but in excellent condition. Not old, he corrected himself, but antique. The house itself seemed to be from another era and was trying to be faithful to those bygone days. He envisioned a bedroom with a four-poster, white gauze mosquito netting and all. Somehow, it fitted.

The housekeeper led them down a hallway with an inlaid teak floor that was polished to a fine gleam. At the third door she knocked and, without waiting for an answer, opened it.

Aaron and Kali entered the room and looked around. The walls were lined with dark wooden bookcases, the shelves filled to capacity.

The floor was highly polished wood with a blue and silver Oriental carpet in the center. A royal blue divan, framed with dark cherry wood, was on one side, and two deeply upholstered club chairs were across from it. In front of a large bay window was a cherry wood federal desk. Professor Gable sat behind it.

"Aaron," the professor exclaimed, standing slowly as a smile spread across his weathered, lined features. A moment later he limped from behind the desk to grasp Aaron's hand tightly.

"And you must be Kali." Gable's eyes roamed over her features, sparkling as they danced over her face. His broad and unfeigned smile made his face appear years younger. "My dear, I feel like my life has been vindicated. Thank you."

Then Gable's eyes looked past Kali and beyond Aaron. "Where is Michael?"

Aaron looked away briefly and swallowed hard. "He's dead."

Herman Gable stared at Aaron, his shoulders suddenly drooping, his face aging before Aaron's eyes. "So young." Then Gable straightened his shoulders, strength and determination flowing back into his face. "Tell me what happened."

For the next ten minutes, Aaron told Gable what had happened that night and also told him about what he'd discovered in the Sperry research computer. When Aaron finished talking, Gable seemed to realize for the first time that they were still standing in the center of the room. Shaking his head, he motioned Aaron and Kali to the divan.

Gable seated himself on the chair across from them. "What about you?" he asked Kali. "What will you do?"

"We have no choice," she said as she reached for Aaron's hand and held it tightly. "We must stop Aldredge from entering my world."

"I've waited all my life to meet you or someone like you. It is the vindication of all my efforts, all my theories, but I'm an old man now. My arthritis has almost crippled me. It stops me from doing almost anything except using my mind. Yet I have no complaint, for it is a blessing in itself. If I had been more active, able to do more physically, I may not have found the way for you to return to your world."

"There is a way?" Kali asked, her hand tightening on Aaron's.

"Possibly," Gable said. "It's never been tested. It's only a theory."

Aaron stated the obvious. "We have no choice, Professor."

"We must go to my lab at the university. I have equipment there that will aid you."

Aaron and Kali stood quickly, while Professor Gable took a little longer to struggle to his feet.

He is in great pain, Kali thought to Aaron. Aaron sensed the sadness she felt for the old man. *He will not live much longer.*

How do you know?

His heart is very weak. He will not be able to withstand any great amounts of stress or shock. His arthritis, too, becomes more painful each day.

Aaron had nothing to say. Kali had told him facts.

They left the rental car in Gable's garage and, a half hour later, arrived at the university laboratories.

Ignoring the students and professors who populated the hallways, they went into Gable's private office. Inside, Gable went to the computer monitor, turned it on and brought up a file.

When it was on the screen, he pushed two keys on the keyboard, and a printout of the file began. While the printer clacked, Gable motioned Aaron and Kali to follow him into an adjoining laboratory.

Inside the room, Gable pointed to three slender and shiny four-foot-high metal poles. Each pole had a transformer attached to it. Wires, all color-coded, ran from pole to pole.

There was a large gas generator with a four-inch hose that led from the exhaust valve to an outlet connection. The generator was hooked to the three poles.

"I had prepared this to use on Michael's doorway. I was planning to go there to see if it was possible to reverse the doorway."

"How would you have known if you succeeded?" Aaron asked, stepping closer to examine the equipment.

"That was Michael's part. He would have gone through. After a prearranged time, I would have reversed the doorway and he would return."

"A dangerous plan," Kali said, turning to face Gable. "How can you be certain that it would be my world that the doorway opened into?"

"We couldn't be certain. That was the problem. It was an experiment. Experiments are, by their very nature, a way of seeking out knowledge of the unknown."

"But if there was someone from my world . . ."

"That's exactly what I've spent my years looking for. Until now there has been no one."

"Professor," Aaron began. A knock on the lab door interrupted his question.

Kali spun, staring at the door. "Two men," she said. *Looking for us,* she told Aaron silently.

Gable started toward the door, but Aaron gripped his thin arm. "They're looking for us."

"I'll take care of them," he whispered. He motioned Kali and Aaron to stand next to the wall. When Gable opened the door, Aaron and Kali were hidden behind it.

"Yes?" Gable asked, his voice laced with irritation.

"Professor Herman Gable?"

"Yes."

"May we have a moment? There are some

247

D.M. Wind

questions we'd like to ask," the Afro-American agent said, holding up his N.S.A. identification card. The lighter skinned man peered over Gable's shoulder into the lab.

"About what?" Gable asked, his voice harsh with irritation as he stepped out of the lab and closed the door behind him.

When the door closed, Aaron pressed his ear to the wood and listened.

"You are acquainted with a Michael Noriss?"

Gable nodded gravely. "A former student of mine—a brilliant psychologist. Is this a security check for a government program? If so, has my highest recommendations."

"He called you nine days ago. What did he want?"

"My calls are my business."

The agent shook his head quickly. "This is a matter of national security. Michael Noriss violated government property. He infiltrated a government research center."

"I doubt that. Michael Noriss is a man above reproach. He's a doctor of psychology and highly respected in his field."

"He's also dead. He was killed while trying to escape from a government installation with top secret documents."

"What?" Gable asked, his voice trembling. Neither agent doubted that the old professor was genuinely upset.

"What did he call you about?" the agent repeated.

Gable shook his head. "He wanted to know about the work of an old colleague of mine, a Doctor Aldredge."

"And?" the second agent prodded.

Gable shrugged. "I told him I haven't heard from Amos Aldredge in over ten years."

"Did Noriss mention a man named Aaron Blaine?"

Gable shook his head again, then looked from one man to the other. "How did you know that Michael called me?"

"After we caught him, we ran our usual investigation of all his business dealings. We traced all the calls he made in the past six months."

"I see," Gable whispered. "What does this Blaine have to do with Michael?"

"He was Noriss's partner. They both attempted the break-in, and Blaine escaped. We're looking for him."

"What did the men steal?" Gable asked.

"We're not at liberty to discuss that."

"I see." Then he exhaled slowly, sadly. "If there are no further questions, I would like to get back to my work."

The dark-skinned agent handed Gable a card. "If you hear from Aaron Blaine, call this number."

Gable looked at the plain white card, which had only the N.S.A. initials on it and one phone number. "I don't see why I would hear from a man I don't know."

"If you do, Professor, it would be best to call us." The two agents stared openly at Gable who understood the warning. "Naturally," Gable murmured.

When the agents were gone, Gable returned to the lab. "I think they believed me," he told Aaron and Kali.

Kali shook her head. "One did, the other wasn't sure. He was thinking about having you put under surveillance."

"You really can read minds," Gable said in an awed voice.

"No, I can pick up active, surface thoughts, but if someone opens their mind to me, then I can read more deeply, although read is not the right word."

"I hope we have enough time before they start spying on me." Gable's voice seemed distracted as he looked at the equipment.

"All I caught was that he would call in his request. That should give us some time."

"At least an hour, if not more," Aaron said. He was familiar with agency practices from his advanced training with the government.

Gable turned to Aaron. "Help me dismantle this, and I'll explain as much as I can."

For 35 minutes, Aaron and Gable worked and talked. When the apparatus was completely taken apart, Gable had been able to convey to Aaron everything he could.

"Bring my car around to the lab delivery entrance. We'll load the equipment there. You'll take my car and leave yours in my garage."

Aaron shook his head. "If they find it, it will put you into grave trouble."

Gable laughed. "What can they do to me. I'm too old and in too much pain to be afraid of them. Besides, you must stop Aldredge and warn Kali's people. Now get my car."

Aaron started to protest again, but Kali's thought cut him off. *He's right, Aaron. We must do it this way.*

I know, Aaron admitted. *But it's dangerous for him.*

He understands. It is his choice, just as Michael had a choice to make.

Aaron left the office, cautiously peering about whenever he reached a corner. When he reached the car and was certain that no one was watching him, he started it up and drove to the loading dock.

In the lab, while Gable took the computer printout and scribbled several additional notes, Kali watched everything he did.

When he finished, he handed her the ten pages of printed information and then went to the neatly stacked equipment. "Let's start bringing this out."

They reached the loading dock just as Aaron drove up. He took the first of the equipment and put it in the trunk. While Kali stayed at the car, Gable and Aaron returned to the lab and collected the rest of the equipment, except for the generator.

"It's too big to put in the car. I'll pick another one up in Arizona."

"The same wattage or higher," Gable said. "The electric force reversal procedure has not been fully tested. There may be errors in it."

"I'll recheck them. I'll go over them carefully."

When the car was loaded, Aaron and Gable returned to the lab, where Aaron interfaced his computer with Gable's and extracted the spatial helix and electromagnetic field information.

"Thank you," Aaron said after closing up his computer and grasping the professor's hand in his.

"Don't thank me. Just do what you set out to do. Stop that lunatic from destroying Kali's world."

"I will," Aaron promised. He wasn't sure that he could do it, but he would try with every ounce of his ability.

And then Kali stepped up to the professor and smiled warmly at him. "We will always be indebted to you."

"Your debt was paid when you walked into my house. My work and my life have been validated. Go now and help your people."

Kali put her arms around Herman Gable, embracing him tightly. And then, without Gable's knowledge, she projected herself into his mind. She was not trying to read his thoughts; rather, she was looking for certain neurological connections.

She found them quickly, and she efficiently went about deadening the pain-carrying nerves that were affected by his arthritis. Fifteen seconds after she'd entered Gable's brain, she began to withdraw. As she left, she constructed a barrier within the old man's mind that would be able to shield his thoughts and knowledge from any intruders.

Herman Gable's arthritis was not cured, but he would never again be bothered by the intensity of the crippling disease's pain.

Even without Gable's offer of the car, Aaron had known that he would not be able to take any form of public transportation. All airports would be watched as well as bus and train terminals.

There was only one way to reach Arizona, and that was by car. Their only advantage, and it was a big one, was that no one had any idea of where Aaron and Kali were going. But, on the off chance that there would be someone watching Michael's house in Arizona, Aaron had decided not to go there. Instead, they would go to an old deserted cabin near the Indian hot springs that Michael had taken him to several times before.

Aaron and Kali had returned to Gable's house to drop the professor off and load their two suitcases. Before they could drive away, Gable had handed Aaron money.

"We don't—" Aaron had protested.

Gable stared unflinching at Aaron. "Take it. You'll need the cash."

Aaron had accepted the $300, knowing that the professor was right. He had a little over $200 of his own money, and he could not use a credit card. That would be too easy to trace. The government would have alerts out on all his credit cards.

They left Washington during rush hour. Gable's car, an '85 Oldsmobile Cutlass, had blended in well with all the traffic. Instead of going via a direct route, which would have taken them within the vicinity of the Shenandoah, Aaron took the old Florida 301 highway.

They drove nonstop, with Kali and Aaron taking shifts while the other slept. They never went above the 55 limit and were always cautious when driving in traffic. They could not afford to be stopped by police or get involved in an accident. When they stopped for food or to use a bathroom, it was never in a large city but always at a fast food place.

For Aaron, the most fascinating part of their furtive journey west was in getting to know Kali. It seemed that with each state they left behind, his knowledge of Kali and her world and her people grew.

It was just outside of Rocky Mount, North Carolina, where they picked up I-95, that Aaron realized that they were speaking more and more with their minds and less with their mouths. All

it took, he realized, was for him to consciously
direct his thought to her.

"It's strange," he said aloud.

"What is?" she asked, turning slightly to look
at him.

When he answered, it was with his thoughts.
*Strange is the wrong word—I meant different. It
takes so little effort to communicate this way.*

*It will become easier. It is the most natural
way.*

"For you," Aaron said aloud, but the thought
he projected to Kali was laced with humor.

*For you, also, now that you have rediscovered
the ability. Remember, it was your forbearers's
choice to . . .* Kali searched for the phrase she
needed. *To embrace the verbal, the technical,
and to forgo the empathetical—*

Which you think is bad, he said, cutting into
her thought.

*Not bad, not good. Your way of evolution
was different from ours, that's all. Your people's
acceptance of the physical sciences set you on a
different path than ours.*

Aaron, Kali added, her thoughts growing
sharper within his mind, *have you not realized
yet that when we speak with our minds, that it
is not language that we use, but pure thoughts
that are readily understood without the limiting
definitions of words?*

Aaron hadn't considered telepathy in this way
before, but as he worked on Kali's explanation,
he realized that when they had communicated

by telepathy, there really were no words in the true meaning of semantics. *Then why do I hear you in English?*

Because your mind translates thought into the easiest method of definition and comprehension. You hear in the language you are most comfortable with.

"Is that how you learned our languages when you first came to this world?"

Kali nodded. *And it is also how I was able to make you see my world, as I remembered it.*

"From what I've learned and seen of your world," Aaron said, "from what you've shown me in your mind, your world and your people have chosen a wonderful path."

Turning from Aaron, Kali looked out the windshield and, in a faraway voice, said, "We are not really different from you."

And then they both fell silent again, in voice and in thought.

At Florence, South Carolina, they left I-95 and turned onto I-20 toward Atlanta. Then they bypassed Atlanta and started toward Texas.

When they were between Birmingham and Tuscaloosa, Aaron brought up a subject he had been avoiding since his and Kali's first meeting on the astral plane.

"On the road, that first night near Sperry Hollow, why were you trying to commit suicide?" Aaron asked.

"I explained that. I was tired of life."

The Others

"You are life." *You're filled with life,* he empha-
sized with his thoughts.

"Now. But then all I wanted was for my life
to be over. I hated myself for not being able
to escape from Aldredge and for being used by
him. And all the years, Aaron, all the lonely
years. They were becoming too much."

"What happened?" Aaron asked, taking one
hand from the steering wheel to reach across
and draw her close.

"You," she whispered.

"How did you survive? How did your people
survive after they came here?"

Kali sighed. "Like all people who have become
the predominant species of their world, our
instinct for survival is strong. We had to survive, and so we did. And you must remember
that at first we didn't realize how different we
were from the natives of this world. But as time
passed, we learned."

*Different mentally, not physically. We are the
same physically.*

Yes, Kali agreed. *Except that in your world,
I cannot grow old. It is a curse, Aaron, and a
terrible burden.*

But you have borne it well, my love.

*I have accepted my fate. There was nothing I
could do to change it.*

"Until now, perhaps," Aaron whispered.

"Until now."

"Michael and Professor Gable believe that it
was . . . is your people who have been mistaken

for the demons in our legends, the creatures who inhabit our superstitions."

Do I look like a creature? Kali asked, a hint of humor underlining the mind link.

A ravishing creature.

"Yes," she said aloud.

"Yes?"

"It was the people of my world, the unlucky ones like myself who were drawn into your world, who became your demons."

"Why did your people become demons?"

"Privacy. When you stay young and everyone you know grows old, you become resented. After a while, we get tired of moving around, of starting yet another life, of learning another language, of trying to blend in and become part of a new culture or yet another civilization. It is a hard life, and it takes its toll." Kali paused, her gentle sigh a whisper of resignation in Aaron's ears.

"It reached the point that to maintain our sanity we had to have roots. We need a feeling of belonging, a sense of home, even though we were living on a world we had not been born on."

"I can understand that feeling," Aaron told her.

I know you can, she replied. She shifted closer to him and placed her hand on his thigh.

"In order to keep the homes we had chosen, we did not mingle with the people of the towns or villages; instead, we kept to ourselves. When we ventured out, it was either in concealment or with great ceremony. I lived for a long time in Eastern Europe. For generations I lived as my own descendant. People will believe what they want to."

"Were you one of the legends?" Aaron asked, not quite sure he wanted to hear the answer.

"In a way," Kali replied seriously. "I never changed my form when others could see, except when I was in grave danger and needed to escape. I never used my abilities to frighten people. I couldn't do those things. When I arrived here, and after I learned what this world was like, I promised myself that I would try to become like the people here.

"But for several others, it was impossible. Many became insane, turning on the people they lived with—killing them or killing themselves. They were the werewolves, the vampires. They were not responsible for what they did, since their minds had degenerated with time and hopelessness."

"What about Langst and the others at the compound?"

"Langst is like your criminals. His mate, Amelia, was the same. Their minds are twisted. Because their mental abilities are so strong, they believe they can do whatever they want. They are cruel. They take what they want, leaving only pain and terror in their wake." *And Aaron, Amos Aldredge's mind is like Langst's, without the metaphysical abilities of my people.*

But even without those powers, he is as dangerously insane as Langst.

"I know," Aaron said just as they passed the first sign for Tuscaloosa.

When they reached Texas, the miles had begun to pile up on the odometer. From Texas, they entered New Mexico.

It was early evening, the sun having set an hour before. Kali had been sleeping for a while and had just woken. She lay still for a few moments, gazing at Aaron's profile from the back seat. A feeling of warmth and love suffused her. She smiled, thinking of how long she had waited to feel those emotions.

Sitting up, she pushed a gentle thought to Aaron. *You are beautiful.*

Taken by surprise, Aaron said nothing.

"Are you tired? Do you want me to drive?" Kali asked.

Aaron shook his head. "Come up front and sit next to me."

Kali climbed over to the front seat in as graceful a way as was possible, which she thought was totally clumsy.

You are never clumsy, he stated.

Kali smiled and drew close to him.

"Why didn't you find one of your people to live with on this world?" he asked, picking up their last conversation about Kali's life.

"There are not a great many of them here. From time to time I would meet someone from my world, but those few I met were either already insane or on the verge. I tried to help when I could, but it did no good."

"But you know so much about what happened to your people here," Aaron commented.

"Most of what I learned was in the past ten or so years. First from Langst and Amelia in California, and then from the others at the research center. What I found out confirmed what I had always thought."

"How did you stay sane?"

I would not let myself be any other way. I could not. I made myself believe, kept my hopes alive, that one day I would find a way to go home.

"Soon," Aaron whispered.

"I want to go home, Aaron," Kali said, her voice choked with emotion. "I . . . I don't want to stay young and watch you die. I want to live my life with you and grow old with you. Is that so much to ask?"

Aaron had no answer for her. Instead, he put his arm about her shoulders and drew her closer. A moment later, she pressed her face against his shoulder and cried.

They turned northwest three hours later, and the next morning they were in Arizona. And Aaron knew that from this moment on, he would have to be very cautious. Aaron pulled into the first truck stop and, as he and Kali ate breakfast, he studied the map and plotted out a circuitous route to Michael's cabin hideaway. It would take several extra hours to reach the cabin, but Aaron knew there was no choice.

Once they were on the road again, Aaron made himself stop thinking about all the people who were after them. Instead, he thought about what the trip had meant to him.

During the almost 2000 miles spent driving and sleeping and discussing Kali and her people, a sense of ease had grown between them. Their bond had grown stronger with every mile traversed.

They had not just talked about Kali and her people or what Aldredge was planning for her world; they'd discussed a myriad of things. These shorter conversations had centered around insignificant things, the sort of tidbits of information that made a relationship solid and taught each one more about the other.

Yet when they entered the dry country of Arizona, tension reared its head and brought Kali and Aaron to a deeper, more introspective silence. Both knew that their escape from reality was over and that the future was at hand for them and perhaps for two worlds.

It was dark by the time Aaron pulled the Cutlass to a stop at Michael's old cabin. Inside, Aaron went to a closet and took out the lantern Michael kept there. He checked the tank and saw it was full. When he lit the lantern, the incandescent ball of the kerosene flame brightened the cabin's interior.

"Voilà," he proclaimed, smiling at Kali.

She returned the smile and then tried to stifle a yawn.

"Let's get the gear out of the car and settle in. I'll go for supplies in the morning."

Forty minutes later they were undressed and lying on the narrow bed. Aaron held Kali to him, relishing the feel of her warm skin on his. He kissed her eyelids, and Kali made a low sound in the back of her throat as she snuggled closer to Aaron. *I love you.*

I know, Aaron thought back. He heard her giggle within his mind and liked the sound.

I'm glad I found you that night, he told her. When he received no response, he tried to feel within her mind. He succeeded, only to find a soothing, peacefulness emanating from her, and realized she had fallen asleep. Aaron joined her shortly after that.

Chapter Eighteen

The Grandfather paced within the confines of his hogan. He looked at the walls and at the contents of his shelves. He was deeply saddened by the knowledge that there was no one left who was fully prepared to follow in his footsteps, no one to teach his people of their mystical heritage and metaphysical traditions.

Nonetheless, the Grandfather was truly a wise man and understood that the days of deep belief were over. His people no longer wanted to remember their proud past. What they wanted was to become part of the civilization that had washed over them, stolen the lands that were their domain, and cast them from their rightful place to the bottom of the dung heap of the white man's world.

The Grandfather knew that it was not their fault, for those of his people who lived today had been taught their indifference by their parents and their parent's parents before them. It had begun when the first white man had come to desecrate their lands and their faith. It had been written in legend that should the Navajo—Dinee, as they called themselves—lose their faith, then one day another civilization would rule the Navajo. That legend was about to come to pass.

Yet it was not too late to help his people, although they did not know they needed help. Only he had seen the writings of the spirits, and only he and Michael had known what the future held. Michael had already made his unselfish sacrifice for what remained of the Navajo nation.

It was two in the morning. Five and a half hours had passed since he'd become aware that they were near—Michael's friend and spiritual brother and the woman whom the spirits protected.

The Grandfather had made his preparations, for he knew that tomorrow he would see the two who needed him as he needed them.

Turning, he went to the far wall of the house. He lifted the old hunting knife from its peg,

D.M. Wind

reverently drawing the ancient blade from its buffalo skin sheath. He held it outward so he could gaze at the perfection of the honed bone blade.

The knife had been handed down from father to son, medicine man to medicine man, and was at least four centuries old. It was a sacred knife, the lasting symbol of the power and might of a vanished race.

Taking the knife to the small table, he placed it next to the three leather pouches that contained his powders. Then he returned to the center of the room and squatted over the sand drawing he had completed that afternoon.

The circle's border was turquoise sand. Bands of red and black alternated inward for six lines. In the center of the sand painting was the sacred mountain. All around the likeness of the mountain were ancient Navajo symbols. Beneath the Navajo writing were stick figures.

This painting, the Grandfather's last, had been started when Michael had taken his white brother to the sacred mountain. It showed Michael and Aaron. It showed, too, the woman in other forms—a bird, a cat, a wolf.

There were other figures—a black and evil predator, a howling animal, a bird. There was another white man with a dark malignant aura created by waves of multicolored sand. This figure was chasing after the others.

The picture was a story, a story not yet fully told.

The Grandfather grunted in approval while he restudied the painting. He reached into the old medicine pouch which hung about his neck and withdrew several buttons of peyote.

He tossed all but one into a boiling pot. Then he sat before the small stove, and as the peyote buttons brewed, he chewed on the one button he'd saved.

Twenty minutes later he shut off the stove. The water in the pot had become a tealike liquid that had no name other than the color that the peyote had turned the water. It was called the Black Drink.

Spitting out the remains of the small peyote button, the Grandfather poured a cup of Black Drink from the pot. He drank it in one long gulp, ignoring the searing heat. A moment later he began to chant the ritual phrases that would allow him to put himself into a special state of semiconsciousness that bordered on life and death.

The Black Drink, so much stronger than a single button, would help him to reach this state. There, he would be able to expand his mind in preparation for the woman. It was important that he meet her on her level, unencumbered by the weightiness of his earthly body. To reach this wondrous state would take a long time, all of what remained of the night and many hours of tomorrow.

But the Grandfather would be ready; it was his fate and his destiny. He had waited almost a full century for this one special moment.

Chapter Nineteen

Kali woke before Aaron. She looked at him, studying his sleeping face; her heart flowed with love. For the long centuries that she had been damned to this world, with no hope of escape and no desire to be a part of what she could not, she had never imagined falling in love with someone from this world.

As she had told Aaron, she had been with many men. Although she'd been wife, concubine and lover, each time it had been in body only, not in heart. She had been with men, sharing their lives when the loneliness of her life had grown too heavy. But she had never stayed with anyone long enough for them to see her stay young while they grew old.

It was different with Aaron. Just as she had

found her life's mate in Aaron that first terrible
night in Virginia, she had realized, too, that
their love was doomed. After endless centuries
of denial, Kali had been unable to stop herself
from loving him, from opening her mind to
him, from giving herself up to him.

The bond they had forged from their love
would live on within her until she died. When
Kali had accepted his love and given her love to
Aaron, she had decided that when Aaron died
so would she die. Her life would be with him
or not at all.

However, with the startling possibility that
Gable's theory to reverse the doorway might
really work, Kali had found herself amidst a
new quandary, one that all her years of life
had left her unprepared for. If Aaron succeeded in reversing the doorway, could she
go through it and forfeit her love? Once again
it was fate that came to the forefront, for Kali
saw that she might have no choice. Someone
must warn her people of the looming danger
of Amos Aldredge, an immortal malignancy if
he reached her world.

And she of all people knew what Aldredge
planned. If the man reached her world, it
and the people who lived upon the gentle
green plains, would perish. While she could
not be certain that everything on her world
had stayed the way it was when she'd been
drawn through the spatial opening, she prayed
that it had remained as she remembered.

The Others

Her world was a peaceful place, where the sciences were of the mind and not of the things that this world had discovered and misused. With Aldredge's knowledge of nuclear physics and the physical sciences, he would rule her world in a short time, along with his alter ego, Charles Langst.

She could not permit it to happen. All Kali could hope for was that a doorway into her world would never be found. Without a doorway, she had but one decision to make—when to die. She had already made that choice. It would be with Aaron, when the time comes.

Aaron shifted, his breathing changing for a moment before settling down again. Kali realized that her thoughts had been strong and unguarded and had reached into his sleeping mind.

She blanketed her thoughts so they would not disturb him. She made herself relax and, at the same time, began to caress Aaron's chest lightly. Desire rose within her as she touched his skin. She turned, lifting her head slightly so that she could better reach him. Her mouth covered his nipple. She kissed the taut skin gently.

Aaron stirred, but Kali did not stop. Her lips and hands roamed over him, gently teasing him awake. A moment later, when he was within her mind, she brought her mouth to his.

Their lovemaking was gentle, passionate and fulfilling. When it was over, and their breathing calm, Kali caressed his face and listened to the steady beating of his heart.

Aaron stroked Kali's lustrous hair and said, "I must get the generator today."

Kali's thought conveyed her acceptance.

"After we buy the generator, we must visit the Grandfather and get permission to go to the sacred grounds."

Will he give it?

Yes, Aaron replied. "He loved Michael, he will do it for him, if for no other reason. We'll pick up supplies and camping gear. Once we buy them and the generator, they'll know we're in this area. But they won't know where to look. Federal authorities are not given much respect on Indian reservations. It will take them a while to find us. With a little luck, they may not find us at all."

"They will, and it won't take them very long."

Aaron gazed at her, puzzled. "How do you know?"

Because of me. Langst will be with them. As I've already told you, our people can sense each other when we are nearby. That is why there is no war on my world. It would be unwinnable.

That's probably what Aldredge is counting on.

"It is," Kali stated.

Aaron sighed. "We'd better get started. The generator will be the last thing we buy. After we get it, we'll go see the Grandfather. We won't come back here."

Two and a half hours later they stopped in

Prescott, which Aaron believed would be far enough away to throw the hounds off their trail.

After having a light breakfast, they went to an auto supply store and bought a roof rack. Once the roof rack was secured on the Oldsmobile, they went to a hunting and camping store, where they bought sleeping bags, a Coleman stove, pots and pans, a percolator, two large kerosene lanterns, and two heavy-duty torchlights with extra batteries. The last thing Aaron bought was a two gallon can of kerosene.

After paying for the purchases, he had a little less than $50 to his name.

What about the generator?

"Credit card," Aaron said.

"Won't Aldredge and the government agents have had your credit cards canceled?" Kali ventured.

Aaron shook his head. "No. Federal procedure for tracking a fugitive is to let the credit cards stay valid so that they can follow the purchase trail. However, all credit card companies have been notified and will report a purchase within minutes." Aaron paused and smiled at her. *That's why I picked Prescott. It is far enough away from our destination to be misleading.*

They stopped ten minutes later at a large recreational vehicle center just outside Prescott. Aaron looked over the five styles of generators the center offered and purchased a Honda

EM3000A. The generator was capable of producing 3000 watts and would run for six hours on a single tank of gas. It was more than ample for Aaron's needs. He bought a plastic five gallon can.

Once the credit card purchase was approved—as Aaron had predicted—and the generator loaded on the luggage rack next to the other purchases, Aaron and Kali started back. On the way Aaron stopped at a liquor store and purchased a three liter jug of Paul Masson Chablis. They had lunch halfway between Prescott and the reservation. After lunch, Aaron pulled into a gas station and filled the car and the plastic gas can.

At 3:00, Aaron and Kali arrived at the Grandfather's hogan. Aaron paused at the door, the bottle of wine in his left hand, Kali's hand in his right.

"We can go in," Kali told him. "We're expected."

Aaron looked at her, shrugged and opened the door. The darkness took him a moment to adjust to. The only light came through two windows and streaked in pale yellow lines to the floor. Particles of dust, stirred by the door's opening, swirled within the bands of light.

The Grandfather was seated cross-legged before a circular sand painting. His back was to them, and he was as still as death. There was an empty pot and cup next to him.

The old Indian did not turn or acknowledge

them in any way for several seconds, but finally Aaron saw the shaman's shoulders lift and fall. "Come, brother of my seedling, you and the woman are welcome," he told them.

Aaron and Kali approached the old man. "Sit," the Grandfather commanded.

Aaron drew Kali with him to one side, but the Grandfather stopped them. "Sit across from me there," he said, pointing a leathery finger to the opposite side of the circle.

Before going to his seat, Aaron put the bottle of wine next to the Grandfather. Without looking at it, the old shaman nodded. "Your memory is good, but it still puzzles me why it was the white man who invented this noble drink."

Kali and Aaron sat. "Grandfather," Aaron began, looking directly into the old man's dark eyes, "he is dead."

The Grandfather's ancient, lined face remained stoical. "I performed the burial ceremony on the night his spirit became one with his ancestors. A lock of his hair and several of his most special possessions were placed upon his funeral pallet. My seedling rests with the gods of our people."

How could he know that Michael died? Aaron asked Kali.

He is attuned to the spiritual world. He is one who has been trained by those who did not walk the path of your physical sciences. I never thought that possible on this world. He uses

*the same drug that you did the first time, to
free his mind and open himself to the higher
levels.*

Exhaling sharply, Aaron turned to the Grandfather. "We are here—"

"I know why you are here."

Aaron glanced at Kali and saw that her eyes
were fixed on the old shaman. *Listen.* It was
not a command but a loving and whispered
suggestion within his mind.

Concentrating, he pushed his senses toward
Kali. The instant he made contact with her
mind, he almost broke the link. The powers
and forces flowing within her thoughts staggered him. A moment later, he realized what
was happening. The Grandfather and Kali were
communicating.

He has always been the one, the Grandfather's thoughts, which were pictures more
than words, were telling Kali. *When my seedling
brought him to the reservation the first time, he
did not know I was near. It was eight years ago,
and I knew he would be the one who was shown
in the paintings.*

He is special, Kali replied.

*He is strong. He has the strength that my
people used to possess. Within him is the will
to do what is necessary, just as Michael had.*
The Grandfather reached into his pouch and
withdrew another small section of peyote. He
placed it in his mouth and chewed it slowly.

He looked at Aaron. "You have learned much.

276

The Others

Now heed my words. When you return to the sacred mountain and do what you have been born to do, I ask you to put my body in the chamber. My funeral palette has been prepared."

Aaron stared at the old man. "But you are alive."

"My time is at hand," the Grandfather stated calmly.

"If I can, I will do as you ask."

The Grandfather nodded. *After my body is lifeless and my spirit has risen, the cavern must be sealed forever.*

It shall be as you ask, Kali intoned formally.

The shaman looked at Kali. *This circle is the last. It is closed and shall never be reopened. I am the last of the guardians. I have waited for you to come. From the beginning of our history, one man of each generation was chosen to watch over the cave of the spirits. When a spirit chose to come to our world, it was a guardian who protected it and took it to freedom. The last spirit came before my time. You are the first I have seen. It is my duty, my life's duty, to protect you from those who would harm you.*

Kali blinked away tears. *My people are grateful for you and your ancestors. Would it were that others of this world understood and accepted.*

Too much of the spirit was forgotten long before man walked on the plains that the gods created for them.

But not your people, Kali stated.

D.M. Wind

The Grandfather's thoughts were heavy when they reached Kali. *My people no longer follow The Way. They too are lost. Michael was the last.*

You are the last, Kali stated.

"I was born seventy years before him. My seedling was the next guardian, the protector of the spirits. He was the last, and he protected you as he was destined to do from birth."

"He knew he was going to die when he went with me?" Aaron asked.

The Grandfather looked at him, his eyes fixed and glassy. "He learned of his fate when he brought you to me."

Then the Grandfather pointed to the sand paintings. "This is you," he told Aaron. "And this, you," he said to Kali. "The others will be here soon—the dark one, the shapeshifter, and the white man. They will have others of the spirit people. Beware the dark one and the white man. It is from them that your lives will be changed forever. It is from them that your destiny will be sealed."

"How?" Aaron asked.

The Grandfather's eyes traveled slowly from the painting to Aaron. "I am allowed to see only matters of this world, not of the spirit world. Be prepared to accept your fate, brother of my seedling. Use your strength to grasp that which is offered, and to flourish where you might. You must both go now. Prepare well and you shall grow to greatness. Be unable to

278

accept that which is offered, and you fail all, both here and on the world from which your mate sprang forth."

As he said those last words, the old shaman closed his eyes. *Kali?* Aaron called.

He has gone into a deep trance. He will not speak further to us. It is time to go.

Rising in unison, Aaron and Kali stared down at the old man and then at the circle of sand for several minutes before they left.

Once they reached the base of the mountain, in which Kali's doorway resided, they spent the remainder of the day carrying the camping supplies and Gable's equipment to the same campsite to which Michael originally had brought Aaron.

When the campsite was set up and dinner eaten, Aaron told Kali that he had to return to the car to hide it.

"I will do that," she offered, standing as she spoke.

"It's too dark, too dangerous. I know the area better than you."

Kali smiled, took his hand in hers and said, "Let me. I can do it faster and better." *Trust me in this.*

I trust you in everything.

"That is what a husband is supposed to do," Kali said, teasingly.

"And a wife is supposed to obey her husband."

"Not on my world."

"Women's lib?" Aaron asked, smiling openly.

"No," Kali whispered. *Women's love.*

"You have all the answers."

"Just the right ones. Rest. I will be back soon." Kali rose onto the balls of her feet and kissed him lightly. An instant later, she released his hand and melted into the darkness.

Aaron stared at the spot from where she had disappeared, knowing that whatever she would do would be the right thing. A few moments later he heard the flapping of wings. An eagle? he wondered, realizing suddenly that this was the first time since he and Michael had broken into Sperry's research center and taken Kali out that he was alone.

Turning, Aaron put more wood on the campfire. Staring at the flames, he thought about Kali and about everything that had happened to him.

Under the clear dark sky, Kali swooped low Eleven minutes after leaving Aaron, she landed next to the Oldsmobile and, a moment later, returned to her natural shape. She stretched and smiled. It had felt good to fly again, to feel the freedom of the air, to taste the coolness of the winds, to gaze down upon the land far below.

Pushing those thoughts from her mind, Kali got in the car and, after taking the keys from the glove compartment, started the engine.

The Others

The road was empty. There were no other vehicles in sight as Kali drove toward the distant, shadowy mountains. She drove for an hour, going directly to the spot she had scouted out before she had gone to the car. Her night sight was good, far better than any people who were born on this earth, and it made things easier for her. She left the road and drove across the bumpy, hard-packed, sandy earth to the very edge of a narrow ravine.

Getting out of the car, Kali stared at the automatic transmission lever and gave a mental push. The car clicked into gear. Once again, she used the power of her mind to push the accelerator pedal down. Ten seconds later the car went over the edge and tumbled to the hidden floor far below.

When the sounds of metal scraping and bouncing against rock ended, Kali closed her eyes and shifted. She spread her wings wide. Moonlight illuminated her golden feathers when she launched herself toward the sky, toward Aaron.

Aaron had been lost within his thoughts. He had replayed all the events since that night in Sperry Hollow, trying to see if there had been a time when he could have done something different, if he could have found some way to make things work out better.

Completing his introspective voyage, he'd come to the inescapable conclusion that there was nothing he could have changed, not even Michael's death.

There was one other certainty within him. He loved Kali and would do whatever was necessary to help her and secure her safety. For Aaron, that was the most important thing of all.

No.

Aaron whirled when he felt Kali's thought. Standing, he gazed into her eyes. "For me it is."

"No," she repeated. "The most important thing is that we have known each other and that we accept ourselves and our fate."

"Kali," he began.

Kali stopped him with a sweeping gesture of her hand. "The Grandfather used a word that is not usually used when describing people. He called me your mate, not your wife, Aaron a mate is more than a wife. A mate is a companion in all things."

Aaron shook his head. "I don't see the difference."

"Feel it," Kali commanded, pushing her emotions into his mind. *We are mated. We belong to each other for as long as we live. That is what is different between your world and mine. We had joked earlier about women's lib. It is not equality or liberation, but the knowledge that we compliment each other, that we are willing to give to each other rather than to take. It is more than just trust. It is tonight when I left you*

*to hide the car. You accepted the fact that I could
do this without asking how I would accomplish
it. It is that and more.*

It is . . . Kali stopped pushing direct thoughts
and drew upon her memories of her world and
the people on it.

Aaron stood transfixed, staring into the gold
flecks of her eyes, as the emotions she tried
to explain filled his mind. He saw everything
clearly, as she carried him upon a journey that
was populated by her memories of her world.
He saw people together, growing old together,
loving and working and laughing together.

He became part of her memories and the
emotions she offered to him. He tried to think
logically, to put each emotion into its proper
place, but he realized that to do so was impossible. He had to accept them for what they were
or not accept them at all.

When Kali withdrew from his mind, Aaron
sighed. He understood more now, much more.

"Make love with me, Aaron," she whispered
when she felt his understanding rise forth.

In their sleeping bags, long after they had
shared body and mind in their unique way,
Kali lay nestled within the crook of Aaron's
arm. She listened to the pattern of his breathing and watched his sleeping form. She felt
protected and loved, but she could not stop
her tears.

Kali knew there was not much time left for
them. She had heard much more than Aaron of

what the Grandfather had said that afternoon. She had looked deeper into the old shaman's mind to learn the truth. Aaron would find the way to open the doorway. Because of that, she was once again damned to spend the rest of her life without the love she had discovered.

She had also learned something else, something that she had never thought possible. Kali had never conceived a child on this world. She had believed that the mating between the people of her world and this one was impossible. Today she had learned that the Grandfather was a hybrid. Within his mind, there was a link to her people.

That was why the Grandfather was able to communicate with her, without ever having the evolutionary mind block released by one of Kali's people. It was also the explanation of why his people had become the guardians of the doorway. A person from Kali's world must have mated with one of the Grandfather's people. Their children were the descendants of whomever the person was who had come through the doorway. It had been that person who had set up the guardianship, so that others drawn into this inhospitable world would have a chance for survival. Michael had to be a hybrid, also. That was why the Grandfather called him a seedling.

Kali sighed, knowing that it was pointless to keep her mind cartwheeling when she needed rest to prepare for what was to come.

The Others

She pulled herself closer to Aaron, and, although he was asleep, his arm tightened around her. Slowly, breathing the scent of his skin, she fell asleep.

Chapter Twenty

From the moment the gray and pink bands of dawn broke over the mountains, Aaron and Kali worked at a furious pace. Both knew time was of the essence and that they had a job that only they could perform. Neither allowed himself time to dwell on the consequences of failure or, conversely, of success. Midafternoon found Kali and Aaron on their first trip inside the mountain, carrying unlit kerosene lanterns. They used their torchlights to guide them, and Aaron, walking next to Kali, watched the way she looked at the Indian petroglyphs that were on all the walls.

Aaron had no trouble retracing his previous steps through the mountain passage. When they reached the opening to the burial cavern, he told Kali what it was. Without looking into the Navajo's sacred chamber, he continued along the passageway toward the spatial field.

"Does anything look familiar?" Aaron asked as they neared the doorway.

"I've spent my whole life trying to remember the exact spot where I had entered this world, but I can't. Everything is a blank. I was frightened—no, I was terrified. One moment I was on my world, walking in the high grass of a valley near my home, and the next instant I was spinning and falling. All I remember was landing. I was terrified. I changed my shape, and I bolted. I don't know how long I flew, but it was a long time. I've regretted giving in to my fear ever since."

"Regretted what? Your natural reaction to something unnatural and unexpected? I can't imagine the disorientation of going through an electromagnetic field and into a different world."

"When you first saw me standing in the road, that was unexpected, but you didn't give in to your fear."

"Different circumstances!"

Different people, she countered.

It doesn't matter! Aaron's thought carried a finality that Kali understood. The subject was closed.

A few steps later, Kali and Aaron felt the first emanation of the spatial field. The closer they got, the more intense the feeling. Their skin

D.M. Wind

prickled. The fine hairs on their arms and legs stood out. The scent of ozone grew heavy in the surprisingly fresh air, something Aaron had not noticed the last time.

Stopping, Aaron put the lantern down, pumped up the kerosene and lighted the wick. A second later the small cavern was bathed in yellowish white light.

Kali looked at the walls and read the drawings. She studied each of them for several minutes while Aaron waited silently.

"They show my people—otherworlders."

"Otherworlders?" Aaron asked.

"Otherworlder is Aldredge's euphemism." Turning, she looked deeply into Aaron's eyes. *Otherworlder sounds so inhuman.*

Alien, Aaron corrected.

We aren't.

I know that. Michael knew, and Gable knows. And the Grandfather. Aaron, can it be done? she asked again. This time she was not able to completely hide the emotions behind the question.

Aaron shrugged. "All we can do is try."

Kali just gazed at him, her thoughts fully blocked by her willpower.

"Touch it, Kali."

Touch it?

The doorway. Feel it.

Kali swallowed hard. She stepped forward, arm extended. The instant her fingertips touched the field, she remembered. Shivering,

288

she started to draw back her hand but could not. When she started to pull away, Aaron grasped her hand and held it tight. Then he pushed hers firmly against the field.

I am with you. There is nothing to fear. Nothing! His thought was as strong and forceful as was the security he offered her.

Kali released her pent-up breath and relaxed her tightened muscles. She bit on her lower lip, while she explored the field with her palm. She did not protest when Aaron's hand left hers.

When she'd roamed over the doorway's field long enough, she turned to Aaron. "I remember this feeling, the pulsing sensation. It went all through me when I was pulled into this world."

Aaron nodded thoughtfully. "Your fear was justified. Kali, on your world there was no electricity, was there?"

Kali shook her head. "Nor was there any here when I arrived."

"If you touched a live wire to an Egyptian, three thousand years ago, how would he have reacted? I would imagine he would have been terrified. You reacted normally when you came through the door. It wasn't just fear, but the fear of something never before known. Now you know it for what it is."

Perhaps.

Aaron smiled. *Trust me,* he told her, reminding her with the speed of a thought that she had said the same thing to him last night.

Always, she replied.

"Good, let's get the equipment."

· It took three more hours to bring the equipment into the doorway's chamber and set it up. When the electromagnetic columns were in place and the wiring connected, Aaron ran the 200 feet of exhaust tubing out of the cavern and into the burial chamber. He was pretty certain that the exhaust fumes would rise upward, exiting the chamber through the small natural rock chimneys that the bats used at night.

He took a moment to look at his handiwork. He laughed, thinking that he had turned the inside of the sacred mountain into a movie set suitable for the remake of a Frankenstein film.

Then Aaron started the generator. Sitting on the floor, with Kali at his side, Aaron turned on his portable computer.

"What are you doing now?" Kali asked.

"When we were at Gable's lab, I used my computer to get the electromagnetic helix configurations that Gable used and stored it on the hard drive. What I'm doing now is bringing up that configuration to see if it matches the field in here."

"I don't understand these things."

"Half the time, I don't either."

That's not true, Kali shot at him.

Aaron shrugged and pressed three more keys. A moment later, a revolving graphic reproduction of Gable's spatial field was on the screen.

The Others

"This is what Gable had determined the doorway's electromagnetic field looks like," he told Kali.

Centered on the green screen was a multitude of curving lines. What appeared to be a flow of current pulsed through each of the helix's lines. The lines that ran vertically curved on top and bottom. The horizontal lines were more diagonal than truly horizontal. Near the center of the spatial field was a circular revolving ball. Within the ball was yet another field, duplicating the larger one.

"Now what?" Kali asked.

"The small box over there," Aaron said, pointing to a cardboard box one foot by two feet. "There's a black meter with two wires running from the front and a single cable in the back with a RS-232 connection. Get it for me."

When she asked what a RS-232 connection was, Aaron gave her a mind picture. Kali went to the box and withdrew the instrument. When she brought it to Aaron, he turned his computer around and, taking the cable from her, attached it to a port.

When that was done, he flicked on the meter, hit several more keys on the computer and looked at the screen. Gable's helix was now smaller and off to the left side; on the right side of the screen was a new configuration.

"Random energy lines of electricity," he told Kali. "Look," he added, pointing to the new

291

picture. "This is the electrical field around us. It's not quite normal, but it's not the doorway's field either." Pausing, he picked up the wires coming out of the meter and handed them to Kali. "Take these leads and hold them to the doorway. Hold them by the rubber backings."

"What will this do?" Kali asked. Still nervous from her experience with the doorway's field, she was far from anxious to touch it again.

"My computer isn't set up like Gable's. It can't get readings from a direct contact. The meter will get those readings and simultaneously transmit them to the computer for analysis."

"I thought you said that nothing can be put into the doorway," Kali commented.

"We're not putting it through the field, only testing the electrical emissions."

Kali gazed at Aaron, her eyes wide.

Aaron smiled confidently. *It won't harm you. You can do it.*

For you, she replied.

Kali went hesitantly toward the field, her hand extended before her. She stopped the instant the first pulsing rippled along her fingertips. *Ready,* she told Aaron.

"Hold the two leads about a foot apart and press them onto the field."

Kali did as Aaron instructed, closing her eyes when the first sparks accented the leads' contact with the field. Then she opened her mind and waited for Aaron's next instructions.

The Others

Good, she heard Aaron think at her, *it's coming in now.* Three minutes later Aaron told her they were finished. "Look at the field."

Kali knelt by the computer. On the screen were two almost identical helixes. The difference between them was in the pattern of energy lines in the circular center field.

On Gable's the pattern was a duplicate of the exterior. On the doorway's the pattern ran in opposition. *Gable's notes?*

Kali handed Aaron the printout Gable had given them. He looked at them and then at the two spatial fields on the monitor.

"Gable's field is from the one he created in the lab. It's the reversal of this doorway, in theory. When we turn on the electromagnetic inducers," Aaron said, his words quickening as he looked at the printout, "they'll react with the spatial field and should reverse the entrance sector. If it works, it will show up on the screen."

"What will happen if it doesn't work?" Kali asked aloud.

It has to work! Aaron declared, unaware that he had slipped into a mind link instead of speaking aloud. He did not see Kali's smile; his concentration was on the screen and the figures that continually flashed across its bottom.

"When will you test it?"

"Now," he said.

Kali reached out and covered his hand with hers.

D.M. Wind

*   *   *

The campfire had died to but a few lonely flames fluttering amidst a bed of glowing coals. Their silent dinner had come and gone hours before. And for Aaron, the beauty of the Southwestern night was dimmed by his feeling of failure.

Kali had done her best to ease his frustration and self-directed anger, but he had refused to listen to anything she'd said and had become uncommunicative.

When she'd tried to reach him on a telepathic level, she'd found his thoughts to be churning and unresponsive, centered around the spatial field and searching for whatever it was he'd done wrong. She'd drawn away mentally, but she stayed silently by his side as the hours grew longer.

Shortly after midnight, Aaron broke his long silence. "I don't understand it," he said as much to himself as to Kali. "I did everything exactly the way Gable told me to. Exactly! It should have worked."

"You're tired. Your mind will be clearer in the morning."

"My mind is clear right now. No, there's a bad hookup, or I did something wrong. I have to call Gable."

Dangerous! They will find us faster.

We have no choice. I must call Gable.

Kali projected another thought. *There is another way.*

294

"What way?" Aaron asked aloud.

With your mind and mine together. Let me go inside your memories. Let me look back to the time with Gable and see if I can learn anything.

Do it!

It is not so easily done, my love. There are so many things in your mind. Memories that can be painful, old hurts, everything you have ever done or have ever been, all will be open to me.

Everything has always been open to you.

Not in this way. What you gave me freely, I took. I have never delved within your memories, for they are yours alone. It is something I could never do. There are risks.

"We have to do what's necessary," Aaron stated. "Whatever the risks are, they must be taken. We can't afford to let Aldredge and Langst reach your world." Then Aaron smiled for the first time since leaving the mountain and projected his thoughts. *I love you, Kali. I trust you.*

Kali gazed at him for several seconds before pushing him down onto the open sleeping bag.

"Close your eyes," she whispered. "I will help you sleep."

"I—"

It is best, she told him, her thought gentle and warm within his mind. A few moments later, Kali reached into his sleep center and nudged him from consciousness.

What she was attempting to do was not something done frivolously, nor would Aaron's being awake help. In fact, it would be just the opposite. She had to go into his deepest memories. When she did that, all of his life would be unveiled, not only to her but to him as well. Early traumas, hidden and healed for years, would come forth with all their pain. She could not, would not, do that to him.

Instead she would find the memories of their meeting with Gable and bring them out with the clarity of something that was happening at this exact moment in time.

When she was finished, she would do her best to make Aaron forget everything that she had brought out. If she was successful, she would retain the memory herself and share it with him in her mind without any other of his memories shadowing the one important memory.

Slowly, with her hands on each side of his temples, she entered his sleeping mind. She wove deep within his thoughts, searching for that one instance, only to find a myriad of others.

Memories were not as easily obtained as were the surface thoughts that Kali could read on any person. Memories were deeper within the core of the mind. They were stored in no specific order. Time held no meaning for a memory. A memory was recalled either by conscious effort, if possible, or because something had triggered its release. A smell, a touch or seeing something that was familiar were the most common forms of release.

The Others

Kali could not use a trigger. She had to search everywhere, locating all of Aaron's memories until she found the one they both needed so desperately.

She faltered badly at one point and almost drew out, but she held herself strong. She relived with him that terrible night on the road when she had gone seeking death and instead had almost killed Aaron.

Within the replay of Aaron's memories, she remembered that first startled feeling when she had entered his mind as he had traveled out of body and toward the next plane of his existence. When she had stopped him from leaving his earthly world, she had been shocked. The instant her mind had linked with his, she had known that she had found her life's mate.

Inside Aaron's memories, she heard herself talking to him, telling him that it was not yet his time to die. She experienced herself pushing him, returning his spiritual essence to his body, along with her own command for Aaron to find her. And although he had not known it, she had stayed with him, caressing him and keeping a silent vigil within his mind, until he had finally regained consciousness.

Kali willed herself to leave that memory and continue her search. A myriad of childhood experiences rose up—the death of Aaron's mother and father in an airplane crash when he was ten, and his terrible grief at their loss. There were many memories of Aaron's brother raising him and guiding him toward manhood.

As Kali worked and grew to know Aaron in a way no other could, she did her best not to see more of his life than she had to. For another hour, Kali sped within Aaron's mind, seeking that which he must have within him until, finally, she found the one memory they so desperately needed.

She entered the memory swiftly, becoming part of it, again living that afternoon with Herman Gable. This time she lived it through Aaron's perspective.

As soon as the important memory was etched in her own mind, Kali began her withdrawal. During the long and tedious process, she carefully resealed each of the memories she had activated, working with a gentle sureness that most neurosurgeons could only dream of. Yet it was a long and strenuous procedure, and by the time she was finished and had left Aaron's mind completely, four hours had passed. Nearing exhaustion, Kali lay down next to Aaron's warm body and fell into a deep sleep.

"What the hell is he doing in Prescott, Arizona?" Aldredge's question was angrily directed to the three men seated across from him at the conference table.

The Afro-American N.S.A. agent, showing no emotion at Aldredge's shouts, said, "Running. I told you we'd find him. We have two teams in Prescott, one of ours and an F.B.I team. We'll have them soon enough."

Aldredge glanced at the black-haired man sitting next to him. When he turned back to the three men across from him, he ignored the two N.S.A. men and spoke to Captain Lowell. "You're the only one who came near to catching Blaine. Do you really think that Blaine and the woman are in Prescott? Do you believe that they managed to drive two thousand miles without being seen, only to use his charge card and make his whereabouts known?"

Lowell shrugged. "He ran out of money. What else could he do?"

"Michael Noriss was from Arizona. There has to be a connection," the Caucasian N.S.A. man said.

"Of course there is!" Charles Langst stated. His intense green eyes raked across the three men before fastening upon Lowell. "I was tracking them. I was close. I almost had them. But you let them get away!"

Lowell stared back at the man. He did not try to stop his loathing of Langst from showing on his face or tainting his words. "Perhaps I did. But then, you weren't there. I'll stick by my report. Lieutenant Meyer was with me and will attest to its validity. We couldn't stop them. They overpowered us."

"You were warned about the woman. You knew what she is . . . you knew her abilities."

Lowell stood and glared at Aldredge. "And I also know what you are." Without another word, Lowell left the conference room. Lowell accepted the fact that there was nothing he could do to stop Aldredge or save Blaine and the woman from the government.

Since Blaine and Kali's escape from the General Lee Motel, he had been under constant surveillance by Aldredge, Langst and the National Security Agency.

However, he had to admit to himself that it was only Langst's surveillance that bothered him.

No more, he told himself. Today he intended to resign his commission and leave the service.

When the door closed behind Lowell, the dark-skinned agent turned to Aldredge. "We found some new information this morning."

"What?" Aldredge demanded.

"For the past three days Professor Gable has been taking a taxi to the university."

"So?" Aldredge said, snorting derisively. He hated even the mention of the name of the man who had tried to ruin him.

"He always drives to work. This morning one of my men went into his garage." The agent smiled, and Langst felt a kinship with the man's predatory grimace. "We found Blaine's rental car locked in Gable's garage. Blaine must have taken Gable's."

"Why would Gable help him?" Langst asked, directing his question to Aldredge, not the agent.

Aldredge met Langst's curious stare. "There could only be one reason. Gable's research and mine have always run along similar lines. Perhaps Blaine went to Gable to see if Gable has made progress in finding a doorway."

"You've never mentioned this Gable to me," Langst said in a low voice. "Perhaps we should visit this Professor Gable," Langst suggested.

Aldredge nodded. "Perhaps we should."

A combination of the sun and the scent of brewing coffee woke Aaron. Stretching languidly within the sleeping bag, Aaron slowly opened his eyes. When he saw the sun, he realized he'd slept late into the morning. Turning, he saw Kali standing by the Coleman stove.

Then he remembered last night. Sitting up quickly, he tossed off the lightweight covering and stood. As he gained his feet, Kali turned to look at him.

"Good morning," she called, a warm smile on her mouth.

"Is it?"

"It is. Every morning with you is a good morning," she told him, turning her back to him and picking up the coffeepot.

Chastised properly, Aaron went to her. Before he could put his hands around her waist, she spun, holding out a cup of coffee for him.

"How are you feeling?"

"Fine," he replied, taking the offered coffee. *Inside.*

Aaron paused. He searched within his mind but could sense nothing different from before he'd fallen asleep. *What happened?*

You remembered.

Again Aaron went inside his own thoughts and tried to bring up the memory of Gable. He found nothing new. "I . . ."

"I have the memory. It is best this way."

"Well?" Lifting the mug, he sipped the hot coffee as he stared over the rim and looked deeply into Kali's eyes.

"There's no rush. Can't we relax and have breakfast, please?" she asked aloud, not willing to trust herself to keep the sadness out of her thoughts. Time, she knew, was running out for them in more ways than one.

Aaron suspected that something was amiss, but sensed that when Kali wanted him to know, she would tell him. "Fair enough."

Chapter Twenty-one

Herman Gable sat at his desk, writing in the longhand he'd almost forgotten how to use. The years of advancing arthritis had made it impossible to write legibly, but ever since Aaron Blaine and Kali had left, his painful condition had not bothered him.

While Gable didn't know how she'd done it, he was certain that Kali Moss was responsible for the easing of his agony. Looking up from his letter, he wondered if they'd made the passage to her world yet.

He hoped so. He depended on the fact that they had. Herman Gable had no choice. Early this morning, when he'd risen from bed at his usual 5:00 a.m., he'd heard something outside and had gone to the window. What he saw frightened him. His first impression was that a thief was breaking into his garage. He'd almost called the police, but something about the way the man was dressed had made him wait.

When the man reappeared with a notebook in his hand and walked quickly away, Gable knew who and what he was—a government agent. Blaine and the woman's head start was over. Aldredge and the government people had discovered his link with Aaron Blaine.

After the man had gone, Gable had dressed. He knew that he could not help the couple physically, but there was something else he could do.

By 6:00 Gable had reached his office at the university. He had worked quickly and efficiently, destroying all his research materials as well as the experimental data concerning parallel worlds. It hurt him, and he grieved for the loss of the last 20 years of his life's work, but it was a sacrifice necessitated by dire circumstances. Aldredge had not yet discovered how to generate a spatial field. Well, he would not learn it from Herman Gable.

When everything had been erased from the data banks of the computer, Gable began to shred his handwritten notes. By noon, he had destroyed everything that was directly involved with his research of parallel worlds.

Refusing to give in to his sadness, Gable concentrated on the job at hand. He was writing a very personal letter to an old friend who was the head of the senate subcommittee which monitored scientific grants given for military defense. In the letter, he outlined Aldredge's plans. He could only pray that his friend would believe him.

When a knock interrupted his thoughts, he looked at the clock on the wall. He had a meeting with a research student in ten minutes. The student was early. "Come," he called, looking down at the letter again.

The door opened, but he did not look up. "Have a seat," he instructed. "I'll be with you in a moment."

"Hello, Herman."

He recognized the voice instantly. When he raised his eyes, he found who the voice had told him it would be. It was Amos Aldredge. Behind Aldredge was a tall, black-haired man.

"What are you doing here?" Gable demanded, acting as though he had not expected to see Aldredge.

"That's not a very friendly greeting for an old colleague."

"You are anything but a colleague. You are an abomination to everything I stand for. Get out!" he snapped, his voice quavering with anger.

Aldredge smiled benignly. "We'll leave just as soon as you tell me where Aaron Blaine and the woman went."

"Who? Aaron who?" Gable asked, his face expressionless.

305

Aldredge's smile widened, exposing yellow tobacco-stained teeth. His thin lips were drawn tightly back; his eyes were flatter and meaner than Gable remembered. "Don't play games with me, Herman. They found Blaine's car in your garage. Where did they go?"

"I won't tell you that," Gable said, his voice steady and low. "But, Amos, you must listen to me. What you're attempting to do is wrong. It's madness."

"Madness? Not at all, Herman. In fact, I am on the very edge of success. Soon I shall be on the parallel world we both dreamed of for so long."

"They will be ready for you. They will have been warned about what you are intending to do."

Aldredge laughed. "Warned? Herman, warned about what? Have you become so senile that you can't distinguish science from some science fiction plot?"

"Not senile enough to let you get away with what you want to do to this world and the other."

The tense lines on Aldredge's face relaxed, and his voice became more gentle. But his eyes never changed, remaining flat and deadly. "Herman, we've been through much together. We've both worked to prove the existence of parallel worlds. Herman, they exist! And I control the powers that will lead us to them. I have the power, Herman. Work with me now and share that power. Think of it, Herman. Think of what it would be like to visit another world!"

Aldredge paused to let the older man ponder his words. When Aldredge judged that enough time had passed, he smiled warmly at Gable. "I can take you to another world, Herman, and all you have to do is tell me where Blaine and the woman are."

Gable stood to face Aldredge. "I will never forgive you for destroying Allen. He was a good man. He trusted you. He was our proof that parallel worlds existed. His mind was able to penetrate the barriers between those worlds, but you couldn't let him do it at his own pace. You used hallucinogenics and burned out his mind!"

Aldredge bent closer to Gable and stared hard into the older man's eyes. "You're wrong about Allen Bachman. He never reached a parallel world. He never left this one. But he did do something very important. He reached an otherworlder and gave me the proof of their existence. He put me in contact with that man. Oh, I forgot my manners," Aldredge said slyly. "Herman Gable, meet Charles Langst, the man who Allen found ten years ago. Charles is not from our world."

Gable looked at the man, taking in Langst's dark hair and deep green eyes. "You trust this madman, this power hungry fool?"

Langst said nothing, he just stared at Gable.

"Come to Sperry with me, Herman, and work with me on Project Doorway. Don't fight me, because you can't win. Where are Blaine and the woman?"

"You're a fool, Aldredge, and I've already taken steps to close you down."

"Perhaps it is you who are the fool, Herman. There are no steps you can take. You can't touch me or stop me this time, you pitiful old man! Now," Aldredge shouted, his lips twisting at the corners, "where are they?"

"Go to hell!"

"That really is beneath you. Herman, please make it easier on yourself. Tell us what we need to know."

Gable shook his head.

With that, Aldredge turned to Langst. "Can you read him?"

Gable listened to Aldredge speak as if he no longer existed and watched Langst look at him. There was a funny sensation in his head. A moment later, Langst spoke for the first time. "No, he has a surface barrier protecting his thoughts."

"We'll go through his files then," Aldredge stated.

"You're too late, Aldredge. I destroyed the files."

Aldredge stared at him. "You what?"

"You heard me. I destroyed all my work on parallel worlds. You won't find anything in my files or in the computer."

"You stupid old fool!"

"Not so stupid, Aldredge. Now get out of here!"

The Others

Aldredge glanced at Langst, who was staring intensely at Gable. "There is another way," Langst stated. Stepping forward, he fixed Herman Gable with a hard, unyielding stare. "Make it easier on yourself, old man. Tell us where they are."

"You don't frighten me," Gable challenged. He meant what he said. He believed himself too old to be truly frightened anymore.

"Do I not? I said I could not read your thoughts, but I can still control your mind," Langst said at the same instant that he projected a thrusting, overwhelming thought into the old man's mind.

Gable stiffened under the sudden attack. His mind blazed with sudden pain; a fire raged in his soul, but he fought against the mind probe that Langst was using until suddenly, within his head, he heard the other man speak. *Tell me, and the pain will end.*

"I have endured worse," Gable stated through clenched teeth.

No, you haven't, Langst told him, his thoughts sharper now, burrowing deep within Gable's mind. He shot a probe into the heart of Gable's pain center.

Gable screamed, but Langst cut off his cry and continued attacking by sending flashes of pain throughout Gable's body.

I can find it without your help. With your help, the hurt ends.

"The . . . there is no . . . no pain!" Gable stuttered, refusing to yield to his tormentor, refusing also to think of anything about Michael, Kali or Aaron.

Is there not? Gable's legs fell out from under him. He struck the floor painfully and stared at the ceiling. His vision was blurred by pain-induced tears; his chest burned as though something were squeezing it and forcing the breath out of his body.

Tell me! Langst accented his command with a brutal attack on the pain center of Gable's brain. Gable gave vent to a horrible cry. Langst eased up, and Gable could breathe again.

Where are they?

Gable took a deep breath. The air hurt his lungs, and ripples of pain raced along his chest. Langst was standing over him, his green eyes glowing insanely.

Once again, the band tightened around his chest. Then Langst bent and hauled him to his feet. *Where?* The projected thought was a physical blow that sent Gable's mind reeling as Langst's anger burst forth physically and sent Gable spinning away from him.

Gable's back slammed against the window sill. His heart throbbed painfully. Instinctively, he clutched at his chest with his right hand. There was a new pain, different, deep inside his arm and shoulder. Within him, he knew that something in his heart had been torn loose.

In took him only another instant to realize what was happening to him. It had happened six years before, when he'd had his first heart attack.

Gable stared at Langst and knew he would win. "They . . ." Gable gasped for a breath, and Langst eased the constricting band. Each word Gable spoke cost him more of his life. Yet he willingly sacrificed it to stop the two madmen. "They . . . are . . . at . . . the . . . doorway," he gasped.

"What?" Aldredge exploded.

Gable's breath rattled in his throat, and he smiled at Langst through clouding vision. His pain was lessening now.

"No!" Langst roared. Before his shout died, Langst's form wavered and shifted. The giant black leopard stood in the man's place, its mouth open in a snarl of defeated rage.

Gable stared at the cat. He was devoid of fear, and, as he felt his life draining away, he also felt a sense of elation that he had finally witnessed a transformation that he had only been able to theorize.

Then, with one quick bunching of its muscles, the cat leapt at Gable. The black cat met the old man with a ferocious charge, the force of its leap lifting the old man off the floor. The leopard's savage snarls drowned out the sound of shattering glass.

Aldredge took a half-step forward but froze. Both the man and the cat were through the window, tumbling toward the ground three stories below.

As he reached the window sill, a large, black feathered hawk flew inside and landed on Langst's clothing. Aldredge turned when the hawk shifted.

Calmly, Charles Langst put on his clothes.

"Damn you, Langst!" Aldredge shouted.

"He was dying. We learned all we could," Langst stated matter-of-factly.

"Gable's files," Aldredge said suddenly, ignoring the sounds of shouts that filtered in through the shattered window.

He reached for the phone and dialed a number. Fifteen minutes later, Gable's office and lab were sealed off by N.S.A. agents while Aldredge went through all the filing cabinets. True to his word, Gable had destroyed everything that pertained to parallel worlds.

Then Aldredge remembered Gable's penchant for keeping records of his graduate students' activities. He found the cabinet that housed those records and began to go through them.

Twenty minutes later his head rose, and a look of victory was on his face. "Michael Noriss found a doorway on the Navajo reservation. There isn't an exact location, but if you can feel out Kali Moss's presence, we'll find the doorway."

"When?"

"We'll leave tonight. We'll bring the others. They can help."

"I don't need any help," Langst stated.

Aldredge nodded. "Just the same, all of your people will go. We are not taking any more chances."

Chapter Twenty-two

"Start the generator," Aaron said.

Kali pulled the cord. The low hum of the gasoline engine reverberated in the chamber. Erratic bolts of blue-white electric arcs radiated out from the electromagnetic columns and into the spatial field. A dozen seconds later the arcs steadied.

Aaron turned on the computer and entered the sequence to call up the spatial helix. Once the helix's image formed on the screen, he entered the secondary numbers to bring up the new field. The computer screen split. Two helixes showed.

Aaron read the numbers blinking on the bottom and then glanced at the images. They matched in every detail.

"You did it," he whispered.

You did it, Kali replied with a warm thought.

Aaron laughed, venting his nervous frustration.

"It was a stupid mistake."

"No, it wasn't," Kali replied. "Gable must have changed the wiring configurations without marking them on the notes he gave us."

"Too simple," Aaron said with a disgusted shake of his head. "I should have tried to reverse the transformer wiring before I gave up."

"You didn't give up, Aaron."

Aaron considered how Kali had drawn him into her mind to show him his own memory. He had studied it carefully and discovered the error. He had connected the transformers of each electrical pole the way Gable's printout had stated. But the way the poles had been wired in the laboratory had been just the opposite. What he'd done had been to reverse the spatial field's external matrix rather than the internal one. He felt foolish for costing them several hours of the precious time that remained before Aldredge and his people would discover their whereabouts.

It's over and done with. Time to move on. What's our next step?

Aaron shrugged. "Test it," he ventured.

"How?"

In reply, Aaron stood and went to the center of the field. He raised his arm and made a fist.

315

Glancing back at Kali, he took a deep breath, smiled and, before she could protest, thrust his arm forward.

"Aaron!" she half-screamed.

His eyes remained fixed on her as his fist reached the doorway. The tingling, pulsing sensations began, but when he pushed forward, no barrier stopped him. When his arm was in and he felt the pulsing reach his shoulder, he stopped.

A light breeze washed across his hand. It was cool, not cold. He unclenched his fingers. Then he became aware of something else. Drops of water splashed on his skin. Turning his palm upward, he let the water fall into it. A few seconds later he closed his fist and pulled his arm back.

When he opened it, his palm was wet.

What?

"Water," he said, extending his hand so that Kali could see. She bent over his palm, touching it with her finger. Slowly, with her eyes locked on his, she licked at her fingertip.

Fresh, she told him. *Rain.*

As she projected her thoughts to Aaron, she saw a smile spreading on his face. *What?*

"We did it!" Grabbing her about the waist, he pulled her to him. He kissed her deeply, passionately, but when he released her, he saw that she was not as pleased as he thought she would be.

"What's wrong?"

The Others

Kali shrugged. "How can you be sure it's my world?"

"It is," he stated. "Look." He walked to the computer with Kali in tow. "See the way both helixes are identical? The electronic flow of the fields are exactly the same, only reversed. According to Gable's notes, if we opened a doorway that did not enter into your world, it wouldn't have the same matrixes."

Kali shook her head. "That's not what I mean. How do we know this doorway led from my world? I can't remember where I arrived."

Aaron sighed. What Kali said made sense. But then he remembered his first visit to these caves and looked at the walls again. "It is your world. Look at the drawings."

Could not people from yet another parallel world do what my people can?

Aaron shook his head. "I don't think so. Michael was emphatic about this. He and Gable believed that evolution caused the creation of parallel worlds. For every evolutionary change, a new world in another dimension is created. If that's true, then there would only be one world like mine and one like yours."

"Aldredge believes that it is the major decisions that creates parallel worlds. He attributes my world's creation to the advent of the belief in sciences and the rejection of the metaphysical arts and mysticism."

Aaron thought carefully about what Kali said before shaking his head. "In either event, the

D.M. Wind

doorway would have to lead to your world. The old wall paintings are too explicit in their depiction of shapechanging."

Kali was not so sure. "Why have no others come in such a long time? The Grandfather says that none came during his lifetime."

"He didn't spend his whole life in this cave."

"He would know, Aaron, and be able to sense one of my people's arrival."

"Perhaps the people of your world found the doorway and blocked it somehow."

"It doesn't really matter," Kali whispered. "What do we do now?"

Aaron gazed at her, and a sad feeling of loss gripped him. He willed the feeling away and almost succeeded, but when he tried to form the words, nothing could get past his emotion clogged throat. *You go home*, he thought to her, drawing upon the logic with which he had always based his life.

Kali closed her eyes but could not close her mind. Tears brimmed and fell to her cheeks making pathways that sparkled in the light of the kerosene lantern.

"Is there no other way?" she whispered.

Aaron did not reply.

Tomorrow, my love. I need to be with you today, to look at you in the sun. Aaron, I need one more night with you.

Aaron shut down the computer. He went to the generator and turned that off, too. When the last echo of the gas engine faded away, he folded Kali into his arms.

Kissing her tears, he spoke softly at the same time. "The sun is waiting for us."

They had made the return trip to the campsite in time for lunch. Neither ate, their impending loss having destroyed their appetites. So they sat in the sun and held each other's hands, the heaviness of their emotions weighing down heavily upon them.

"What's it like?" Aaron's words were startlingly loud in the silence they had created.

Kali's eyebrows arched as she touched his mind briefly, but she spoke aloud. "To change shape? To be anything you want?"

"Yes."

"You already know the feeling of telepathy. We've shared it, and now it's as much a part of you as your voice. Shapeshifting is . . ." While Kali paused to search for the right words and her eyes grew distant, her voice remained warm and close. "To change shape and to be free of this form and assume another is . . . Aaron, there is nothing like it. Nothing!"

"Does your mind change? Do you become your shape?"

Kali's tinkling laugh sounded good to Aaron's ears. "Oh, Aaron, that's your people's legends—werewolves and vampires. Please," she added, still laughing and shaking her head.

Then she settled down, smiling gently at him. Aaron, it's hard to explain. You don't become

your shape, yet you become more than your
shape. You have your own mind in a different
outward covering."

"I wish I had the ability."

Would you like to join me?

The thought staggered Aaron. He stared hard
at her, his mind spinning with both the certainty that it would be impossible and a growing
sense of excitement. "How? I'm not from your
world."

*You cannot change your own body, but you
can come into my mind. Come with me, Aaron,
and we will run free together!* "Look into my
eyes, my love," Kali whispered.

The golden flecks within her green eyes
glowed. Aaron was pulled into them, and,
at the same instant, there was a twisting
sensation and the weight of his body was
gone. Before anything else happened, he felt
the familiar caressing touch that told him his
mind and Kali's were one. Soon after that, he
realized that they were rising.

Quickly, Aaron settled himself within her
mind.

You fit so well, she said.

We are one, he replied when a sensation of
floating replaced the twisting weightlessness
seconds before.

*Open your thoughts. Look through my eyes,
feel with my body, breathe with my lungs.*

Kali's thoughts were as much an order as
they were a plea. Aaron obeyed her unspoken

commands and saw, felt and breathed with Kali. They were high in the sky, soaring upward one moment, floating in a lazy circle the next. When the wind whistled by him, he tasted the coolness of the high currents without feeling any chill.

What are we?

Free, she responded, her thought carrying a loving yet teasing quality. A moment later she added, *We are an eagle. Now relax within me and let me take you to where you've never been.*

Aaron did what Kali asked. He suspended any disbelief, refusing to think of anything other than what was happening. Logic was no longer a ruling part of his mind. He rested within her mind, feeling the security of her thoughts while he experienced those things that no man had ever lived through before.

He gazed upon the mountain peaks in the far distance and saw everything on them. His eyes were those of an eagle's, sharp and precise. The power of the golden feathered wings was awesome. The feeling of freedom, combined with the pure ecstasy of flight, was almost too much to bear.

But bear it he did, with unfeigned enjoyment. They flew for an endless amount of time, gazing out at the magnificent land that spread a mile beneath their soaring pathway.

Aaron saw things differently from ever before. It was not the same as looking through an airplane's cloudy window. The magnificence of the land and the crystal clarity of the sky were visions he had never truly witnessed. And as Kali flew, covering great distances, Aaron was able to view his world in a far different light.

Below him were small specks that were people. He saw the dirty, polluted areas that they lived in and the yellowish, bubble-like haze surrounding Phoenix.

Tasting the clean air of the upper atmosphere, he knew that for as long as he lived, he would never be able to breathe city air again without knowing how badly humanity had fouled it.

They flew until the sun was almost gone and returned to the ground when it became littered with shadows. Aaron had not wanted it to end, but all things must come to an end at some point, as did his hours as an eagle.

When they were on the ground, Aaron withdrew from Kali's mind. When he opened his eyes, he found Kali standing above him, her body unclad, her mouth curved into a smile.

"You flew well."

Aaron shook his head. "I'm a good passenger." His stomach rumbled. "And a hungry one."

Langst tried to ignore the contact he was experiencing in his mind. He could not identify the one who was trying to reach him and that disturbed him.

It was not a familiar touch. He was certain that it was not Blaine, for he remembered Blaine's touch on the plateau.

Standing, he left the motel room and went out into the night. Seconds after the door closed behind him, he was 500 feet up in the sky. He did a wide turn and began to follow the seeking thought wave.

As he flew, he let his own mind range. He attached a part of himself to the other's probe and tried to follow it to its source.

Before he reached the sender, the thought ended. Langst gave vent to a shriek before collecting himself and wheeling high in the night sky.

He searched everywhere, using the sharpness of the hawk's sight. Then he felt the thought again. He chased it, attacking quickly and savagely. The thought led to the sender.

The image he got was of great age. The sender was an old and withered man. He was the other one's mentor. This man had trained the one who had killed his Amelia.

He almost descended in attack but stopped himself. He did not want to give things away. He turned back to the motel, and as he flew, he began to plan out exactly what he would do— to the old man, to Blaine and to Kali.

The Arizona sky was a glowing pattern of stars; a three-quarter moon hung just above Aaron's shoulder. Kali sat next to him, her hand securely gripped by his.

She had seen a change come over Aaron shortly after they had returned from their flight. Intuitively, Kali had not tried to learn what Aaron was thinking. She sensed that when the time was right he would speak his mind. For the moment, she was content just to be near him and spend this special time with him.

Closing her eyes, Kali leaned her head on Aaron's shoulder. "I love you," she whispered.

Aaron gently squeezed Kali's hand. Within him, tension built. It was a feeling that grew stronger, as the certainty that what he and Kali had been sharing for the last six months was nearing its end.

Aaron was confused. For six months he had accepted the impossible, believed in things that could not happen, and learned first hand that they could indeed happen. His years of adhering to logic and to scientific principles had been shattered when he'd met Kali.

His love for Kali had deepened with each day. That love, he believed, was proof enough that parallel worlds and the people of those worlds existed. For the first time since he'd begun his odyssey into the unknown, he made himself face reality.

Kali's shapeshifting and their voyage in the sky had been the catalyst that opened his mind and allowed him to see just how different he and Kali were. He understood that Kali and he were human, but at the same time he realized they were of different branches of humanity.

Aaron perceived yet another truth as he stared at the flames of the campfire and listened to the soothing sounds of the night animals. His love and Kali's had been doomed from the start.

Why had it happened at all? he asked himself, already knowing that there could be no answer.

You knew, didn't you? Aaron silently asked Kali, reinforcing his question by opening his mind and showing her his thoughts.

Kali entered his mind gently, caressing him without hiding her emotions. *You had to learn this for yourself, my love.*

"Is there no other way?" he asked.

Kali shook her head slowly. "I can't see any."

Aaron released her hand and then cupped her face within his palms. He drew her to him, lowering his mouth to hers. When they parted, their eyes were covered by a film of mist that did not hide their faces from each other.

It is not an easy thing to love someone and know that you must lose him. Kali's thoughts were but a reflection of Aaron's.

Aldredge does not know how to set up a doorway, and he doesn't know of this one's existence. If we go back and convince Gable to destroy the information about the doorways . . .

Kali's thought interrupted his own. *If one man can learn their workings, cannot another?*

Aaron knew she was right. "But if we stop Aldredge now . . ."

"Langst is immortal on this world. He can wait until another scientist discovers the doorway home for him."

Again Aaron knew she was right. There was only one road for them to take. "The only way is to send you to your world and warn them," he said at last. And for me to try and stop them here, he thought to himself.

No!

Kali's silent shout startled him. He hadn't meant for her to hear that. Shrugging, he looked at her. "I have to. After you're back on your world, I'll destroy Gable's apparatus and wait for Aldredge and the others to show up."

"That is suicide!"

Aaron took a deep breath. "It's reality. It's what neither of us wanted to admit to."

Kali looked away, her thoughts shielded. "There is no other way?"

"I wish there was," he whispered. "You'll go home in the morning."

Kali closed her eyes and squeezed off her tears. Her shoulders trembled. Standing, she moistened her lips and walked to the sleeping bags, conscious of the way Aaron's eyes followed her.

When she reached her destination, she turned back to Aaron. Tears streaked her cheeks, moonlight accenting their wet paths. Her eyes locked on his, and she raised her hand. Slowly, she unbuttoned the checked top and shrugged it off. Her jeans followed.

Aaron gazed at the perfection of her breasts and at the subtle play of her muscles whenever she moved. When she lay down on the sleeping bag and raised her arms to him, Aaron went to her. By the time he reached Kali, he was as naked as she.

Their mouths came together as Aaron lay down next to her. The kiss deepened. Their hands roamed each other's bodies, their passions exploded, and they came together in a mixture of love, desire, and, ultimately, desperation.

Just as their bodies joined and their minds blended together, so did their tears. Long after they had reached a shattering climax, they held each other tightly, unwilling to be parted for even a brief moment. When they finally fell into a troubled half-sleep, both were aware that this night would be their last together.

Aaron, holding Kali tightly and smelling the fragrance of her hair, was unaware of the large black hawk circling high above them, watching the two lovers entwined together.

Because Kali's mind was overloaded with sadness and her dreams were filled with visions of Aaron, she did not pick up the satisfied and momentarily unguarded emanations radiating from Langst's mind when he discovered them.

A few moments later the hawk wheeled in the sky and flew back to the motel where Aldredge and the other three people from his world waited.

When he landed and changed back to human form, a smile was etched on his mouth. The N.S.A. agents were not around. Before they

had reached Arizona, Langst had convinced
Aldredge that it would be in their best interest
for the N.S.A. men to be sent on a wild goose
chase.

Silently, the five men got into the rental car
and drove from the motel. They would reach
the sacred mountain and the doorway before
sunrise.

The Navajo wise man closed the door of his
house, took several deep breaths and adjusted
the ancient bone knife within its sheath. Without a backward glance, he started toward the
mountain. His jaw worked methodically, chew-
ing the peyote that would give him the strength
to complete the journey that had started with
his birth.

Looking at the stars, the Grandfather gauged
the angle of the moon. He knew he would arrive
precisely on time. That, too, had been in his
sand drawing, as well as deeply set within his
mind.

At 4:35 Kali sat bolt upright. Her sense of
danger had set off an alarm inside her mind.
Her breathing came in sharp gasps. She looked
around, extending her senses and feeling for
those who were coming.

"What?" Aaron asked, wiping the sleep from
his eyes.

Kali held up a hand to forestall his words
while she continued to search for what had

disturbed her. When she started to sense another's mind and touched that well-remembered thought pattern, she exhaled sharply.

"They are here," she stated.

"Aldredge?" Aaron asked quickly.

Kali nodded. *Aldredge. Langst. The others.* She paused, her hand again rising. *There is another, also.*

Who?

Kali shook her head. "I'm not sure. His mind is shielded, but there is no danger."

"How close are they?" Aaron asked.

"A half hour—maybe closer."

Let's go! came Aaron's silent command.

They left the sleeping bag, dressed and started up the mountain.

They're at the campsite, she told Aaron when they reached the entrance.

"It doesn't matter," he said, gently pushing her ahead of him and into the mountain.

When they reached the fork in the cave at the opening to the burial chamber, a dark shape stepped into their torchlight beams.

Kali froze, her hand tightening on Aaron's arm, while Aaron instinctively drew his service revolver. He pointed it at the intruder and prayed that he would not have to use it. For all his bravado, the pistol was useless. The danger of a ricochet was too great in the confines of the stone tunnel. An errant bullet might conceivably kill him, or worse, it could hit Kali.

"The time has come for all our destinies to

329

D.M. Wind

be completed," the Grandfather intoned.

Aaron's breath exploded outward. He holstered the pistol. "Was it he you felt before?" Aaron asked Kali.

Yes. I should have recognized him.

Three strong now, they went to the far chamber. Working silently, Aaron started the generator and checked the wiring connections.

With that done, he turned on the computer and repeated all the steps he'd followed yesterday, willing himself not to speed up. Aaron knew that everything had to be right the first time. There could be no mistakes today.

He glanced at Kali. *I love you.*

And I you, she whispered in his mind.

Aaron, feeling the strain and nervousness rising within Kali's thoughts, stopped working. *You are strong, and you will do what must be done.*

For you as well as for my world, she replied. *They are almost here.*

Aaron turned on the switches of the field generator. Blue lightning erupted across the spatial field's surface. A few seconds later the arcs settled into a smooth pattern.

Aaron checked the computer screen. The two helixes matched perfectly.

The doorway's ready, he told Kali as he stood. Behind him, the Indian stepped back, pressing himself against the wall, blending into the shadows.

Kali looked from the electrical arcs that

330

marked the doorway back to Aaron. Then she went into his arms. Tears fell freely; her moist mouth met his.

You are my mate, my only love, she cried within his mind.

Aaron held her tight; he could say nothing at all. Instead, he stared at her, drank his fill of her magnificent beauty, and then did the hardest thing he'd ever done in his life. He pushed Kali away from him.

Go! he commanded.

Kali reached toward him, her arms extended, her fingertips outstretched.

Aaron stared at her entreating hand as the darkness of his loss swept through his mind.

"How sweet," Amos Aldredge said as he stepped into the chamber. Next to him was Charles Langst, and behind Langst and Aldredge were the otherworlders.

Chapter Twenty-three

"Did you really think you would get away?" Aldredge asked. "Especially you!" he snapped at Kali.

Knowing that his pistol was almost useless in the cave, Aaron ticked off the variables. Behind him, the doorway hummed patiently. Realizing that Langst might be able to read his thoughts, Aaron forced himself to erect a barrier to shield them. As he did, he felt Kali's familiar touch and knew she was aiding him.

Judging the distance to the doorway, Aaron wondered if he could push Kali hard enough and fast enough to reach it before Aldredge or Langst. Paramount in his mind was the fact that someone must get to Kali's world.

Before he could thrust Kali at the spatial

field, Langst stepped forward. His green eyes were dull, no emotion showing on his face. "Amelia is dead," he told Kali.

"I know," she said aloud.

"You will join her. And you!" he stated, pointing a long-nailed finger at Aaron.

"Listen to me!" Aaron shouted, ignoring Langst and looking directly at the three behind Langst. "I can send you back to your world," he told them.

Langst laughed. "Do you think we're all emotional cripples like this one?" he asked, flicking his finger toward Kali, although his eyes remained fixed on Aaron. "And you? What exactly are you? A glorified computer operator? If Aldredge has been unable to send us home, what makes you believe you can?"

"He's telling the truth," Kali said to the otherworlders. "He has done it. The doorway home is there," she pleaded, motioning to where the electromagnetic poles sent arcs of blue lightning into the spatial field.

The three otherworlders stepped forward. Aldredge, his eyes suddenly wild, whirled on them. "Stop! They're liars! They're trying to save themselves. Get them! I will find your world for you. I am almost ready."

The people of Kali's world looked from Aldredge to Langst to Kali. Their expressions were puzzled, but their eyes were hopeful.

Trust us. We are not like them, Kali projected to the three. *He can send you home. You can*

*be free to live and to die among your own kind.
Don't let them steal this from you. Don't let them
destroy our world. They cannot control you any
longer. Be free!*

As the three otherworlders started forward,
Langst stepped between them and Kali.

No! came his command. The power behind
Langst's thought was like a primordial scream.
His form shifted suddenly. The maddened
snarls of a hunting leopard reverberated in
the chamber.

The otherworlders backed away. Even Aldredge stepped back when Langst reverted to
his animal shape.

Then, as Langst turned, the old wise man
emerged from the shadows to step between the
cat and Aaron and Kali. His voice rose high in
an ancient chant. The words were sonorous
yet unintelligible, directed solely at the coiled
cat. The Grandfather's old arms, bedecked with
symbolic bracelets of turquoise, wove patterns
in the air.

Watching the scene, Aaron realized that
because the shaman was a hybrid, he was
using his mind as well as his words to hold
Langst still.

Aaron watched the cat's head move from side
to side, following the motion of the Grandfather's hands. The leopard's green eyes were
frozen on the old man's hands; the cat's powerfully muscled body trembled as it fought against
the medicine man's mystical entrapment.

Seeing that the old man's actions were buying them the time they needed, Aaron turned to Kali. *Move back toward the doorway,* he told Kali. Hesitantly, she took a single backward step.

The instant she did, Aldredge stepped forward with a government issue .45 in his hand. "One more step and I'll kill her!" The pistol's barrel was aimed at Kali's head, and Aldredge's finger tightened on the trigger.

Suddenly, the barrier that he and Kali had been maintaining to shield his mind broke when Kali directed a forceful mental command toward Aldredge, holding him back and doing her best to stay his hand. Slowly, Aldredge's arm dropped, even as his features twisted in his battle against Kali's control.

Aaron knew that while the two agents of death were being held at bay, they were just as trapped now as they had been minutes ago. If the Grandfather stopped his mind-controlling chant, Langst would attack. If Kali broke her control of Aldredge, the scientist would shoot.

And so amid the ethereal tableau set within the mountain chamber, Aaron searched madly for a means of escape for Kali and defeat for Aldredge. Then he remembered Kali's descriptions of the otherworlders whom Langst had snared for Aldredge.

Weak, almost helpless. They are bordering on insanity. They can be molded by Langst and

Aldredge and are controlled by them.

Aaron stared at the three pale faces that looked so troubled and doubt-filled. They were the answer and the hope. Aaron sensed that if he were to speak aloud, they would not listen to him; instead, he used his mind the way Kali had taught him. Building his thoughts into energy, Aaron attempted to reach the three. He directed his thoughts to them, pushing with all his mental might.

Be free of them. Go through the doorway. Go back to your world! Aaron stared at them, but they gave no sign of having heard. *Go before it is too late. We cannot hold these two back for much longer. Go,* he pleaded.

The three looked at him and then at each other. There were no returning thoughts, no answers. The three otherworlders started forward. They moved so slowly and cautiously that Aaron had to use all of his resolve to stop himself from shouting for them to run. When they were opposite Kali, one of the otherworlders stumbled. As he tried to regain his balance, his shoulder struck Kali.

Knocked off balance, Kali could not hold the mind link with Aldredge. His arm rose again and his eyes narrowed. *Run!* she ordered her people as the chamber broke into a frenzy of kaleidoscopic action.

The otherworlders rushed in unison to the doorway as Aldredge shouted frantically and fired his weapon. The bullet missed Kali, striking the wall behind her. The pinging whistling of a mad ricochet resounded in the chamber just as the otherworlders reached the doorway and jumped through. A brilliant flash lit the chamber, blinding everyone within it for a split second.

The black leopard gave vent to an angry roar as the Grandfather's spell was broken. In the same instant, Aldredge moved his pistol, centering it on Kali again. His finger tensed.

Before he could fire again, the old Indian spun faster than anyone would have thought possible and motioned with a closed fist toward Aldredge. When his hand opened, he released a white powder into Aldredge's face.

Screaming when the white powder struck his eyes, Aldredge fired wildly. Again the sound of a ricocheting bullet caromed in the confines of the cavern.

Langst snarled and shook his muscles free. He slunk forward, his eyes fixed on the Indian.

Aaron, his mind strangely calm, pushed Kali toward the doorway, blocking her body with his as he kept track of the players in this insanely impossible game.

Silence filled the chamber as Aldredge wiped the powder from his half-blinded eyes. He raised his pistol. The Grandfather drew his bone blade knife and, ignoring the leopard, launched himself at Aldredge.

Before he reached the scientist, Langst swiped his mighty forepaw at the Indian's side. His extended, unsheathed claws knocked the old man off target.

But the medicine man was not that frail, and, as his lunge carried him past Aldredge, his knife flashed out and the ancient bone blade met flesh. Aldredge screamed as he tumbled to the floor with the medicine man.

Langst's enraged howl echoed horribly in the cavern. His feline body tensed again, its powerful muscles bunching to spring at Aaron.

Aaron released Kali, pushing her sideways rather than at the doorway, and drew his service revolver. His eyes locked with the cat's green ones, and he saw both Langst's insanity and his own mortality within them.

Aaron took another step back, his eyes never leaving the leopard's. The sound of electricity behind him grew louder. An instant later the pulsing of the spatial field rippled along his back.

And then everything seemed to freeze in time as Langst's leopard eyes glowed briefly. Aaron's pistol flew from his hand. He heard it hit something metallic and, at the same instant, felt the spatial field tremble for a split second before it steadied again.

Langst leapt, another horrible growl heralding his attack. Aaron kept perfectly still, his muscles taut. Adrenaline pumped into his bloodstream. His heart pounded fast in the face of the hurtling black ball of death. Staring into the green eyes of death, Aaron remained immobile. He knew that there was only one chance, and he had to take it. When there was but two feet between him and the airborne leopard, Aaron dropped to the floor.

A whoosh of air passed a hairbreadth above him, followed by a sudden flash of light. Aaron lay on the floor, gasping and trying to ease his frantic breathing.

He had escaped. The heavy scent of ozone told him that Langst had gone through the doorway and would not return.

Sitting up, Aaron looked around. Aldredge lay unmoving on the floor. The Grandfather was near him, also lying still. He looked for Kali and found her sitting on the chamber's stone floor, her eyes fearful, her hand covering her mouth to hold back a scream. He rose slowly, went to her and helped her to her feet. Drawing her into his arms, he held her tight against him.

I . . . I thought he would kill you. What happened? she asked with her mind.

He's gone forever. Your other people will be able to stop him now. Without Aldredge, Langst is only a criminal, nothing more.

Aaron . . .

"It's over, Kali," he reassured her.

"The hell it is!" Aldredge screamed.

Turning, Aaron realized that Aldredge was far from dead. He was sitting up now; his weapon was once again leveled at Aaron and Kali. Aaron's mind was calm, too calm, as he stared

D.M. Wind

into Aldredge's insane, hate-filled eyes.

Aaron held Kali tightly, imperceptibly turning her out of the line of fire. The instant he saw Aldredge's finger squeeze the trigger, he pushed Kali away and ducked. This time the pistol's loud explosion was not accented by a ricochet; rather, a low flash erupted from the spatial field when the bullet went through it.

Aaron glanced quickly at Kali. He saw she was lying on the ground near the joining of wall and floor. His breath caught as he realized that he must have pushed her too hard and she'd hit her head on the rock wall. Turning back to Aldredge, he controlled the anger that festered in his mind and threatened to break through.

"It's finished, Aldredge. It's over," Aaron told him in a tight voice.

"You meddling bastard!" Aldredge shouted. Then his voice grew strangely calm. "The only thing that's over is your part in this," he stated, still holding the gun at Aaron.

Slowly, Aaron took a step to the side.

"Don't move!" Aldredge ordered.

"There's nothing you can do now."

"Isn't there?" Aldredge asked, his eyes widening to expose red-veined white around coal dark orbs. "You're an ass, Blaine. Do you think I'm about to waste all the years I've spent finding these people and their world? Especially since you've given me a way into that world?" Aldredge paused, his lips forming a disquieting

340

sneer that was supposed to be a smile. Carefully, Aldredge raised his left hand toward the handle of the knife which was still embedded in his shoulder.

Aaron watched him, ready to move the moment he had the chance, but Aldredge's eyes never wavered. The scientist winced when his hand covered the handle. He gave vent to a low grunt as he pulled the knife from his flesh and threw it to the ground.

"I'm going to kill you, and then I'm going into the other world. I won't have my equipment or my notes—" Aldredge bit off his words as his face twisted with pain. His left hand returned to his shoulder to press against the open wound. "But I won't need them. I never did. I have my mind and my memory, and I will create the physical sciences in a metaphysical world. I will control that world!"

Aaron shook his head. He saw that Aldredge was getting weaker. He had to keep him talking, stall him, and then stop him from going over.

"You're too late. The first three are already on their world. They'll raise the cry and warn their people about you and Langst."

Aldredge shook his head. It was a gesture that combined a clearing of his mind with the denial of Aaron's words. "They're too weak. They are half-insane. No one will believe them, no one!"

"You can't be sure of that, can you? It's a

different world. Your logic and principles don't apply there. You won't know what will happen to you once you get there."

"I know enough to be able to control any who oppose me. Langst taught me enough. And I will find him there."

"Aldredge—"

"Enough! You should have listened when you were told to forget the accident."

Aldredge advanced. His step was weak, but he did not falter. When he was standing two feet from Aaron, he motioned Aaron back. Their strange shuffling dance took an eternity to complete. When it ended, Aaron was still facing Aldredge, who now had his back to the doorway.

"Good-bye, Blaine," Aldredge said with a smile as he drew his finger back on the trigger.

A loud screeching cry shattered the tense silence. From the corner of his eye, Aaron saw a golden blur strike Aldredge's head.

There was no time to react. Before the eagle's scream faded, a sharp flash erupted within the spatial chamber.

It took a few seconds for the afterimages of the dancing lights to wash from Aaron's eyes. When he could see again, he looked around the cavern and his heart grew heavy with the final knowledge of his loss.

Kali had saved his life by knocking Aldredge through the doorway. She had sacrificed herself and their love to do it. But Aaron realized that Kali had only done what they had known all along would be necessary to do.

Closing his eyes, he pictured a naked Kali standing before him. In his mind, he went to her, held her close and kissed her deeply. *Goodbye, my love, my mate,* he told the image that was all that remained of Kali.

Aaron set the sadness from his mind for the moment and rose from the ground. Turning, he saw the Grandfather was still lying on the rock floor, ten feet away. He went to the man who had played so important a part in this drama. The Indian's chest rose and fell unevenly. Aaron choked back the bile, when he looked at the Grandfather's open side. His blood flowed out, seeping into the crevices of the rocky floor.

Aaron knew that death was coming fast. Reaching out, Aaron cradled the ancient head and blinked away his tears. He blamed himself for the old man's death, just as he had for Michael's.

Surprisingly, the Grandfather opened his eyes. A smile formed on his wrinkled lips. His voice, when he spoke, was low, but Aaron could hear every word.

"Do not regret what has happened, brother of my seedling. Everything is as it was meant to be."

"Aldredge went into the other world," Aaron said. "He is with them."

"No, he is not." The Grandfather paused for a gasping breath. "Nor will he live long. I was

granted that true vision by the spirits." Aaron
neither doubted nor believed. All he knew was
that Aldredge and Kali had left his world.

When the Indian spoke again, his voice was
weaker, but his words were clear. "I have
waited all my life, prepared myself for this
one day. I am the guardian of the spirits,
and I have lived my life for them. It was a
good life, a full life. Your destiny, Aaron," he
said, using Aaron's name for the first time, "is
still before you. Remember your promise to
me," the Grandfather added as he closed his
eyes for the last time.

"I will not forget." Aaron held him tightly for
a long time, while the realization that he was
alone built within him.

He rose some time later, remembering his
promise to the Navajo wise man as well as
his obligations to Kali and her people. He
would bring the Grandfather's body to the
burial chamber and place it on the funeral
palette. Then he would return to the spatial
cavern, dismantle Gable's apparatus, and seal
the burial cavern and the spatial chamber, so
that no one would ever find them.

Aaron went to the field generator. There, he
looked down at the pile of clothing on the
floor—Kali's clothing. A wave of sadness closed
his throat. He swallowed hard and reached for
the switch. He put his fingers on it and started
to shut the generator off, but could not.

Staring at the arcs of blue/white electricity,

he found himself wondering if he should cross over.

The logic that had always stood him in good stead came forth to taunt him when his fingers tightened on the switch. Logic made Aaron look deeply into his mind and heart, giving him the ability to discover the true paradox that had damned both Kali and him. If Kali had stayed on this world, he would lose her at the end of his life. If he went to Kali's he would still lose her, but at the end of her life.

Aaron was willing to accept that, but there were other problems to be faced. Could he live on that other world? Could he survive in a metaphysical society? And above all, could he retain his sanity in a world where he would be immortal, outliving all others?

"Possibly," came Kali's throaty reply.

Whirling, his fingers releasing the switch at the same instant, Aaron stared at what he thought had gone from him forever.

"You . . ." *You went through the doorway.*

No, my love. I pushed Aldredge through. I stayed. "I had to wait," she said aloud, her words filled with emotions. "I had to see what you would do."

Aaron took her hands in his and squeezed them tightly. "I love you, Kali. You are my life, but . . ."

"But you are uncertain, afraid," she finished for him.

Aaron looked deeply into Kali's eyes. "Yes."

"So am I."

"Of what? It is your world that you will return to."

"I am afraid of the unknown. Is it my world? It has been almost three millennium since I walked upon its surface. And I am afraid of losing you. Aaron, my love for you is a strong force within me. It gave me the courage to face Aldredge and Langst and to help you stop them." *And,* she added with her mind, *I cannot go on without you.*

"Are you saying that you want to stay here with me?" Aaron asked, his hands again tightening on hers.

Kali closed her eyes. *That must be your decision. What do you want? Can you accept me as I am, and watch while I stay young and you grow old? Can our love survive knowing that when you die, I shall live on? Oh, Aaron, I know too that you will make me promise not to end my life when yours is over. I will promise that to you, and we will both know it to be a lie. What will that do to our love?*

"I don't know," Aaron admitted.

Slowly, Aaron drew her naked body against his clothed one. The heat of her skin penetrated his clothing as he kissed her. When their lips parted, he took a slow breath. "All that I know is that I love you, and that by knowing you and who you are, it has changed me. I can never go back to what I once was."

"Then you will cross over with me?"

The Others

"Would I fit into your world any better than you did in mine?"

Kali gazed at him through the moisture that filmed her eyes. *We would have each other, no matter what world we lived upon.*

Aaron started to shake his head but stopped. A shadowy smile etched its way onto his lips as the realization struck him that Kali had given him the only possible answer. "No matter what world we lived on." Why not both worlds?

Turning, Aaron and Kali looked at the doorway. *I would like to see your world,* he told her.

Thank you, my love, my mate. Her thought was more than just words, it was a promise of things to come.

It took Kali and Aaron two hours to bring the Grandfather to the bottom of the burial chamber, place him on his pallet, and consign his soul to those spirits who had given him life.

When they climbed the 900 steps to the entrance, Aaron looked around for a means of blocking it off. Kali, it turned out, was the means. She pointed up at the interlocking rocks of the passageway's ceiling and drew Aaron back with her. She stared at the ceiling for several seconds. First one rock fell, and then another. Thirty seconds later, the entrance was blocked by a thick wall of rocks.

Impressive, Aaron said.

When we are on my world, I will teach you

how to build all your mental powers. You have them, Aaron. All of your people do, but they are dormant, atrophied by neglect.

Once they were back inside the doorway's chamber, Kali sealed that entrance in the same manner as she had the burial cavern. Then, with her hand in Aaron's, they walked toward the doorway. Just before they stepped through, Aaron paused.

What? Kali asked, suddenly afraid that Aaron would be unable to join her.

I will never willingly be apart from you again, no matter what the risk or where I must go. His reassurance was strong and firm within her mind.

What is wrong then?

"When Langst attacked me, he used some force to take my gun away," Aaron began as he looked at the chamber's floor. But the gun wasn't on the floor. *Where is it?*

There! came Kali's sharp thought.

Turning, Aaron followed Kali's pointing finger. The gun was stuck on the third pole of Gable's electromagnetic field generator.

Kali released his hand and started toward it.

"No!" Aaron commanded with the sudden flashing memory of the way the spatial field had fluctuated when his back was against it, just after Langst had pulled the gun from his hand. "Something's wrong," he told Kali. Grasping her hand, he took her with him to the computer.

The Others

Both their gasps echoed within the chamber. On the screen, the left helix, the doorway's helix, was revolving perfectly. But on the right side of the screen, the reversal of the doorway had changed.

"It's . . ." Kali could not speak.

Aaron's stomach twisted painfully as he studied the new helix's configuration. "It's not your world on the other side," Aaron said, stating the obvious.

We almost went into it.

Aaron laughed suddenly. *Langst and Aldredge are there, but they aren't on your world!*

Kali shook her head, trying to accept Aaron's words. Then a smile lit her features. *My people went through before the gun struck the pole. My people are safe.*

I hope I can't say the same for Langst and Aldredge.

"Wherever they are, destruction will follow," Kali said.

"Perhaps," Aaron said in a low voice. "Perhaps not. The Grandfather told me something before he died. He said that his spirits had granted him a vision. Aldredge would not live long on his new world."

Kali held Aaron's gaze. *I pray to his spirits that they spoke true.*

Aaron walked to the pole and looked at the pistol. Reaching down, he tugged it free. In response, the spatial field fluttered for an instant.

"The pole is magnetized," he told Kali. "The magnetic field held the gun across the transformer. The metal bridge made by the gun may have changed the voltage configurations of the doorway. Look at the computer now."

Kali studied the split screen while Aaron returned to her side. "Identical," she said.

Aaron went to the generator and opened the gas tank. "There's about a half hour of fuel left. When the generator stops, the field will reverse again."

"Then there will be a way back."

"Yes," he said. "If we want it," Aaron told her. *Come, it is time.*

Aaron and Kali went to the doorway. At the very beginning of the spatial field, they paused and turned to face each other. Their mouths came together, and their hearts beat as one. *I love you,* they thought at exactly the same time.

Then, hand in hand, they stepped into the doorway's spatial field.

Epilogue

When Langst landed—sure-footed even though his eyes were flashing from the explosion of light that marked his passage through the doorway—his paws sank into soft sandy earth. His nostrils picked up strange and unidentifiable scents.

Shifting quickly, he rose to his feet, his body once again human. Sweat broke out from every pore. The heavy oppression of swamp-like humidity attacked him ruthlessly.

He looked quickly around. Everywhere his eyes went, strange sights greeted him. This was not his world. It had never been his world. He was standing on a small sandy island that was bare of vegetation. Surrounding the island was a thick and darkly viscous swamp. Bubbles rose on the swamp's watery surface, breaking open randomly and discharging gaseous vapors.

To Langst's left, separated by 20 feet, was another small island. It looked similar to the one he stood on, but its surface appeared darker and grainier.

In the distance, he heard strange, wailing cries. Closer, he spotted a large dark form floating in the air. Never before had Langst seen its like. It was dark brown with wide wings flapping mightily. A long, sharp bill stretched out two feet from the huge bird's weirdly shaped and spiked head.

From above and behind him came a low muffled explosion. Whirling, he watched Amos Aldredge appear five feet over his head.

Aldredge fell straight down, just missing Langst. His cry of pain rang out loudly in the humid air. When he shook himself free of the gritty earth and looked up, Langst was standing above him.

Aldredge's grip tightened on the pistol that was still in his hand. "Where are we?" he asked Langst in a croaking voice. Sitting up, he felt the blood running from the open wound and once again tried to staunch it with his hand.

"In your hell, I would imagine. This is not my world."

"But . . ."

"But what? We were tricked!" he shouted,

propelling flecks of spittle in the air between them.

Aldredge shook his head and tried to stand. Loss of blood forced him back.

Suddenly, the sun was blotted out. Aldredge looked up. Gasping loudly, he stared at the impossible sight and shook his head in wonder and fear.

"What?" Langst demanded.

A loud roar shook the ground. Langst spun and froze. Rising up from the mire, not 15 feet away, was a long sinuous neck topped by a gigantic head. The beast's mouth opened to reveal three rows of sparkling, razor-sharp teeth.

"Aldredge, what is it?"

Aldredge stared at the beast. His head moving from side to side in total disbelief of the nightmare he found himself in. "It can't be! It can't be!" he mumbled.

"What can't be?" Langst roared, terror propelling his words. Bending, he grasped Aldredge's shirt and pulled him to his feet. "Damn you, tell me!"

"I was wrong," Aldredge whispered. "Dear God, I was wrong."

The giant bird dove.

Langst released Aldredge and shifted instantly, springing frantically away. His leap carried him across the 20 feet to the island he had seen earlier. The diving bird swerved when Langst leaped and then rose into the air again. Langst, in leopard form again, watched the unbelievable sight.

Aldredge paid no attention to Langst or the bird; rather, he was still staring at the beast that had risen from the mire. It was coming toward him, growing larger. His hand shook as he raised the pistol. Looking into the small, beady eyes of the gargantuan, he shivered.

He had been wrong. It had never been mankind's decisions that had created parallel worlds. And Gable had been right—it was evolution itself that created new worlds, evolutionary change, evolutionary adaptation. Extinction on one world was creation and evolution on a new world. When the dinosaurs died on earth, a new breed arose on this world. A breed that would survive, because they were smarter, larger and totally carnivorous instead of herbivorous.

Those thoughts were Amos Aldredge's last, as the huge dinosaur's four foot mouth opened, and bit the would-be world-ruler in half.

Charles Langst watched Aldredge die. Then he looked up and saw the giant pterodactyl diving once again. He had been so frozen by his terror that he had not realized that the ground beneath him was not solid, and he was slowly sinking into it.

When he tried to move, he could not. Each motion he made sent him deeper into the viscous quagmire. The giant flying lizard was almost on him when he instinctively changed shape again. He became a hawk, but he could not get free. The thick ooze coated his wings. In flashes that were too fast to see, Langst changed from form to form, fighting against the death he had never before thought possible. He had been immortal for almost 4000 years. He could not accept the end that was finally upon him.

When the pterodactyl struck, Langst's defensive form was an elephant, a beast too large for the monstrous bird to lift. But when he changed, his weight altered, and his 2000 pounds accelerated the quicksand's pull.

The ooze covered his head, clogged his breathing passages and blinded him. He changed back to his human form only to feel the long claws of the pterodactyl digging, penetrating deeply into his shoulders and back.

Charles Langst opened his mouth to scream. Nothing came out. The quicksand filled his mouth and his lungs, suffocating him while the pterodactyl fought mindlessly to pull its dinner from the earth.

Charles Langst never knew whether he became the prehistoric bird's dinner.

As Aaron and Kali stepped into the spatial field, the generator sputtered, but it was too late for Aaron to get them out. The doorway itself sucked them deeper within. Darkness surrounded them. Electricity pulsed through their bodies while they twisted and spun inexorably toward their new world.

Their hands stayed locked together as the

electromagnetic forces vibrated through their bodies until, suddenly, cool air washed across their faces and golden sunlight half-blinded them. Then they were falling.

The fall was only three feet, and after they realized they were unhurt, Aaron stood up, drawing Kali to her feet. They looked around and saw they were on a level plateau. Directly across from them, a half mile in the distance, rose the foot-hills of a mountain range. The air tasted clean and fresh. Scents of flowers were carried on cool breezes. The grass abounding on the plateau was a deep emerald green. The earth beneath their feet was soft.

Home? Aaron asked, remembering the coughing sputter of the generator when they'd stepped into the doorway.

Kali turned to him, her eyes wide. She shook her head slowly. *I feel no presence. No emanations. Aaron, this is not my world. What happened?"*

"I don't know. When we entered the doorway, I heard the generator skip. If I'm right, I believe the spatial matrix was changed again."

Neither spoke for a moment as they took stock of their situation and continued to gaze at the beauty of this strange new earth they had arrived upon.

Kali bent and grasped a handful of grass before straightening up again. She held it to her nose and took a deep breath. The light scent of the grass was a pleasant perfume that told her that this world was healthy and not like Aaron's earth.

Aaron looked at the mountain range, trying to see if it held any similarities to anything he had ever seen before. But all he discovered was that on this world the environment and erosion had not produced the southwestern deserts of Arizona. Here the land was more like California's flowing mountains and green valleys.

"Where are we?" Kali finally asked aloud.

Aaron looked around again, his arm tightening protectively about Kali as he saw the silhouette of a man in the far distance. "I don't know, but perhaps he does."

Kali looked to where Aaron pointed and saw the man. As they waited for him to come to them, Kali projected a careful, scouting thought toward the man.

I get nothing, she told Aaron. *Which does not mean anything. The people of this world may not be telepathic, but even so, you must listen to his mind, not his words,* came Kali's cautioning thought. *When you speak to him, project your thoughts even when you speak aloud. You will understand him, and he will understand you.*

Aaron nodded, remembering their conversation about telepathy and language when they had driven across the country.

The stranger reached them ten minutes later. He was a handsome man, tall, almost six feet, with wide shoulders and a well-defined physique. The man had shoulder-length dark hair that shone with health. His brown eyes were open and friendly. He wore leather sandals, and a short kilt-type garment was fastened to his waist by a leather belt tied in a double knot. His hands were open and empty, and he wore no recognizable weapons.

"Welcome, travelers," came the pleasant thought that danced on the surface of Aaron's and Kali's minds.

"We thank you," Aaron replied, using his voice while projecting the same thought to the man's mind.

Good, Kali whispered within his head.

"I am Abraham, second son of Josef, King of Edean," he informed them.

"Edean," Aaron said, thinking of another word that sounded almost the same.

Aaron looked at Kali, who sent him another thought. *Is not the Garden of Eden, where Adam and Eve were cast out, one of your people's myths?*

Aaron nodded. *But that's impossible.*

Nothing is impossible, my love. Look at where we stand now.

Aaron realized her truth and something else also. Gable's theory was not completely right. It was not just evolution that controlled the creation of parallel worlds. Mankind's major decisions were also a factor in creating parallel worlds. Leaving the fabled Garden of Eden had been one, long before true written history had come into existence.

Aaron turned back to Abraham. "We are honored to meet you," he replied. "I am Aaron. This is my wife, Kali."

"A fine old name is Aaron. Welcome to the Kingdom of Peace. Although one never knows how long it shall remain that way."

Kali dipped into Abraham's troubled mind for just an instant, careful not to leave any traces of her presence. When she withdrew, she sent a guarded thought to Aaron.

He is a gentle man. From what I saw within his mind, the people of this world are kind and innocent and deeply rooted in their traditions, yet I sense trouble here.

"Have you journeyed far?" asked Abraham.

Kali and Aaron looked at each other and were unable to hold back their laughter. "We've traveled the distance of the world," Aaron replied.

Abraham smiled. "Then you must rest. Come, my home is not far."

Aaron smiled back at him. He liked this man, and he liked this world.

As do I, husband, Kali told him, her grip tightening upon his.

They started off with Abraham, the son of Josef, the King of Edean, and Aaron glanced back, marking the spot where they had entered this world and firmly fixing it in his mind.

Kali, if this is not your world, and it certainly

isn't mine, will the same laws that governed your life in my world effect us?

Kali pondered Aaron's question for several seconds before responding. *I don't see why they wouldn't.*

Aaron smiled broadly then, stopped walking and faced Kali. He embraced her, lifting her off her feet. From the corner of his eye, he saw Abraham stop to watch them.

Then we're both immortal?

Yes, Kali replied, matching his smile with her own.

I love you and will love you for as long as we have together.

A long time, my love, a long, long time.

Don't miss these gripping tales of
HALLOWEEN TERROR

Hell-O-Ween by David Robbins. On Halloween night, two high school buddies decide to play a joke on the class brain, intending only to scare him to death...but their prank goes awry and one of their friends ends up dead, her body ripped to pieces. Soon seven teenagers are frantically fighting to save themselves from unthinkably gruesome ends.

_3335-6 $4.50 US/$5.50 CAN

Pranks by Dennis J. Higman. It is Halloween night and the kids of Puget Sound are dressed to kill. All they want is a little harmless fun—a little revenge against the uptight citizens who look down on them. But as it grows darker, their pranks turn meaner and nastier. Driven by mindless bloodlust, the children go on a rampage of death and destruction. Murder becomes their favorite trick, and their victims' only treat is to die...

_3521-9 $4.50 US/$5.50 CAN

LEISURE BOOKS
ATTN: Order Department
276 5th Avenue, New York, NY 10001

Please add $1.50 for shipping and handling for the first book and $.35 for each book thereafter. PA., N.Y.S. and N.Y.C. residents, please add appropriate sales tax. No cash, stamps, or C.O.D.s. All orders shipped within 6 weeks via postal service book rate. Canadian orders require $2.00 extra postage and must be paid in U.S. dollars through a U.S. banking facility.

Name _____

Address _____

City _____ State _____ Zip _____
I have enclosed $_____ in payment for the checked book(s).
Payment <u>must</u> accompany all orders. ☐ Please send a free catalog.